TO DESTROY,
I LOVED MEETING
YOU. KEEP MY NIECE
ON HER TOES.
- Jason

25 4

Around the Corner from Sanity

Tales of the Paranormal

Jason A. Kilgore

Jason A. Kilgore

D1739105

Dedication

For Mom, whom bad spirits could never touch.

Acknowledgments

Original cover photo by Matt Voorhees.

"Catherine's Locket" was first published on *The Harrow* online magazine, 1999.

Edited by Donovan Reves of Bloomsday Editing & Proofing (bloomsday.net).

And my everlasting thanks to my writer's group, the Village Peeps of Corvallis, Oregon,
who help me take my writing to the next level.

Table of Contents

Purgatory's Price

Norman Wimperlick stood in the remains of his house, his face limp with shock, his arms hanging listless at his sides. He had been asleep only moments before when a terrible jolt threw him from the couch. The next thing he knew, he was standing in the midst of shattered lumber, exposed wires, and broken plumbing spewing water from his walls. Yet all he could think was, *How the hell am I going to clean this up before Marilyn gets back?*

There was a knock at the front door. Without thinking, Norm walked over to it and forced it open against fallen paneling and a torn hinge.

The sight of the man on the other side was almost as shocking to Norman as the destruction of his house. The man was tall and blond, completely nude and devoid of body hair, and sported an immense pair of ivory wings nearly as large as he was. His body glowed with a light so glaring it was hard for Norm to look at him directly.

"Norman! Welcome to Purgatory's Price!" the winged man said, his voice deep and glib like a radio announcer. "I am Azrael, your post-passing agent and Purgatory negotiator. I'm also tonight's host!"

A spotlight suddenly beamed down on Azrael as game show music blared from some unseen source.

"What?" Norm asked. Mild laughter rippled through an invisible audience.

"I'm sorry to have to tell you this, Norm, but the time has come for you to pass on."

Norm looked at him, dumbfounded.

"Let me put it another way, Norm. You're dead. And you're tonight's contestant on ... Purgatory's Price!"

Applause rang through the shattered home.

"I'm dreaming," Norm mumbled, turning to find his couch. Laughter erupted from somewhere, like the laugh track of a prime-time sitcom.

"No, Norm, you aren't dreaming! This is the bomb, baby! This is the real thing!" Azrael put his hand on Norm's shoulder and pushed into the house. "Just look over there." He pointed to a collapsed portion of the living room where rafters had fallen. Norm saw a foot sticking out of the rubble – his foot. "You see, Norm. You've finished your life here! You bit the big one! You've passed on the ol' flame! You've...."

"You mean I'm dead?"

A wave of laughter passed through the invisible audience.

Azrael leaned against a bookshelf, careful to avoid a smashed lava lamp. "Norm, remember when you bought this place three years ago? Remember how you thought the side of the mountain gave you such a view? Well, you forgot to ask the realtor about the stability of the cliff face. All the recent rain brought it down!"

Norm raised his hand to his lips. "It can't be! How could I die now? I'm in the prime of my life!"

"Actually, Norm, you would have died next year from mad cow disease, anyhow. It's better this way. At least you went out sleeping. Besides...." Azrael pulled a big box out of thin air, wrapped in gold foil and an oversized bow. He handed it over to Norm. "You've just won a consolation prize!

"Gabriel, tell us what he's won!"

"Well, Azrael," a deep-voiced announcer said from somewhere, "Norm has won a collection of Cloud 9 Cosmetics." The audience cheered. "These fantastic products combine the pleasing fragrances of earthly pleasures with the soothing touch of angel tears. The skin cream has an added ingredient of aloe to ease the pain of those pesky Purgatory fires! You'll feel fine with Cloud 9, by Angelco! Back to you, Azrael!"

"Let's all hear it for Norman, everyone!"

The audience applauded loudly, cheering and whistling.

Holding the golden package in one hand, Norm stared forlornly at the splintered walls and furniture, trying to make sense of the situation as pungent mud oozed through the shattered living room window.

The applause died down to an expectant murmur. "So, Norm," Azrael said, "any questions before we begin?"

"Begin what?" Norm's eyes were wide and tearful.

"Purgatory's Price, of course. The ethereal game show which pits the recent dead against the fiery torment of Purgatory!" Azrael raised his hands. Suddenly the room was filled with ecstatic synthesized organ music and canned sound effects. Disco lights danced on the splintered walls, and the crowd clapped and whooped in anticipation.

"A game? Now?"

Azrael waited for the applause to die down. "The rules are simple, Norm. For each point you earn you'll be rewarded one prayer. The more prayers you get, the fewer eons you'll have to spend in Purgatory."

"Purgatory?"

"Someone hasn't been a good Catholic!" Azrael said, raising an eyebrow and eliciting laughter from the audience. A dictionary appeared, falling into Azrael's arms. "Let's see.... Ah, here it is! *Purgatory.* 'A place of spiritual cleansing for those dying in the grace of God but having to expiate venial sins, et cetera.' Do you have any venial sins, Norm?"

"I don't even know what 'venial' means."

The dictionary disappeared. "Oh, you know, they aren't the 'mortal' kind. They're pardonable, given an eon or two of torment. You ready to start the game?"

The music started again.

"Now, it's easy to play," the angel said. "I ask you a series of questions, and if you get them right, you get a prayer. Ready?"

"How many questions?"

"Just sixteen-hundred!"

Norm's jaw dropped. "Are you serious? That'll take forever!"

"That's why it's called eternity, Norm!" More laughter. "Then there's the Bonus Round!"

"What sort of questions are these, anyhow?"

"Simple stuff. What is the average rainfall in Paraguay? Who is credited with the invention of the tube steak? What chemical laxative is appropriate for use with hedgehogs? That sort of thing...."

"Couldn't we make it simpler? I mean, I don't know those things! Couldn't we just play Scrabble or something?"

The audience oohed and awed.

"Well, I don't know.... We haven't done that sort of thing since Richard Nixon challenged me to a game of golf."

The crowd started chanting "Do it. Do it."

"All right. All right. I think we can bend the rules...." The crowd erupted into a frenzy of applause.

"What happened with Nixon?" Norm asked.

"The old chap was doing pretty well. He was one under par at the 216th hole when he hit a horrible slice. Went over the rough cut glass and out into the ever-burning forest. He started cursing a blue streak. That's when he used the 'G' word in vain. Too bad! Oh well, we all knew where he was headed, anyhow!

"Okay, Norm, get your Scrabble board!"

Norm rushed over to the closet, now exposed with its door blown off, and shuffled through the games that had fallen to the floor. Finding his target, he carried the time-honored board game over to the akilter kitchen table and set it up.

"I've got to warn you, Norm, I was the three-time Scrabble champion at the All-Seraphim Challenge last epoch!"

"I'll keep that in mind...," Norm mumbled.

Norm drew the lowest letter to start. But the board suddenly quadrupled in size as he started to place his first word, *gumbo*.

"Oh, I forgot to tell you. There are a few minor modifications to the game." Azrael's voice suddenly sped up. "The board is four times larger, there are four times more letters, and there are an additional twenty I's, eight fewer U's, and six extra Q's. Of course you can't look up words unless they've been played, and any phony word is a lost turn. There's also a two-minute time limit per play. Every point you earn is another prayer. We'll keep it in English, just to be fair. Agreed?"

Norm just stared back, still holding his G tile for *gumbo*.

"Great," Azrael concluded. "Let's begin."

The two played at a feverish pace. Each word ended with a thunderclap. The audience cheered each move. Azrael had pulled far ahead after two-thirds of the tiles had been used.

"Your move, Norm. Time's almost up on this move!"

"I know, I know!" Norm put an *x* on a double word space, simultaneously joining an *a* and an *o* to make *ax* and *ox*. "Ah ha! Twenty prayers!"

Azrael smiled and put all of his letters on the board.

"*Ouguiya?* What's that?" Norm asked.

"That's the monetary unit of Mauritania. Twelve prayers -- including a double letter score -- times three for a triple word makes thirty-six, plus fifty for using all my letters, plus two for the word *aa*, makes eighty-eight prayers. That brings my total prayers so far to 2400. You have 1253."

"I thought we couldn't use foreign words!"

"An ouguiya is an ouguiya no matter what language you speak."

"And dare I ask what an *aa* is?"

"That's a type of lava, Norm. You'll be seeing plenty of it soon."

The game continued, and Norman's muscles hurt from the tension. He started sweating despite the chill from the muddy floor. The crowd had started applauding again, with the occasional cheer or whistle.

"Azrael? What is the point of all this?" Norman asked. Azrael looked up from the seven-letter word he had laid down, *sjambok*. The audience suddenly got quiet. "I mean, how is playing a game supposed to have value in the afterlife? Why not judge me on the virtues I had when I lived? I did a lot of things I'm proud of – helpful things. Don't those carry any weight?"

Azrael's wings fluttered. The room was completely quiet except for the creaking of boards and the splashing of water from busted pipes. Suddenly Azrael jumped up, lights flashed, and the audience went hysterical with cheering. "You've just won the main round, Norm! Congratulations! Realizing the importance of life is the first step toward Heaven!

"Gabe, tell him what he's won!"

"Norm, you've just won an all-expenses paid trip to Heaven!" The crowd stepped up its applause. "Accompanied by all the family and friends you've missed since they died, you'll enjoy ten days and nights of tranquility aboard the H.H.S. Chastity. Following Purgatory, you and your deceased loved ones will sail through the Pearly Gates in style with ten restaurants, shuffleboard, and two Olympic-sized pools! Enjoy a wide range of exotic foods such as ambrosia and manna and view your life on the oversized screen that comes with your luxury suite! Enjoy your cruise, Norm!"

The audience began whooping and cheering again.

"You mean I'm not going to Purgatory, now?" Norm asked.

"Well, possibly, Norm, you still need prayers. But you haven't played the Bonus Round yet!" Just then the lights came back up and dramatic, synthesized music echoed through the room. "Are you ready for the next step, Norman?"

"I guess so."

Azrael took Norman's hand and dematerialized with him, the house vanishing around them. They re-materialized in a cathedral full of people dressed in black. The duo hovered near the ceiling, and Azrael pointed toward a coffin.

"My ... my funeral?" Norm said.

"That's right, Norman!" There was a distant *ding ding ding ding ding* in response.

Norman looked down at Marilyn and their daughters. "I'm so sorry, Marilyn." He whispered and looked around. "Everyone's here! All my family. All my friends from my old home in Kentucky. And there's Coach Barrick. I didn't know he was still alive!"

"Not for long, Norm. Ready for the Bonus Round?" Norman nodded. "The object of the Bonus Round is to gather as many prayers as you can get. You only need 330 more to get out of Purgatory, Norm. Just a few more, now!"

"How do I do that?"

"It's simple. All you have to do is close your eyes and think of the good things you've done for people. At that moment, those people will remember them. If they decide to pray for you, you get their prayer plus *five* bonus prayers! But you only get one hour. Ready?" A digital scorekeeper appeared over Norm's head.

"Ready."

"Go!"

Norman shut his eyes and began remembering all the good deeds in his life as the heavenly audience began shouting words of encouragement. Norm remembered when he asked Marilyn for her hand in marriage. He had gotten down on one knee and produced the ring from his leisure suit pocket. It was the cheapest diamond he could find, but it put them in debt for a year. Just then Marilyn began praying, her head lowered behind a veil. The scoreboard dinged.

Norman was strengthened and thought about the birth of his children. Unprepared for their appearance after delivery, he saw them as they came out and pronounced, "Oh my! We've given birth to aliens!" in a weak attempt to inject humor. *Lucky Marilyn didn't remember that!* he thought. But it was one of the happiest days of his life. The twin girls had been born healthy. To his surprise, his daughters began to pray with their mother, something Norman had never known them to do.

The digital readout dinged again and read eighteen. "That's eighteen prayers, Norm! Keep going!"

Norman was surprised at how fast the memories were coming: the elderly woman he volunteered to take care of who always called him "sonny boy," the scout troop he led (and got lost) in Yellowstone, the friend he helped move to Duluth, the cousin he took to the hospital when he Super Glued his hands together, the homeless man he gave his umbrella to before he realized it would hail. The prayers were rolling in, and he was up to two-hundred.

"You're doing great, Norm! Ten more minutes!" The audience was cheering loudly now, drowning out the funeral ceremony below. Norman thought hard to get more prayers, thinking back to his childhood: saving his friend's pet turtle from bullies with BB guns, swimming across Mary's River to rescue his neighbor's terrier, fixing his sister's Wet My Undies doll.

The readout read 324. "Only six more prayers, Norm! One more memory!" The audience began counting down in unison: *ten ... nine ... eight ...* Norman thought really hard. He was out of memories and grimaced. He couldn't think! *four ... three ... two ...*

"My birth!" Norm yelled as a buzzer went off, "I was my own gift to my mother!" He remembered the scent of his 10th birthday cake from his boyhood kitchen. *Come and get it,* she had said.

Far below, Norman's 80-year-old mother was weeping, her head bent low in prayer.

"You've won, Norman! YOU'RE THE NEXT WINNER OF PURGATORY'S PRICE!"

"I am? You mean I'm not going to Purgatory now?"

"That's right! Let's hear what he's earned, Gabe!"

"Norm, you're the winner of *Peace of Mind!*" The audience went wild, finally appearing in vast, translucent bleachers around the ceiling of the cathedral. "Peace of Mind is from God & Son, makers of the hit emotions Happiness, Sympathy, and many others! You'll enjoy an eternity of easy thinking, truth, and no worries as your destiny comes to face you. You'll bask in the warmth of knowing that all major needs and ambitions have come to a close with no loose ends! Enjoy your Peace of Mind, Norm!"

The crowd went wild again as the cathedral faded away. A glowing gangplank appeared, leading up to a radiant doorway crowded with the ghostly figures of long-dead loved ones.

Azrael gestured toward the gangplank and motioned for Norm to go up it. "That's right, Norm. You're the winner! Enjoy your prizes!" Norman smiled shyly and walked slowly up the plank, golden box of Cloud 9 Cosmetics in hand, until he was swallowed by the luminous doorway.

"Thanks again for watching, folks!" Azrael said to the unseen audience as the scene shifted to a burning car on a road lined by corn fields. "Our next player is Alice Schwartz of Iowa. Her Tesla exploded! Alice! Welcome to Purgatory's Price...."

Catherine's Locket

"It's beautiful," Hanna Walker proclaimed. The golden locket in her hands had fine filigree woven onto its surface, tangled into intricate patterns. The chain attached to it draped over her palm to hang like a lock of braided hair.

"It's for you, my dear," her Uncle Fletcher said, his crow's feet compressing into a smile. His deep voice emanated from the thick, gray web of mustache and beard. "I picked it up in St. Petersburg. A Russian colleague of mine is having financial problems. He's from a very noble and respected family in Russia, but he's gotten on the wrong side of Vladamir Putin. I helped arrange for a rather substantial loan, interest-free, and he repaid me with the locket, among other things."

David, Hanna's teenage son, leaned over and examined the locket. "Is it real gold?"

"Absolutely," Fletcher answered. "It belonged to none other than Catherine the Great." Her uncle paused, graying eyebrows raised. "It's true. You're holding jewelry that graced the neck of an empress. And like all priceless artifacts, this one has a rather interesting story behind it."

"Tell us," Hanna said. Her husband, Tim, sat beside her. Unused to stay up to this hour, his eyes drooped. David, on the other side, sat forward on his chair, the firelight sparkling in his earring.

Fletcher smiled and sipped at his brandy. The moment of silence accented the thumping of a wooden gate out in the garden. The New Hampshire winds were strong that night.

"Well?" Hanna urged.

"Open the locket," Fletcher finally said. Hanna did as told. The interior revealed a tiny gem encased in a depression.

"A diamond?" Hanna said. But then the shape didn't seem right.

"Wow, really?" David exclaimed. Tim's eyes opened wider.

Fletcher smiled. "No, honey. Just glass."

Hanna sighed. *Silly*, she thought to herself.

"But don't be disappointed," Fletcher said. "The story is about that little sliver. Catherine and her husband, Czar Peter III, hated each other with a passion. He was dim-witted and despised his Polish-born wife. Catherine grew bored and lonely, so she had an affair with the handsome court chamberlain, Sergei Saltykov. Catherine would spirit away from the palace to be with him. Together they would go riding in the forest and end up at a smaller palace on the grounds, called Mon Plaisir."

Hanna leaned forward. Fletcher's plain brown clothes and tousled, silver hair faded away, replaced by emerald forests and marble palaces.

"They would love each other in secret there," Fletcher continued, "surrounded by intimate wood paneling and

12

Dutch tiled floors. Perhaps it was the spell of the wind in the forest or the music of the fountains around Mon Plaisir, but their love grew to a roaring fire. Soon she became pregnant with Sergei's child. Fearing their secret love would be discovered, they parted. But the handsome chamberlain died a year later under mysterious circumstances, and the child he fathered was taken from Catherine by her husband's family. Naturally, Catherine was heartbroken beyond comforting."

A moment passed as Hanna considered the story. Her uncle could weave one hell of a tale, but they always turned out to be true -- with a little stretching here and there.

Fletcher took another drink of brandy as Tim shifted into a more comfortable position, head against the red velvet back of his chair.

"Sergei was a player!" David said, eyes alight. "How'd he die? Was he ... assassinated?" He said assassinated with a slither of tongue.

Fletcher smiled devilishly. "I don't know, David, but it's rumored."

"How tragic," Hanna whispered, breathless. "So how does that relate to the locket? Did Sergei give it to her as a present?"

Fletcher shook his head. "Czar Peter was murdered shortly thereafter, when Catherine took his throne by force. After things returned to some form of normalcy, she had a handmaiden contact a Gypsy medium. Meeting with the Gypsy at Mon Plaisir, she demanded the medium help her contact her dead lover. The Gypsy was said to have agreed, casting a spell on a mirror near the bed where they had loved. 'Whenever you wish to be with him,' she told the Empress, 'you need only look in the mirror and see him watching over you.'"

"Did it work?" David asked.

Fletcher shrugged. "She seemed to think so. She would often go to Mon Plaisir to gaze into it. Servants were afraid of the mirror, saying that ghosts would leer out of it, watching them from the other side. Years later, the son, Paul, was being groomed to succeed his mother. He was raised as the son of Catherine's dead husband, Peter, but there were always whispers about his true parentage. He grew to hate the rumors. Anxious to erase all trace of Sergei, he shattered the mirror and had the servants cart away the remains. Catherine rushed to Mon Plaisir when she heard, but she was too late. The only remnant of the mirror was one, tiny sliver of glass, overlooked in a corner – the very sliver in the locket. It's said that she wore the locket whenever she became lonely for her long-dead lover."

The wind shook the shutters as Hanna carefully closed the locket.

"It's a riveting tale," Tim said, yawning.

Hanna nodded in agreement, wide-eyed. "Imagine, a love so strong that even death couldn't separate them."

"Well, it's a story, anyhow," Fletcher answered. "I wouldn't put much faith in it. Russians are great at telling tales! My Russian colleague may have just picked this up at a market and pawned it off to me as something of value."

"Well, I think it's lovely," Hanna said. She hugged the old man. "Thank you, Uncle Fletcher, I feel like an empress already." She gave him a peck on the cheek. Returning to her seat, she turned the locket around in her hands. Reflections of her and her family burned in the golden glow of firelight in its surface.

* * *

Hanna turned the page of an old National Geographic. The slick paper smelled of plastic and solvent, new, unread. Catherine the Great's portrait lay next to a photo of the cathedral where she was entombed. She was old, in her late fifties, according to the figure caption, and looking very grandmotherly despite imperial dress. Her mouth hinted at a smile, but her eyes were pools of fatigue and mental burden, and they were sad, so sad.

A slender necklace ran down Catherine's neck to disappear under the lacy collar of her red, silken robe. Could it be the same necklace? Hanna touched the locket at her neck, wondered if Catherine had felt its cool touch against her skin as she did at that moment. Hanna had worn it since Fletcher left two days before, unable to part with it from morning to night, feeling an attachment to something stronger, more noble, higher in purpose than the dishes she washed or the secretarial work she did.

"What are you doing?"

Hanna jumped. "David! You startled me." She stopped to take a breath. The fire crackled against the momentary silence. "I'm just reading up on Catherine the Great, seeing if I can find anything on the locket that your Uncle Fletcher gave me."

David looked over her shoulder. "Hmm." He plopped onto the sofa across the room and draped himself over it. "How come Uncle Fletcher never stays long?"

"He's a busy man, David. He travels all over the world making big deals for oil companies."

"So? Aren't we important too?" Hanna didn't know what to say. David continued, "How come you got that cool necklace and all he gave me was a bunch of stupid wooden dolls shaped like bowling pins?"

Hanna closed the magazine. "Those are valuable too. Very old. Handmade. Russian nesting dolls are symbols of a very rich tradition in that country."

David shrugged again. The chains on his black leather jacket jingled. "At least *he* gives me stuff. What I really want is a driver's license. When are you and Dad going to teach me to drive?" He rolled his tongue against his cheek and briefly stuck it out, exposing that damned silver tongue ring. She heard it tap against his incisors as he pulled it back in.

Hanna closed her eyes and sighed, placing the magazine on the coffee table. "We've been through this before, David. We don't feel you're ready for the responsibility yet. You're only fifteen and you were in that fight at school last month...."

David bolted upright and glared at Hanna. "I am too ready! Jeremy's parents are teaching *him,* and he's three months younger! I'll be sixteen in only a couple months. And you *know* I didn't start that fight!"

"The answer's no, David. We'll give it until your birthday and then we'll see."

David jumped up and stormed from the room. "Screw it! You guys are always putting me off. I wish you would just go away like Uncle Fletcher!"

Hanna wanted to grab David's arm as he rushed by, but she stopped herself. "Not ready," she muttered and shook her head.

She sighed and opened the National Geographic back to the page with Catherine's portrait, bent over it, looked closer for a bulge in the robes where the locket might be.

* * *

Hanna and Tim raked leaves in the shadow of their Victorian house. Missed leaves skittered across the brown grass with each gust of frigid wind. The rhythmic scrape of the rakes and the occasional discordant twang of metal from the prongs were like a dirge for summer.

16

Sweaty despite the chill in the air, Hanna stopped for a moment to wipe her brow. "Time for a break," she said to Tim. "Care for some cider?"

Tim just waved his hand at her without looking up.

She set down the rake and walked the twenty yards to the house, absentmindedly stroking the locket at her neck. Hanna admired the house, remembering how meticulously her father had maintained it. "A happy house is a well-kept house," he would say offhand as he cleaned a gutter or applied a new layer of paint. They had put their handprints in the cement of the driveway when she was David's age. The imprints were still there, and she was always careful to clean the dirt and debris from them. Her father had died three years ago, linked up to respirators and heart machines. A heavy smoker, he had been fond of thick cigars and filterless Camel cigarettes. Sometimes he even rolled his own filterless cigarettes like *his* father had taught him. *What a shame*, she thought, *that he didn't value a well-kept body as well.*

Hanna paused a moment at the stairs to the back door and looked toward Tim. She wished life could be as good as when she was growing up. Somehow the old place had been livelier then, festive even. And her father's strength and presence had extended to every corner of the property. Now there were only shadows.

She crossed her arms against a chill breeze, remembered the funeral, the viewing, the months of depression.

Hanna turned and ascended the stairs, careful not to slam the screen door as she entered. The house echoed with the base thumping and growling of David's favorite rock singer, some guy dressed like the dead with a name to match. Was his troublemaker friend Jeremy up there visiting again? She would try to ignore the noise for the few minutes she would be inside.

Hanna stopped in the bathroom on the way to the kitchen, opened the mirrored medicine cabinet for a jar of lip balm, closed the cabinet.

She gasped, dropped the balm into the sink basin with a clank. The mirror. Behind her, the reflection of an older man. Balding. Cheeks sagging. Sad eyes pleading for release.

"Daddy!" she cried, turning directly around. But there was only empty space and the open door into the hallway. Holding her breath, she glanced again into the mirror. The apparition was gone.

* * *

That evening, Hanna went to the living room after dinner. Tim was watching a sitcom. David had gone to his room again, blaring his rock music, his favorite singer screaming. The wind had died down. She took a seat on the couch across from Tim's recliner and watched him intently.

"You've been quiet tonight," he said after a pause.

Hanna nodded. "I had a strange thing happen today when I came in for cider."

Tim looked up in concern but waited patiently.

"You see," she continued, "when I looked into the bathroom mirror I saw.... Well, I thought I saw my father standing behind me."

Tim's eyebrows tensed. He exhaled sharply without speaking.

"I know. It's weird," she said, "but he was there, just as he had looked in the hospital. When I turned he was gone."

Tim raised his eyebrows, taking a moment to respond. "Honey, maybe you should take a couple days off. You've been working pretty hard, lately, and I think all that office

18

work of yours is getting to you, especially with the recent layoffs."

"Yeah, I know," she replied. "Maybe you're right. I'll talk to the boss this week."

The living room grew quiet save for the hollow laugh track of the sitcom and a bass beat from upstairs. But Hanna paid little attention. She stared, instead, at the decorative mirror over Tim's head. At her angle it showed only the ceiling. But she wondered, if she stood up, would she see her father staring back at her?

* * *

Days passed, but Hanna still avoided mirrors, combing and fixing her hair by touch alone. Yet she knew she had to face her fears. She had taken Tim's suggestion and stayed home that Friday, calling in sick. She slept in while Tim went off. David was probably at school, if he hadn't skipped again. She cleaned house, ate a quick lunch, and took care of several little chores. Something about being home alone scared her, even if it was the spirit of her father haunting the house.

Hanna remembered back to age sixteen. The canoe trip down the Saco River. They had overturned. She and a friend had nearly drowned in the rapids, crawling out of the river a quarter mile downstream. "I'll never go in water again," Hanna told her father. He had sat her down in the living room, eyes focused, lips taut, and said, "Darling, you can't spend your life afraid of something. It'll haunt you, search you out, come to you in the dark. You get back on that river as soon as you can!" She followed her father's advice, and the fear had subsided. How she wished she could be as good a parent as he had been.

At one o'clock, Hanna took her place in front of the living room mirror, eyes closed and hands trembling.

Fiddling with the locket out of nervous habit, she opened her eyes. All she saw was her own ashen face staring back at her. The reflection showed oddly combed hair and wide, brown eyes. She softened and took a deep breath. Laughing at herself, she moved away.

But the laugh caught in her throat. A different angle. The reflection of a figure by the recliner. Half-hidden by shadow, a man, tall but stooped over.

"Daddy?" Hanna called to the reflection, her voice meek and squeaking.

The figure coughed soundlessly and looked toward the mirror. The deeply shadowed face was clearly her father's. The tubing was gone. He put his hand on the recliner as if to steady himself and smiled up at her. *Baby*, he mouthed, but no sound escaped the mirror.

Hanna's eyes welled with tears. "Daddy," she said, and turned to see. But there was no one where the reflection had shown. She looked back at the mirror, expecting him to have disappeared as before, but he still stood there, eyelids sagging as if he had just endured a long sleepless night. Then he slowly moved his head to the right, then the left, in a slow and deliberate shake. Something was wrong.

"What is it, Daddy?" she said.

He moved closer, stepping out of the shadows until he stood directly behind her. She expected to smell the cigarettes, feel his breath down her neck. But there was only a chill rippling down her back. She shook so badly she could hardly move, yet she wanted to turn and wrap her arms around him again.

"Daddy? What is it?"

David, he mouthed.

Hanna looked away, then back up. He was fading. She could see the recliner through his image. "I'm sorry,

Daddy. I'm doing the best I can. I'm ... I'm not as good as you were."

He shook his head again. He was almost gone now. *David*, he said again. His mouth moved once more, but she couldn't make out his words. Then he was gone.

Hanna moved from side to side, looking through the mirror to get different angles on the living room, but he was nowhere to be found.

* * *

Hanna spent the rest of the evening alone with her thoughts, sitting in the little sewing room where she kept the family photo albums. She propped up every unfastened mirror in the house around her, waiting for her father to appear. But the glass was empty save for her own reflection.

Her plan had been to lure her father to her with old photographs, and she pulled out some of her as a child, her parents in there with her. But she found herself, instead, listening to the sounds of the house. It groaned and settled with a life of its own. Before long David, and then Tim, arrived and moved through the rooms beyond the sewing room walls. Tim called for her, but she ignored him. She heard them as they stepped across hardwood floors and closed doors with squeaking hinges. A plate clinked. David turned on his music, and Tim turned on the television. Outside, cars came and went along the main road.

She felt like a ghost herself, spying on the living from some secluded dimension. She wondered if that was how her father felt, trapped behind the mirrors, somehow squeezed between photons and the silver backing behind the glass. It was a lonely feeling as the darkness settled around her with the setting of the sun. Still she sat there as the music pounded through the rafters and a distant TV sent muted laughter along lumber that was twice her age. Finally she couldn't stand it anymore. She fled to her bedroom to cry.

* * *

Lying next to Tim in the quiet moments before sleep, Hanna waited to tell Tim about her father. The light of a waxing moon lay draped across the covers at their legs.

David's music still dimly thumped through the hallways.

Tim sighed loudly. "I'm about to go smash our son's stereo. Are you going to go tell him to turn it off or am I?"

"Tim, I saw my father again today."

Tim moved in surprise but said nothing. The never-ending wind rattled the shutters bolted outside the window.

"I think it's that locket that Fletcher gave me. I was wearing it both times I saw him. It's like what happened with Catherine the Great. You know?"

Tim nodded slightly. "And you saw him in the bathroom mirror again?"

"No. This time it was in the living room mirror."

There was a long pause as she waited for him to speak.

She lay there watching Tim's half-shadowed face. He blinked, eyes gleaming in the moonlight, seeming to search her eyes for reason.

"Well, let's say I believe you," Tim said. "Why do you continue to wear it?"

"I don't know," she answered. "I guess I *want* to see him. I miss him, you know?"

Tim nodded.

"I'm wearing it now, even," she added.

"*Now?* In bed?"

The phone rang, startling them both. It took a couple rings before Hanna got up and walked out to the hallway table to answer it.

"Hello?" she asked, unwrapping the phone cord from her purse strap.

"Is this Hanna Walker?" A man's voice. Deep. Authoritative.

"Yes," she answered. People were talking in the speaker's background. She heard an intercom announcement.

"Ma'am, I'm Deputy Daniels with the Sheriff's Department. Do you have a teenage son named David?"

"Yes I do."

"Who is it?" Tim yelled out, but Hanna ignored him.

"Ma'am, I'm calling from Saint Joseph's Hospital," the deputy stated in a nervous monotone. "Your son has been involved in an auto accident."

Hanna held her breath for a minute. "But David's home tonight," she finally blurted. "You must have the wrong...." But the car keys were missing from her open purse. And she hadn't seen her son all evening. Hadn't she heard him in his room?

"Ma'am, according to a friend of his who was also involved ... a boy named Jeremy ... they decided to go on a joyride. They were hit from behind, and your son suffered serious injuries to his head and chest. The ambulance reached the scene in only ten minutes, but.... You're going to have to come to the hospital. He's in surgery now. I'm afraid it doesn't look good."

"Oh God...." Hanna dropped the phone. Her mouth was open. She was unable to focus. *How, Lord, how could this happen?*

There appeared a reflection in the hallway window. The figure of a boy materialized, transparent and warped from the glass. Blood covered the front of his shirt and forehead. His badly cut face was a pale white in the wan light of the moon.

Mom, the reflection of her son mouthed. His eyes and brow moved as if to beg forgiveness. He reached out a torn hand to touch fingers against the glass.

"David! *David....*" Tears came. She gazed at the reflection, longed to run and grab him in her arms, but David faded away like a fog burned by the sun.

"Honey?" Tim muttered from the bedroom doorway.

Sobbing, Hanna lurched forward to place her hand on the window where David's hand touched it. The glass was cold and empty. All she saw was her own image, thin and translucent, a gleam of gold upon her chest.

Rabbit Cry

ONE

Joanne bolted awake. A sound had rushed into her sleep like a tornado, roaring through the window with promises of pain and destruction. The swaying shadow of an elm on her bedroom wall seemed to rise and fall with a wavering, high-pitched cry that echoed through the night. Her eyes widened further as she understood the sound. Her back stiffened. Someone's screaming. A young woman? No, higher pitched. A child? Not a movie scream, or a startle scream, but a wracking cry, octaves above the norm. It was the mindless cry of trying to get away, and Joanne's mind conjured up the image of a thrashing victim ripped by the jaws of wolves.

God, let it stop! she thought. Yet the screaming continued, unrelenting. The pitch of it got higher yet, and the constant shrieking gave way to mindless jabbering and squealing.

And then it stopped as suddenly as it had come, leaving Joanne sweating and paralyzed. Her heart beat against the silence. *Skip!* she thought and threw off the covers. She ran to her son's room in seconds, throwing open the door and flicking the light switch on.

The boy groaned and threw his arm over his eyes. "Momma?"

Joanne turned the light off and went to her seven-year-old's bedside. "I'm sorry, honey. My mistake. Go back to sleep."

"Why'd you do that?" Skip asked, his words slurred. A mop of straight, brown hair had fallen over his squinting eyes.

"I'll explain tomorrow. Now go on back to sleep."

Skip turned over and buried his head in the covers. Joanne pressed the back of her hand to her forehead and let out a sigh. Turning, she felt her way back to her bedroom.

Joanne looked through the window past the elm. Lit by the waning moon, a stately pecan out in the yard was dressed in dark shades of gray and blue, a circle of five stones at its base. The fence line and tool shed on the west end of the property were hidden in the darkness cast by a row of pines. A light breeze gently blew through the trees, their limbs moving gracefully in sync with one another.

She wasn't sure what she was looking for. She expected to see some slumped figure come limping toward the house with hatchet in hand, or the remains of a hapless victim ripped to pieces by a mountain lion. But there was only the trees and yard as she had seen them last.

Joanne wondered if she had imagined it all. The digital clock at her bedside read 3:32 AM. She had had nightmares a couple times in the last days. The move from

Newark last month had been stressful, and things were still being sorted out. Stress always caused nightmares for her.

She turned back toward bed, sweeping aside a lock of wet, brunette hair that had fallen across her eyes, but she stopped midway. The air was split by another scream as it rocketed into the night, moving in tiers from one high note to the next, a squeal of utter pain and torment. She threw the window open and gritted her teeth, trying to pinpoint the source. The cries jerked in and out, each pause long enough for an echo to be heard. Once again the images came, of muzzles with rows of teeth searching deep into living bodies for soft tissue, the beasts shoving themselves forward into their screaming prey.

The neighbors. It was coming from their property. She was sure of it.

Oh my God! She backed away in terror and reached for her cell phone.

"Hellohello?" she stammered at the 911 operator. "Hello? This is Joanne Crowley. There's someone being murdered at my neighbor's. You gotta send someone right now!" Joanne paused, dumbfounded, grasping in the air in a moment of panic, "Um ... Oh! Twenty-nine eighty-three Valley Lane." The cries increased in crescendo, then suddenly stopped. Joanne unconsciously held her breath, straining to hear. "Oh," she said, startled by the voice on the other end. "Did you hear the screaming? Could you hear it? You have to send someone right away! Okay. Okay. This is the second time I've heard it tonight. No, I didn't see anything, but I think it was coming from my neighbor's.... He's on the west side of me. Okay. All right."

Joanne shook so much that it took three tries to hang up. *The operator said deputies are coming,* she thought, *but Lashanda says there aren't many of them in this county. Still, they must surely be on their way, lights and sirens going.*

Joanne sat on the edge of her bed. *Maybe the poor soul's still alive. Maybe it's not too late.... Who's next?* Joanne shook her head. *You've got to stop thinking like that! You're scaring yourself.*

She jogged to each window, engaged the window lock, peeking outside before pulling the curtains. The doors were locked, but she checked them anyhow.

Twenty tense minutes passed before the deputies arrived. Joanne had waited for them in the living room, peering nervously out the side window toward her neighbor's. The sheriff's cruiser drove up silently. Leaving the car running, two deputies stepped slowly toward her porch.

She opened the door before they knocked.

"Joanne Crowley?" a deputy asked, his voice deep and resonating. He was easily a foot taller than her, with dark brown skin colored a wan yellow in the light of the porch. Another deputy was in the shadows looking toward the neighbor's. Her gun was drawn.

"Yes," she answered, breathless.

"I'm Deputy Harlan Groves. This is Deputy Barns. You said you heard screaming?"

"Yes, but it stopped while I was talking to the operator. I heard the screaming twice. It was horrible. Someone was being murdered over there. I'm sure of it."

"Where?"

Joanne pointed toward her neighbor's house. "I'm certain it was coming from over there."

"And you called during the second episode?" he asked. Joanne nodded. "Ma'am, we're going over there to check things out. Do you know your neighbor at all?"

Joanne shook her head and crossed her arms against her robe. "My son and I just moved here a month ago. I've seen a couple people over there, but I don't know anything about them. It's pretty run down."

"All right. You stay here and we'll be back in a bit, okay?"

Joanne nodded, and the two deputies moved away from the porch. Their forms faded into the darkness as they rounded the hedges along the road.

She watched from the living room window, listening carefully for gunfire or shouts. The neighbor's porch light winked on at a deputy's knock, followed by a couple more lights within the house. Another cruiser had pulled into the neighbor's driveway with red and blue lights circling. The lights flashed off the surrounding trees like some eerie discotheque or UFO landing site. Minutes passed, and she thought she saw the beams of flashlights around the back of the neighbor's house. But no gunshots echoed through the valley. No screams for backup filtered through the night.

The deputies returned about an hour after they had left her, guns holstered and walking normally with flashlights.

"Mrs. Crowley," Deputy Groves said, "your neighbor is a man named James Tate. He and his family run a small rabbit farm back there. Now, I know it's a strange question, Ma'am, but have you ever heard a rabbit being slaughtered?"

Joanne shook her head.

"Well, if it's not done real quick, the rabbit screams bloody murder. Sort of a... *squeal*. It seems they decided to slaughter a couple rabbits tonight, and they showed them to us. We suspect the screams you heard were the rabbits, Mrs. Crowley." The deputy paused for a moment to allow her to speak, but she didn't take the opportunity. "Now, you have the option of charging Mr. Tate with disturbing the peace, but he promised us that he will only slaughter the animals during the daytime from now on. Would that work for you, Mrs. Crowley?"

Joanne glanced down. "Okay. Isn't it cruel, though? Why can't it be more humane?"

Deputy Grove nodded. "We'll be reporting this to the animal cruelty unit, but it may be some time before they make it out here. Though to be honest, I doubt they'll come at all. There are a lot of rabbit farmers in these parts, Ma'am, and Mr. Tate hasn't done anything out of the ordinary other than choosing three A.M. for his activities." He paused for a moment, then added, "Let us know if there's anything else we can do for you, Mrs. Crowley, all right?"

Joanne nodded. "all right." The deputies left.

She spent the rest of the night in the recliner, nodding, lights off, watching the locked front door and glancing nervously out the windows. *Silly,* she thought. *It's just rabbits, that's all.* But the memory of those terrible cries kept coming back, jolting her awake. Dreams of tormented creatures hounded her. Shadows crept in the corners. Hunched beasts swayed with the moonlit trees. She could almost hear their talons clacking against each other, eager for the kill. And she knew, somewhere out there, out there in shrubs and brush piles, small animals were hunkered against the darkness, afraid for their lives.

TWO

Joanne stared at the bramble of greenbrier and blackberry with a sense of hopelessness. She could just make out the outline of a concrete compost area through the chinks in this natural armor. The short, brown spikes of the blackberry seemed to her like barbed wire, and the wide, gently sloped greenbrier thorns looked deceptively tender. She might as well try to cut her way through an iron gate.

"It'd take all day to chop through that mess," she mumbled. She thought clearing the compost area would be a quick project, something to take her mind off of last night.

Joanne glanced toward the east side of the house. Skip was there, climbing a huge, gnarled apple tree. Normally she would have called him down, but she let him be. Better he fall from a limb than wander in boredom toward that awful Tate place.

She looked over at the neighbor's. A rusty fence line separated her mowed yard from the chaotic overgrowth of Tate land. A disembodied fender, rusted to an orange-brown and surely older than she was, peeked through the briers. Bald and half-stripped tires lay piled off to the side, covered in honeysuckle. Joanne shivered at the thought of poisonous snakes hiding in them. Copperheads. Rattlers. *At least it's not kudzu*, she thought.

Their homes were along a ridgeline of one of the gentle, sloping hills that defined the region. Her yard sloped generally downhill toward the back and to the west, then up again into the Tate property such that Tate's home sat slightly higher than hers.

She looked back at the muss of vines over the compost. Could there be a cottonmouth in there, ready to strike? She sighed. "Must everything be so damned overgrown in this state?" she asked the vines. "If only you'd clear your own damned selves from the stupid compost!"

She heard a vehicle slow on the road and then rumble up her gravel driveway. Relieved to put off her chore, Joanne recognized the car, smiled and stepped toward the visitors.

* * *

"I don't know, Lashanda. It's all so strange. You wouldn't think I grew up here, the way I've been thinking, lately."

Joanne and her lifelong friend sat on Joanne's front porch. Ice cubes popped in the freshly made sun tea. A large pitcher of it, brimming with tea bags, sat on a stack of cut fire logs. The sweet scent of mimosa blossoms drifted past them.

"What do you mean?" Lashanda asked. Gold loop earrings dangled against her dark skin, brushing her neck with the breeze.

"Well, I guess I've just been out East too long. I haven't been back to Arkansas since Mom died, you know." Joanne flashed a cautionary glance at Lashanda, a sign to avoid the topic. She sipped her tea. "This is a world of grits, and of barns with old, gray wood. I never noticed a Southern accent until I moved to Newark. People made fun of me, so I lost it. Now it just sounds sorta backwards, you know?"

"I'll try not to be takin' no offense, Ms. Crowley," Lashanda said, purposely twanging her voice, laying it on thick like the maid, Mammy, in *Gone With the Wind*. She rolled her eyes and patted her afro.

"Sorry. I don't mean *your* accent." Joanne smiled, suppressing a laugh. "Okay, maybe I do." The two women chuckled at each other.

"Give it some time, Joanne." Lashanda waved away a mosquito. Copper bracelets jangled. "You've been in real civilization too long, that's all. It's time to get countrified. Sit down to some biscuits and gravy. Go fishin' for catfish. Walk around in that fine yard of yours without your shoes on."

Joanne grinned. "That's not how *you* live."

"Honey, *I* ain't country!"

"And I am?"

"Sure, Joanne! You wouldn't have moved back if you weren't, now would you?" She batted away a fly. "Shoot, I'd have moved to Atlanta by now if it weren't for my good-for-nothin' ex and his parenting rights."

Joanne paused to drink her tea and listened to the wind as it caressed the pines. Lashanda's twin daughters, Destiny and Kayla, ran with Skip through the yard, identical in clothing and appearance except that Destiny had beaded braids that clacked when she moved her head and Kayla's hair was in two large puffs on either side of her head. Their breathless giggles swept with the breeze and played in the bamboo wind chimes. Joanne closed her eyes and breathed deep. On days like this, at Skip's age, she and Lashanda and a flock of other country kids would run through the woods or fly kites down at the dairy, barefooted, overflowing with the energy of the young.

But that had been twenty years ago. Lashanda was the last of her childhood friends to stay in touch. *BFFs, as girls say nowadays.* She hoped Skip would make such friends.

Joanne set the tumbler between her legs. She watched sweat roll down the glass to wet her jeans. "I guess I just feel this way because of what happened the other night."

"Honey, don't let it get you down. Don't let some redneck scare you. Why, they're probably nice folks. You just have to meet 'em is all. You know as well as I do that most people out here are nice once you know 'em."

Joanne nodded. "Yeah, just like Old Man Beaux. Remember him?"

Lashanda snorted. "Do I ever! He cussed up a storm when the Harvey brothers spray painted his cows pink!" Both women laughed. "But he never locked his door. He was always quick to say hello and offer some iced tea or cookies."

"And he helped Dad fix things, too," Joanne added. "Hell, he saved us a fortune by digging that root cellar."

Joanne took a drink and savored the sun tea -- something she hadn't tasted the whole time she was out East. "There's a lot of weird things about this place, too, and not just because of the whole Southern thing." She regretted saying anything the moment she said it, though.

An awkward moment passed as she hoped Lashanda would just let it go, but she didn't. "Well?" Lashanda said. "Such as?"

Joanne shook her head. "I mean, besides the whole killing of rabbits thing, there's just this ... vibe ... like I'm being watched or something." She emitted a nervous titter and smiled at her friend. "Stupid really. Probably came from what the real estate agent told me about the previous occupants."

"What? Did someone die in the house?" Lashanda's eyes got big. "Or maybe they were in a cult?"

"No, no one died here ... that I know of!" Joanne chuckled. "But you're not far off with the cult thing. She told me they proudly professed to being Wiccans and invited her to one of their coven rituals. She declined."

"Wiccans? Aren't those, like, witches?" Lashanda's hand went up to touch the little golden cross that hung from her neck.

Joanne shrugged. "I'm not sure they like the term. But from the bit of stuff I've read, I think they cast spells to harness positive cosmic energy or give thanks to nature gods or something. On the other side of the house, under the big pecan tree, there's a circle of stones and cleared soil. I wonder if they did their rituals there. And I've found little stone statues hiding in the underbrush around the property. They're sorta cool-looking, like something from ancient England."

"Honey, that's just sacrilege," Lashanda said, somberly still touching her cross. "If I were you, I'd just haul those things right out of here."

Joanne laughed. "Well, it's not like I believe such superstitious nonsense." *Or* your *religion, either,* she thought, but that she kept to herself.

The girls ran by, screaming with excitement, sticks stuck in their hair like antlers. Skip came running after, streaks of clay soil on his cheeks as war paint, a turkey feather in his hair. He brandished a toy bow -- time for the hunt!

"Your boy's really grown since we visited you in Newark, Joanne."

"Yeah. Too fast. Another reason why I came back. I need to slow down. The hustle and bustle of Newark tore me apart – the shootings, the gangs, rude drivers. The bosses were meaner. The winters were lots colder. I think it all made *me* colder, too. And it was so much more expensive. Maybe I do have country in my blood, like you said." She looked down at her lap and picked at her nails. "Living in a big city was too much. Too much for me. Too much for Peter. I guess that's what pulled us apart, in the end. I didn't want Skip growing up in that environment." Joanne slid her thumb up and down the glass. Cold sweat from its sides pooled at her nail. She had bitten it down to the quick. "Dad was part of coming back, too, of course."

Lashanda nodded. A moment of silence passed before Lashanda said, "You haven't shown me your yard, yet, honey. How about a walk?"

"You bet," Joanne answered. A quick look at Skip told her he was safely away from the Tates, so she got up and took Lashanda by the shoulder, leading her around the porch toward the back of the house. "You can see we have some marvelous flowers planted around here. The realtor said there were daffodils, but I got here too late to see 'em.

There's iris, and peonies, and, of course, lilac. Can't do without lilac, you know."

"I know already!" Lashanda rolled her eyes and laughed. "You've only bragged about them since you came back. And don't tell me again how the butterflies flock to them. It would be the trillionth time!"

Joanne shrugged. "Can I help it if I like butterflies?" She led Lashanda past the house toward the back fence line. "And back here we have a walnut...." Joanne gasped.

"What, honey?" Lashanda asked, looking around.

Joanne stood still, mouth agape, arms slack at her side. She felt the blood drain from her face.

In front of them lay the compost, fully exposed. The tangle of vines had been neatly parted, woven like a Celtic knot, undamaged. The spectacle looked wreath-like, like the crown of thorns turned on end.

"Oh, Joanne, that's beautiful!" Lashanda remarked.

Joanne snapped out of her shock. "But ... I didn't do it. It would've taken days for this! It's been no more than half an hour." She looked around in a panic. This was an elaborate trick, it had to be, but no one was around. The kids had been in sight the whole time, as had Lashanda.

"Well, honey, whoever – or whatever – did this, it's still beautiful."

Joanne didn't feel so sure.

And just inside the woven vines, staring out though the greenery, Joanne spotted one of those wiccan stone statues: a bearded man sitting cross-legged with deer antlers sprouting from his head and a moss-covered staff in his hand.

* * *

Shaken, Joanne ended the tour. Returning to the porch and keeping an eye on the fence line, Joanne fell back into an uneasy semblance of friendliness, chatting about the past with Lashanda and listening to the laughter of their children.

A couple hours later, Joanne asked them to stay for dinner, but they had to go. They walked slowly toward the driveway, side by side, calling to the girls that it was time. There was no hurry. Nothing seemed to hurry anymore since leaving Newark.

Skip and the girls finally came running up just as the women arrived at the car. "We'll come by next weekend and check up on y'all," Lashanda said.

Lashanda and the girls drove away as the cicadas started up, metallic and scraping. Dusk had come. The birds grew quiet, their nests swallowed by shadow.

Joanne turned from the driveway back toward the porch but stopped abruptly. An ember burned at the fence line some fifty yards away. A cigarette. A shadowy figure stood there smoking it, watching, bald head reflecting red with the growing sunset. Joanne raised an arm to wave, weak, like a child unsure of an answer. But the neighbor didn't move. The cigarette glowed again.

Joanne walked quickly to the porch, head down and tilted to hide her face with her hair. Once in the lap of her living room, she peeked out the window.

The man was gone.

* * *

The next morning came with a list of cleaning chores, and Joanne got to work at it. It had taken half an hour of struggling to pull the big kitchen stove from the wall and counters. Observing the mess beneath it, she was almost in tears. Beneath the appliance was a black crust, decades of filth caked on by time and untold generations of roaches. Undaunted, she got on her knees, pulled the soap bucket closer, and began scrubbing with a metal brush. Black clots came off in waves with each scrub, revealing flakes of ancient food and dead insects. She had only just exposed the linoleum beneath when a knock came from the front screen door. The loose wood banged against the frame with each beat, its wire mesh rattling.

"Momma, someone's at the door!" Skip yelled from the living room.

"Hello-o?" a woman sang.

Lord, what timing! Joanne thought. Her hands and chest were covered with debris and soap suds. "One minute," she yelled back and rushed to wash her hands in the sink.

Joanne turned the corner to see Skip standing in profile, looking toward the door. His face and arms were slack. He glanced back at her with the same skeptical look he'd had on his first day of school. Then she saw why.

"Hello, dear!" a woman said through the screen. She was short and squat with wide hips. Her hair was in a high, tight bun, and she wore a very plain, blue dress that hung loosely down to her ankles. She stared through the screen with wide eyes. Her nose was twisted as if it had been broken and never set correctly. Her gaping mouth revealed irregular and missing teeth.

"I'm Damsel Tate. Thought you might like a housewarmin'."

Joanne remembered her manners and approached the door. Damsel was holding a pie. Steam rose through the lattice crust on top.

"I'm glad to meet you, Mrs. Tate. I'm Joanne Crowley." She opened the door and held out her hand.

"Mind if I come in, dear? This pie's a bit hot!" Damsel replied, ignoring Joanne's hand.

"Of course." Joanne opened the door wide. The air was thick with apple and cinnamon. *Silly,* she thought, *she can't shake with a pie in her hands.*

"Moab!" Damsel grunted. "Come along!"

Joanne noticed a lanky teenager fidgeting at the edge of the porch. Just old enough to have peach-fuzz on his lip and an array of pimples, his hair was black and greasy. He wore a faded and ripped red tee-shirt, wet at the armpits, and frayed cutoffs. The boy shuddered at Damsel's command and slunk past Joanne into the living room.

"I apologize for my appearance," Joanne said. "I'm busy cleaning this morning."

"Oh, no matter, neighbor." The woman wore no makeup or jewelry. Hair grew thick on her upper lip. Damsel placed the hot pie onto the dining room table.

"Wait!" Joanne yelled. Damsel picked the pie back up in a huff. "Sorry," Joanne said. "The heat will damage the finish. Let me get a hot pad." Joanne rushed into the kitchen and returned with a potholder. "Here, this'll work." Damsel set the pie down on it.

"I'm Skip," Joanne's son said to Moab, but the teenager just flashed a smirk and returned his gaze toward Joanne's plate collection on the wall. He started to reach toward one but stopped, glancing sharply toward his mother.

"Would you like some tea, Mrs. Tate?"

"Yes, that'd be fine. And please, call me Damsel."

Joanne smiled, then popped into the kitchen, hastily grabbed pie plates and utensils, and returned to put them on the table.

In the moment before she disappeared again into the kitchen to get the tea, she saw Damsel jab a finger toward Moab and then point at the couch where Skip had sat down. Moab immediately dropped his eyes and plopped onto the couch next to Skip.

Joanne returned with the iced tea and poured a cup for Damsel.

"And what's your name, boy?" Damsel asked Joanne's son.

"Skip!" he chirped

"Is that a nickname?" Damsel replied.

Skip blinked and cocked his head. "No, that's my name."

"He's named after an uncle," Joanne said. "Here's your tea. Hope you like sugar in it."

"Of course." Damsel said it as if there were no other way.

"Would you like some pie?"

Moab looked up, eyes excited.

"No, no. We just ate." Damsel smiled and sipped at her tea. Joanne leaned against the wall. There was only the recliner, occupied by Damsel, and the couch where the two boys sat.

"Who's your favorite baseball team?" Skip asked Moab, but the teen just rocked back and forth, staring at the ceiling and picking his nose.

"Moab," Damsel said sternly, "be nice to the boy!" Moab immediately stopped rocking and looked down at Skip.

"Wanna see my rabbits?" Moab drawled. The words spilled from his slack mouth like syrup. Sores glared red and festering on his lips.

Skip answered slowly, glancing toward Joanne. "Okay."

"Um, maybe later, son," Joanne responded, remembering the other night. The cries echoed in her memory. "Right now you need to stay home."

Moab resumed his trance-like rocking.

"So tell me, Joanne," Damsel said, "where you folks from?"

"We just moved down from Newark."

Damsel stared without recognition.

"But I grew up in Masith," Joanne added.

"Oh!" Damsel remarked. "Just down the road! But you don't sound at all like you're from here."

Joanne smiled. "Guess I've been living with the Yankees too long, huh?" she said. Damsel smiled and nodded. "Damsel is such a charming name," Joanne added.

"It's from the Bible," Damsel answered, her head high, "King James Version, Book of St. Mark, Chapter Five, verses 38 to 42: 'And Jesus cometh to the house of the ruler of the synagogue, and seeth the tumult, and them that wept and wailed greatly. And when he was come in, he saith unto them, *Why make ye this ado, and weep? The damsel is not dead, but sleepeth.* And they laughed him to scorn. But when he had put them all out, he taketh the father and the mother of the damsel, and them that were with him, and entereth in where the damsel was lying. And he took the damsel by the hand, and said unto her, *Damsel, I say unto thee, arise.* And straightway the damsel arose, and walked; for she was of the age of twelve years. And they were astonished with a great astonishment.'"

Joanne listened patiently. Damsel recited the verses with all the vocalization of a preacher, staring off into the distance. She said "Jesus" with the accent on the first syllable, drawing out the second with a soothing tone like a young mother talking to her baby.

What a zealot, Joanne thought. "That's very interesting. So you were named after a girl who was brought back from the dead?"

Damsel took another drink, but she stopped abruptly. "Moab!" Joanne jumped at the sudden change in Damsel's voice. "Put your feet down. Ain't nice to put your feet on coffee tables!" She glared at her son, and the boy shifted and stared at his feet.

"So," Damsel said, back to her pleasant tone, "what denomination are you and your husband?"

Joanne blinked. "Um, we don't really go to church much. But I went to Masith Baptist Church as a girl."

Damsel lowered her glass. "Well, you can't be raisin' a young'n without our lord Jesus Christ lendin' a helpin' hand, now can you? We go to Faith Hill Evangelical, just over by Lawton Pharmacy. We'd be happy if you'd join us this Sunday. James will be leadin' prayer. Maybe you and the husband can meet some friends."

"Thanks," Joanne said. She smiled, lips tight.

"I didn't quite catch your husband's name, Joanne. And what does he do for a livin'?"

A moment of silence passed, accented by the couch springs as Moab rocked. "I'm recently divorced, Damsel. Peter's still in Newark."

Damsel's smile disappeared. She set her drink down on the floor and got up. "Well, it's been real nice talkin' to you, young lady, but I have to be movin' on. James'll want to take his lunch soon."

Joanne got up as well. "Um, well, it's been nice talking to you, too, Damsel."

"Mrs. Tate will do, dear. You can have your boy bring back the pie pan when you're through. Come along, Moab!" Damsel walked briskly through the door with Moab on her heels. The screen door slammed.

Joanne caught her breath as they left; there were red stains on the seat of Moab's pants. She looked quickly at the couch. Blood stained the fabric where the boy had been rocking.

THREE

"You unpacked yet?" Joanne's father asked as he cut into his steak. The meat was well done. The dull, serrated knife cut back and forth, sawing the flesh with wet rips. Charlie Hill's face was as gray and lined as his food. His faded blue eyes stared, half closed, at the meal he ate every Tuesday. His scarred table and dusty dining room seemed to reflect him. He hadn't looked the same since the heart attack a year ago. It was part of the reason she moved back.

"Not quite," Joanne answered. She sat at the other end of the table, hands folded, plate empty. "Still have boxes stacked in the closets. Probably stay that way a while. There are so many things I have to do! And I'm worried about the place in general. My neighbors are Southern stereotypes in the flesh. Trees threaten to fall all around my house, and the house itself is an inferno waiting to happen, what with all the 1930's wiring and old wood. Starting my job at the health clinic is hectic enough without having to worry about unpacking."

"Uh huh." Charlie continued eating without looking up. "So you think you're a nurse now?"

Joanne tensed her eyebrows. "Just a receptionist, Dad."

Charlie gulped his beer and ripped off another piece of meat. Dragged it through steak sauce. "So, where's Skip?"

"Lashanda's looking after him for a bit. She keeps him at her place during the days while I work. But he'll be with her a little longer today. Thought maybe we could spend a little time together, just you me, since you won't come out to see us. You know, it would do you good to get out to the country for a change."

Charlie sat up straight and stared at her, still chewing. "I get enough of the 'country' at the sawmill." He returned his gaze to his steak. "B'sides, who the hell are you to be tellin' me what's good for me? What do you know about the 'country' anyhow? You're just another one of them damned Easterners, movin' here to get away from it all. Hell, you ain't even talkin' like us anymore." Charlie ripped off a chunk of meat and shoved it in his mouth. A wad of fat clung to his lips before he sucked it in.

Joanne felt the heat rise in her neck. "Damn it, Dad! I came back because of you. Don't you get it?"

Charlie slammed his utensils down on the plate. Joanne flinched. "Because of me?" Charlie yelled. "Well ain't that a heart warmer! You go away for twenty years and now you want me to open my arms, is that it? I didn't hear from you for half those years! Came back because of me.... Well welcome back, Joanne Hill Crowley. Now my life's complete!"

Charlie resumed his meal.

Joanne fought the urge to wipe her eyes. Her lower lip quivered. "At least I've kept in touch the last few years. You know I care!"

"You called me once a month. It was always the same damned conversation. How's Skip? Fine. Did well in school. How's the weather? Gee, a bit colder here, isn't it? Peter's job is doin' fine. My work's goin' great. Okay. Gotta go. All my love."

"Well now I'm here, damn it! And you can see firsthand!" Joanne's words came out wet, pouring forth with renewed energy. "Skip needs you. *I* need you."

Charlie pointed a fork at his daughter. "I warned you twenty years ago not to run off with that yuppie, but you didn't listen. And where'd it get you? Meanwhile I'm left at the homestead, alone and watchin' my grandson grow up in pictures." Charlie wolfed down another piece of steak, chewing as he talked. "Now that yuppie's left you like I said he would and you come crawlin' back to me. Well I'll help you, Joanne, 'cause that's the way of things, but don't expect me to be forgettin' anytime soon."

Charlie took a long drink from his beer as Joanne wiped her eyes, sniffling. Charlie scowled. He handed her a napkin to blow her nose.

"Why the hell don't you get somethin' to eat? There's another steak in there, you know."

"I'm vegetarian, Daddy. I haven't eaten meat in years."

* * *

Joanne got home at seven o'clock. A storm was brewing fast. Wind had knocked down a number of tree limbs in the dozen miles between her father's and home. The usual smells of clay and pine were replaced by the pungent scent of ozone. Branches waved madly at her. Debris fell. Wind whipped at her hair. Everything had an odd, greenish tint.

Tornado weather. Turning on the car radio, her fears were confirmed when an emergency bulletin announced a tornado warning. She had to get to shelter in the middle of her home.

Lashanda was to drop Skip off around eight, so as soon as she pulled into the driveway, Joanne rushed toward the house to call and tell them to stay put.

But she stopped at the porch. A lean and lanky figure stood in the yard beneath a row of pines, seemingly impervious to the maelstrom of wind around him.

"Moab?"

The teen stood his ground and smiled, arms behind his back.

Joanne glanced at the front door but changed direction toward the boy. "Moab?" she called again, half trotting.

Pebbles of hail fell, and she shielded her face with her arm. Moab remained motionless.

Joanne got within touching distance and stopped. "Moab? What're you doing out here?" Joanne had to scream to be heard above the din.

Moab's smile widened. "Wanna see my rabbits?" he drawled.

Joanne cocked her head. "What? Moab, there's a storm coming! You need to get inside. I'll see your rabbits another day."

Moab moved his head slowly side to side. His smile was undiminished. "Ain't no better time for cleanin' rabbits." He leaned forward to the point where Joanne was sure he'd fall into her. "Pa cain't hear 'em scream." His eyes gleamed. Joanne was sure he chuckled, but it could have been the wind. She backed away. He took a step toward her.

Oh God! "Another time, Moab." She picked up speed as she retreated. The hailstorm increased. The hail crunched as she stepped. "I have to go, now. You get inside, okay?"

Moab pulled a rusty hand hatchet from behind his back.

Joanne gasped. She turned and ran to the porch. She couldn't hear anything over the wind and hail, but she didn't dare look back. She heard the ground crunching behind her. She felt the boy's breath at her back. She screamed and lunged onto the porch, grabbed a fire log and swung it behind her.

But no one was there.

Fighting for breath, Joanne brushed away her bangs and looked back toward the row of pines. She saw Moab climb over the fence and disappear into his family's land, swallowed by the wind-lashed bushes and underbrush.

She started to turn toward the door when she heard a loud crack over the wind. The crack was followed by another, and then a third. A huge limb crashed down in a hail of twigs and needles, smashing into the ground where Moab had been only moments before.

* * *

Hail had given way to driving rain by the time Joanne said goodbye to Lashanda. She kept the call brief. The reception kept cutting in and out, but she managed to say a few reassuring words to Skip to calm his fears. There certainly hadn't been tornadoes in Newark. She hung up and stood looking around the room. The electricity had flickered a couple times and gone out while they were talking. She thought briefly of checking the old fuse box, but the lights were off at the Tate's, too.

A huge thump came from the roof. Joanne jumped. *Branches*, she thought, *from the trees. Yes, that's it, from the elm or one of the pines behind the house.* But she stood still, silent, listening. There was only the constant pecking of the rain against the windows and the occasional whistle as the wind whipped around the corners of the house. The thin branches of a lilac scratched at a bedroom window, rhythmically, like a trapped animal.

Damned drafty house, Joanne thought. She couldn't stop imagining. Things were jumping on the roof, peeking around dark corners. And somewhere behind the neighbor's house a teenaged boy was probably hacking at rabbits with a rusty hatchet. She could almost hear the screams in the wind.

Joanne shivered and shook her head. She felt around in a couple drawers for some candles and matches. She knew the flashlights were stupidly still packed away in one of the closets. There was only a short, squat, aromatherapy candle her Aunt Margaret had given her for Christmas. She set it on the dining room table and lit it.

47

Soon the room smelled of vanilla and some fruity concoction. Shadows danced with the flame, growing longer and more animated the farther they were from the table. She sat in a stiff-backed chair and wrapped an afghan around her, listening to the fury outside, wishing she weren't alone. She pulled out her smartphone and tried to distract herself on the internet, but the glare from the screen seemed to make the shadows grow around her, and the connection was awful here without the wifi.

The house looked solid enough, but Joanne knew it was in a state of constant flux. Her mother would have called it "settling." The hardwood floors beneath the linoleum creaked with every step. The walls moaned and groaned with the wind. The windows shook, rattling the panes with every gust. The house was nearly a hundred years old. She sat there listening to these sounds and wondered why the whole house didn't fall down. *Maybe it will*, she thought. She wondered how many other people had lived in the house in all those years. And how many had died there.

Joanne wished that Skip were home, despite the weather, despite the tornado which Lashanda had said touched down twenty miles to the north. This wasn't a good night for loneliness. Her shoulders felt naked without Peter's broad hands to caress them. Now they were caressing someone else. Someone young and pretty who didn't live in a rundown shack in a rundown state.

Tears welled up and she started sobbing. She held her head in her hands and cried aloud for the first time since Peter had said, *I'm sorry, Joanne. I never meant to hurt you.* Tears came in a rush, spilling from the depths of her heart. *She works in the office*, he had said, *You don't know her.... Wish I could undo what I've done....* She still felt him squeeze her shoulder, trying to stop the tears. The touch had been as empty as their last years together. *I never meant to hurt you.*

She cried herself out and sat there, rocking slowly, listening to the rain die away.

But others had comforted Joanne before Peter. When the lights would go out as a child, her mother would light all the candles and gather the family close. "It's time to sing, now," her mother would say, and they would sing quietly, some church hymn. The monsters would slink away. Her parents would tell them stories about how they had grown up out on the farm, the "homestead" as they called it, milking the cows in the morning and going to sleep with the sun. Joanne would forget about the darkness, lost in their stories of Beatlemania, young sweethearts, and working their family's fields full of watermelons. She would be transfixed by the golden light of candles glittering in her parents' eyes.

"Momma, I wish you were here...." she whispered and pulled the afghan closer.

FOUR

According to the radio, the storm left behind it a hundred miles of destruction. A tornado, strong and early for the season, had destroyed the small town of Pine Meadows to the north. Examining the damage to her own property, Joanne wondered if it had not touched down in her yard as well.

"Lashanda," Joanne yelled. Her friend was across the yard, yanking at a branch that had fallen across the south fence. "See if you can find the saw. It should be in the back of the tool shed." Lashanda nodded and went toward the house.

49

"Hell of a storm," Joanne mumbled. She watched the kids play by the porch as she fumbled with her work gloves. The storm had lasted all night, and a number of large limbs had fallen on the house. A leak had developed under one of them, and she tried not to dwell on the cost of repairs. The yard was strewn with branches. A quaint little bird house that she and Skip had hung on the pecan tree had been smashed by a branch. It now lay in a heap of debris, four nestlings squashed beneath it. They lay one over the other, mouths cocked, eyes forever searching for Momma.

She stumbled on one of the rocks in that Wiccan circle under the pecan. Five large stones arrayed equidistant from one another around a cleared circle of soil pounded bare by constant usage, wide enough, she imagined, for one person to stand on each rock and not quite touch each other with arms outstretched. The thought conjured a picture of robed figures doing just that, chanting some mystical rites and calling to ... what? Spirits? Gods and goddesses? She didn't know.

She didn't want to know.

Joanne walked to the burn pile and threw the chick corpses and an armful of branches into a burn pile before the kids could find them. She doused the pile with gasoline.

She was about to light the pyre when she heard hammering from the Tates'. She spotted her balding neighbor across the fence. The man was rebuilding a rabbit hutch that had fallen over. One of a score of cages built at the base of a hill at the back of the Tate property, the little cage had been so ratty and rotten that Joanne had been sure it was abandoned.

Joanne heard sawing behind her from Lashanda, so she turned and joined her friend.

"I'm not very good with these things," Lashanda said, getting the saw stuck in the limb. Her right eye was bright red. Seeming to notice Joanne's gaze, she said, "I tried to pull off a green limb. Damned thing slipped out of my hand and whipped me in the eye."

"Sorry. I appreciate the help." Joanne added after a moment, "I've got a question for you."

"You ask me anything you want, girl." Sweat glistened on Lashanda's brown skin. She wiped her forehead with the back of her sleeve. "Shoulda worn short sleeves. Didn't know you'd be workin' me to the bone today! You owe me big-time, honey!"

Joanne smiled. "You know those crazy neighbors of mine?" Lashanda nodded. "Well, I think that's the husband right over there. Think I should tell him about his son?"

Lashanda raised her eyebrows. "That boy's dangerous. And that twisted little you-know-what prob'ly got it from his daddy. Lord Jesus! I think you'd better let it lie." She paused, then added, "Given what you told me about him and his momma, I think maybe you'd better forget what I said before about giving them the benefit of the doubt."

Joanne put her hands on her hips and licked her lips, tasting salt. She looked toward Tate. "I don't know. Never met the guy. But I think he ought to know his son's running around with a hatchet and hanging out on my property in the middle of a damned tornado!"

Lashanda shrugged. "Ain't my neighbor. You got my opinion." She went back to struggling with the saw.

Joanne walked toward the west fence without looking back at Lashanda. "Mr. Tate!" she yelled, waving. "Hey!" James Tate stopped hammering and looked toward her. Though far away, Joanne felt his eyes turn on her, burn into her, like a cattle brand into flesh. She shook her head. "Mr. Tate! I need to speak with you."

Tate walked the fifty yards or so toward the fence line, occasionally looking up at her. Joanne sensed an undefined threat with each step he took toward her. His heavy boots smashed through the bramble, crashing like a titan through a forest. He walked with his arms hanging limp. The hammer in his left hand hung down at an angle, the claws sharp and reflective. Sparrows that had flitted through the overgrowth now flew out of the man's path, shrieking warnings and carefully watching him with dark, reflective eyes.

Tate stopped about five yards from the fence. Bottomless eyes. Stained overalls. He stood still and silent, staring at her, unblinking, moving a plug of chewing tobacco from one cheek to the other with his tongue.

"Mr. Tate, I wanted to tell you about your son, Moab." Joanne's throat constricted. Her stomach quivered. Tate remained silent. Lines were deep on his face, and his skin hung loose from his neck and jowls; he looked to be a good twenty years older than his wife. "Um, last night, when I got home, the storm was just hitting. You see, Moab was just standing there, in my yard, getting hit by rain and hail." She pointed to the area. "He ... you see, he wanted me to see his rabbits. He had a...."

"What's the matter with standin' in your yard?"

"Well, it wasn't the standing in my yard that bothered me, though I was concerned he'd get hurt. It was the fact that he had a hatchet and wasn't responding to me. He was threatening me. I think you need to talk to him about this."

"Woman, you don't need to be tellin' me how to raise my son." Tate's words were heavy, deep, the voice of a prison guard.

"Um, no, of course not! I wouldn't presume.... I ... I just wanted to say that, last night, he brandished the hatchet and said...."

"I don't give a rat's ass what he said to you, woman." Tate let the hammer swing back and forth like a pendulum. It glittered in the noontime sun. "Moab ain't got sense God gave a goose. But I'll raise him how I see fit, understand?"

Joanne started to speak but was cut off.

"He don't need no schoolin' puttin' crazy ideas about people comin' from apes," Tate continued, "and he don't need no Yankee big city woman and her nigger friend tellin' me how to raise him, neither."

She put her hands on her hips. "Excuse me?" Blood rushed into her face. "Don't talk about my friend that way!"

Tate switched the hammer to the other hand. The tips of a couple fingers had been cut off at some point and healed over. "Now, Moab ain't s'posed to be comin' over to yer property. It won't be happenin' again, you hear? He'll be gettin' his lickins."

Joanne gasped. "Mr. Tate, it wasn't anything worth whipping for. I'm just concerned...."

Tate took a couple quick, heavy steps toward the fence. Joanne shut up and stepped back. "You don't worry yer little head, woman. It's all in the family." Joanne caught a whiff of the man, a mixture of sweat, tobacco, and motor oil. "But I cain't expect you to be understandin' the importance of family, now can I? Given how you run off and left your husband and your Godly vows, Jezebel. My wife told me about you."

"Now listen here!" she said, pointing at him. "You don't know jack shit about me."

"And foul-mouthed to boot." He spit tobacco juice onto the ground between them and wiped his mouth with the back of his hand. "I feel right sorry for that young'un o'yours, growin' up without his father. No man in his life to guide him in the ways of Jesus."

What a bastard, she thought. "Tate, you just keep your kid off my property and away from my son. Got it?"

"An' you just mind yer own business o'er here," Tate said. They stared at each other for another moment, then he slowly turned and lumbered off, mumbling, "Twern't nothin' to call the sheriff for."

Joanne watched after him, breathless, feeling dark clouds had lifted only to hang at the horizon. "Good fences make good neighbors," she muttered. But the heaviness of the moment continued to weigh on her as she turned, walked to the debris pile, and lit an oiled rag. The gas-soaked pile exploded in a burst of raging reds and yellows, crackling in anger as rain-soaked limbs burst open. Sap from pine branches screamed and bubbled out of the wood, burning away to sooty smoke. The little bodies of the chicks turned black in the sudden heat. She shuddered and looked up through the flames toward the house, watching Skip as he sat on the porch swing, his image warped and twisted by the heat.

* * *

Joanne stood in the doorway of Skip's bedroom. The room was lit only by an antique desk lamp in the corner. A Russian egg sat beneath it, sweeping circles and flowers painted on its surface. A memento from Peter's trip to Moscow two years ago, it was an island of radiant elegance amid kids' books and Star Wars action figures. Skip lay in bed, half-covered. Mickey Mouse danced across his pajamas.

"Ready for bed so soon?" Joanne asked. "Don't you want to read with me first? Tonight's *Bunnicula* again!"

Skip hunkered down and shook his head.

Joanne sat on the corner and tucked him in. "What's wrong, kiddo?"

Skip shrugged.

"Aren't you happy here? You've got a big yard to run in, a big room, and woods all around to explore, just like Davy Crockett."

"Who?"

"Nevermind."

"It's okay here, I guess," Skip mumbled.

Joanne rubbed her aching back. "You miss Daddy, don't you?"

Skip nodded.

"I do too, kiddo, I do too." Joanne lowered her head. She had Skip call Peter at least once a week.

"I wanna go back to Newark," Skip said. "I don't like it here. I miss my friends. I miss Daddy."

"You've got friends. What about Aunt Lashanda's girls, Destiny and Kayla?"

"They're just kids."

Joanne suppressed a smile. Lashanda's twins were only a year younger at six years old. "School will start in about a month. Then you'll have more friends than you know what to do with."

Skip nodded. "Sure. Beats Moab." The boy shivered and pulled the covers closer.

Joanne's smile died suddenly. "Have you been playing with him?"

"He took me to see his rabbits a couple days ago when I took back that pie plate. He's ... weird. Keeps all his rabbits in tiny cages full of poop." His voice dropped to a whisper. "He doesn't like them much. *Not at all.*"

Joanne swallowed hard. "Then why'd he take you to see them?"

Skip paused and pulled his pillow to his chest. "He wanted to show me how to clean them. They needed it! They were all muddy and covered in poop and had flies all over them." He scratched his nose and sniffled. "He went into a little building, and I figured he'd get a washcloth or something, but he came back with a saw. 'What are you going to do with that?' I asked, and he said, 'Cleanin' time. Keep an eye out for my pa.' He took a rabbit out of a cage, then he said, 'Get a listen to this.'"

Skip looked away and started shaking. His eyes glazed over.

Oh God, she thought. *Not that. Anything but that....*

"Skip? Tell me, son."

A tear rolled down Skip's cheek. His lip began to quiver.

"Did he.... Did he hurt the bunny?"

"He started sawing, Momma, right into the little bunny!"

Joanne reached out and pulled Skip close. He sobbed into her shoulder. "The bunny was crying, Momma! She was crying ... and kicking ... but Moab just smiled and sawed. He wouldn't stop, Momma, he wouldn't stop!"

"Shh, Skip, it's all over now.... You don't ever need to go near him again."

"I ran back, momma! But he yelled at me that I'd better not tell you or anyone or he'd clean me too!" Tears rolled down his cheeks and he squeezed her. "I wanna go home!" His crying took on a desperate keen. "I wanna go home!"

Joanne held the boy close, shielding him against the shadows. The wailing from her son turned her cold inside. Her eyes narrowed. She felt the darkness invade her. She patted Skip on the back and looked out his window at the inky darkness.

FIVE

Joanne had always dreamed of owning a garden. The townhouse that she and Peter had in Newark had nothing more to offer than a couple window boxes and some shelf space for spider plants. Here there was room for the sort of garden her mother had maintained, so wide that it took all day just to hoe it all. Joanne didn't have time for that. Right now, she'd be happy with a couple rows of okra and peas. The only okra she'd had in Newark was almost always frozen in bags, since it couldn't grow well that far north. Her plants were doing well, but weeds were making another stand at the base of the stalks.

Joanne paused in her weeding to wipe her brow with the back of a sweaty hand. Earth crumbled beneath her knees. As she wiped her head, she saw one of those stone foot-high Wiccan statues sitting off to the edge of the garden, half-covered by honeysuckle vines. This one was a big-breasted lady with a crescent moon on her forehead. Joanne couldn't tell if the statue lady was pregnant or just chubby, but the look on this one's face was contented. Lashanda may have thought these statues were evil, but Joanne got a good feeling from this one.

She turned her attention over to her son, who was a few rows away. "How's it going, Skip?"

"Fine, Momma!" he called back. He didn't bother to look up from the strip of carrot seed he'd been laying in a furrow. *Put in, cover, pat...* he mouthed as he performed the actions, covering the seeds with a thin layer of dirt just as his mother had told him.

Joanne returned to her work, pulling a large stone out of the reddish, clay-rich soil and tossing it aside. She plunged her hand into tilled soil and pushed some into the stone's hole. She inhaled its scent, organic and moist, and smiled. There was something satisfying about dirt under the fingernails, sweat from productive labor, the promise of sustenance from well-tended earth. She had forgotten the feeling.

Joanne moved to pull some more weeds. "Oh, shit," she whispered. Inches from her face was a cluster of small, black insects in the crook of an okra stem. "Aphids!" She reached out and smashed the bugs with her thumb. A goo of black bodies and sappy guts clung to her fingertips, making mud of the dirt there. Joanne stood up and inspected the plants. Nearly every one had a colony or two of the incessant pests feeding off the plants' sugars.

"Damn. Damn, damn, damn!" She smashed colony after colony, but there were too many. "What I'd give for a healthy dose of ladybugs!" She didn't want to use chemical pesticides. Resolving to order some ladybugs to kill the insects, she returned to her weeding, yanking the succulent plants out by their roots. Each came out with a rip and earthy crumble, the sound of biting into corn on the cob. She threw their ragged carcasses into a wheelbarrow by the handful. But the thought of the aphids kept returning. The weeds she could control. The aphids ... even big-time farmers with expensive pesticides couldn't control their populations.

Joanne ripped the weeds faster and faster. Grass. Henbit. Wild morning glory. Sweat rolled down her face, soaked her collar. Her armpits were drenched. Her back was wet. The weeds came out in twos, then threes, then handfuls at a time, turning the earth as they were uprooted. But the aphids were still there, mocking her, greedily sucking the sap from her winter meals, her harvest, her promise of sustenance. She could almost hear them swarming, crawling over each other, piercing the stalks with their needle-like mouths, bleeding them dry....

"Momma?"

"What is it!" It was a shout, the spawn of her anger. She shook her head, softened the lines of her face, exhaled. "What is it, honey?"

"Momma, why do these bugs like me so much?"

Skip stood about a yard away, half hidden from Joanne by okra stalks. But she saw little blips moving on his arms and clothes.

"Momma?" His voice was urgent, unsure.

Joanne stepped quickly through the okra, ignoring the irritating pricks of microscopic thorns on the stalks, and approached him. More insects flew around them, buzzing, landing on their pants and sleeves. Skip furiously brushed them off, breathing heavy.

Joanne also beat at the insects, but she stopped abruptly. They were beetles. Red, glossy, with black dots.

"Ladybugs!"

"Mom!"

The beetles were flying in and landing on everything, hundreds of them. Joanne grabbed Skip's flailing hand and led him away from the garden. "It's okay, honey, it's all right." She squatted to his height and brushed some of the insects off the panicked boy's face and arms. "It's okay. They won't hurt you. They're going to eat all the bad insects. They're our friends."

Skip pulled off his shirt and brushed the beetles from his chest. "I hate them!" he yelled, stomping on his shirt. "I hate them! I don't ever want to garden again!" He ran off toward the house.

Joanne sighed heavily and, standing, picked up the shirt. She wiped her brow and turned to look at the peas and okra. Ladybugs scurried over leaves and stalks, little tigers on the prowl in the garden jungle, eating aphids with powerful jaws, ripping apart juicy abdomens with mandibles as sharp as saws.

So much for Skip's interest in gardening, she thought. *When the gods wish to curse you, they answer your prayers.* "Must've been a big hatch, lately," she said aloud. She exhaled sharply and shook her head. *So weird. I was just thinking about ladybugs!*

Joanne looked at her watch. Two o'clock. They were an hour late to visit her father. She looked up a moment more to wonder at the sight of all the insects before following her son to the house, leaving the jungle to the tigers.

* * *

"There's my boy!" Charlie said, and held his arms out to his grandson. Skip ran across Charlie's living room into the old man's tight embrace. "Good to see you, son!"

"Good to see you too, Grandpa."

Charlie's living room was dusty and forlorn. Mementos sat piled on yellowed doilies around the room.

"You like it out there in the woods? Huh? Better than a big, polluted city, isn't it?" Charlie took a drag from a Marlboro and blew the smoke out the side of his mouth.

"Sure, Grandpa." Skip looked away from Charlie's eyes, shuffled his feet, stuck his hands in his pockets.

"Come now! I bet you've been exploring animal trails and climbin' trees, huh?"

Joanne sat in the corner of Charlie's living room, watching impassively, fading into the couch.

Skip shrugged. "The woods scare me, Grandpa."

"That's just 'cause you been in the city too long, is all. Now the *trees* are your skyscrapers." Charlie raised his hands high, imitating a canopy. Light filtered through faded curtains. A layer of smoke hung ghost-like in the air.

"Well ... it's like when I'm outside and I know Momma's watching me. I can feel her doing it, you know?" Skip explained, glanced up, returned his gaze to the floor. "Well it's like someone's watching me like that. And the woods are so ... empty. Back in Newark we'd go to the park, and all the animals would be there. But here all the animals run away. The birds stop singing. And it's like I'm walking through a big room, like my old school's cafeteria, only no one's there. It's just me and...."

Skip glanced back at his mom.

"It's all right, kiddo," Joanne said. "Hey, if I remember correctly, seems like Grandpa said he'd get you some chocolate chip cookies next time you came."

"Really?" Skip's eyes opened wide. He turned toward Charlie, smiling.

"You bet, my boy! What ya say to checkin' out the ol' cookie jar, huh?"

Skip ran off toward the kitchen. Porcelain clinked.

"Have all ya want, buddy," Charlie yelled.

"Okay, Grandpa!" came the muted response, mouth full of cookie.

Charlie's smile faded. "What's going on, Joanne?" His voice was low, gruff, demanding.

Joanne sighed. "I'm worried, Daddy." She felt as if the shadows engulfed her. "It's the neighbors. I don't dare let Skip go in the woods anymore. Not without me. Frankly, I don't let him run around in the yard without staying in sight of the windows. He's already having nightmares every...."

"Can I go pet the dogs, Momma?" Skip yelled from the kitchen.

Joanne paused. Charlie answered for her. "You bet, my boy! Take 'em some dog biscuits, too!"

"Thanks," Skip yelled back. The back screen clanged; its springs vibrated wildly like a clock thrown to the ground.

"Last night I heard the rabbits again," Joanne continued. "Skip heard them, too, so I had him listen to his music with his earbuds on." She pulled at a loose thread on her blouse. "I've called the sheriff, but they just said they'd look into it and get back to me."

"You've always been so damned sensitive, Joanne, just like your momma."

"What the hell's that supposed to mean?"

"Remember when I was on the road, truckin' that summer? That dog came and kilt a dozen chickens? What did your momma do about it?"

"We called animal control."

"And what came of it? Nothin'. And the damned mutt did it again. *You can't count on folks takin' care of your problems for you.*" Charlie ground the cigarette into an overflowing ash tray. "When I came home I marched straight over to Bill McCain's place and told him his dog was a killer. Stopped the problem, then and there."

"And they killed the dog, too."

"There's a reason, Joanne. Once a dog tastes blood there's no stoppin' it. It's just the nature of a dog. People ain't no different."

"What? You're telling me I have to kill my neighbor before he kills me? Is that it?"

"Of course not! Damn, you can be so dense!" Charlie shut his eyes, squeezed them tight. "What I'm sayin' is that you have to walk your little butt over there and talk to him. Your neighbor ain't gonna stop his boy 'til you reason with him."

"I've tried, Daddy! Damn it, I've tried! I already told you what he's like. He's just so...." Joanne shut her eyes and fought the urge to scream.

"Then I guess you'll just have to do a better job of convincing the Sheriff." Charlie stood up. His thin, sleeveless T-shirt hung loose from his bony shoulders. He turned to leave the room but stopped.

"And don't think I haven't noticed how you've lost your accent. Maybe you'd feel better here if you just admit your roots."

Charlie walked out of the room, creaking the wood floor with each step. The smoke followed in maddened swirls, like the souls of the lost.

The back screen clanged again. "Hey, my boy!" Charlie's voice called out, distant, fading. Bloodhounds bellowed in excitement.

Joanne reached out and took the cigarette butt, placed it in her mouth, inhaled deeply. "Admit my roots," she mumbled, closing her eyes. She exhaled a plume of smoke. "I'll be more comfortable when those damned neighbors are gone." She took another drag. "Yeah, when they're gone. If I just had proof of the rabbit killings."

Joanne opened her eyes wide, fixed on the distance. "If I just had the proof...."

SIX

Joanne dropped her coffee as she heard the first scream. The cup smashed to the floor. Steaming droplets flew. Shards scattered. But the sound of the crash was overwhelmed by the rabbit's desperate pleas for release. The wracking cries rose and fell as if the poor beast were being skinned alive in spurts of slicing. Maybe it was. The screams tore through the chill morning breeze, stood the hair on Joanne's arms.

Joanne acted fast. She had prepared and waited for days. She bolted out the door, grabbing her digital camera on the way out. Fresh from the shop, the camera and zoom lens cost her a precious $700.

The sun peeked over the eastern horizon as Joanne sprinted to her back fence and climbed over to a pasture. The cry hounded her, begged her to run away, escape, hide behind the nearest bush. But she ignored the jabbering, halting squeals as saw met bone or hatchet met tendon. *Stay focused*, she thought, and ran around a patch of poison ivy toward the back of Tate's property. But James Tate's words hung in her brain. "Moab ain't s'posed to be comin' over to your land.... He'll be gettin' his lickins." Joanne shuddered. *What lickins will I get if* I'm *caught?*

The route was planned. She would go in through the back of the Tates' and hide amongst the rabbit hutches until she got a clear shot. *A clear shot. Proof! Then that little bastard Moab will get his just rewards! The Tates'll be taken away, and the rabbits will be released.*

She climbed another fence, Tate's property. Her jeans caught on a line of rusty barbed wire.

"Damn it!" she cursed under her breath. With a yank she was free, ripping a two-inch gash in her jeans. Her leg stung, but she ignored it. Before her lay a low hill with scattered trees and brambles growing over her head. *Just over that hill,* she thought. *Then I'll get to the rabbit hutches.*

The screaming grew in pitch and volume, wavering, echoing. Joanne had just started through the brambles when it stopped suddenly. She stopped too, and all was silent.

Damn! Joanne thought. *I'll never catch him. But maybe I'll get a pic of the aftermath.* She continued more carefully through the undergrowth. Blackberry thorns tugged at her shirt. Sparrows jumped from vine to vine to avoid her.

Joanne finally came to a small animal trail winding through the brush. She followed it, bending low to fit through its confines.

It took longer than she thought, but she finally neared the top of the hill. A ramshackle shed sat buried in the brush, leaning heavily on termite-infested supports. The roof was made of rusted tin sheets. An ancient layer of dull paint had all but flaked away from the walls, exposing gray boards beneath. But she caught her breath as she saw a window in the side of the outbuilding. All six of the warped panes had a bloody handprint pressed on them from the inside, brown and clotted with age. The prints were deliberate, fingers splayed -- an advertisement of murder. She took a picture.

Stepping closer, she dared to look through the dark, open doorway of the shed. The smell of rot hung heavy in the air. Fat flies buzzed in the fetid atmosphere. The morning sunlight slanted into the building, showed a massive, decaying pile of furry bodies. Dead bunnies. Hundreds of them, in various states of decomposition. She brought up her camera and snapped several pictures of the open doorway and the wretched charnel pile.

A man-made trail stretched north away from the outbuilding toward the Tate house. Joanne moved to follow the trail but stopped. Moab emerged over the hill, walking toward her, following the path to the shed.

She rushed back into the cover of the bramble.

He carried in his hands the bloody and mutilated remains of a rabbit. Fluffy white hair was drenched with crimson. An eye stared sightless from the flesh. Blood dripped from Moab's hands, covered his shirt and pants, glistened on the handsaw hanging from his belt. A smirk played on his lips.

Joanne considered running, but Moab slowed as he approached the shack. She decided to hold her ground, invisible in the undergrowth. Fighting the urge to vomit, she remembered her mission. With shaking hands, she raised the camera and snapped a couple pictures through the brush.

Moab stopped at the doorway of the shack and tossed in the remains. She heard the body hit the pile with a thump. "That's a good bunny!" he chirped. He turned back and crouched, facing away from Joanne. "Who's next? Here, bunny bunny bunny. It's cleanin' time!" He reached to his belt and drew out the handsaw. "Gotta flush you out!" He sprang like a leopard and ran along the path and over the hill. His footfalls faded and disappeared.

Joanne still shook. *God! What a fucking nutcase!* "Got the picture...." she whispered to herself, but she knew it wasn't enough. Those photos wouldn't prove he did it. They would only show he carried the rabbits afterward. "Gotta catch him in the act. Gotta get proof!" She stepped out of the brush and followed Moab.

Once over the hill, Joanne could see the Tate property laid out. Moab was maybe sixty yards down, past the rabbit hutches. His family's house stood just north of him, sheltered by trees. Joanne's house lay behind some trees and fence line off to the right.

She moved stealthily, head low. Her heart raced. Her leg and arms stung as sweat settled into her cuts.

Joanne came to the cages. The wood was rotten. The wire was rusted. And inside sat scrawny, mangy rabbits, covered in feces, infested with disease. Joanne looked away, but she looked back again through the camera lens and pressed the shutter release. Tears threatened to cloud her vision, to blot out the insanity. The rabbits merely looked back, glassy, and huddled in the dark, fungal corners of their hutches to await their fate.

A squeal rose up, not of death, but simply of escape. *He's grabbed another!* Joanne rushed down the path toward the noise. It led to a cleared area off to the left of the house. Reaching the Tate house, she crept along the back wall, stepping over bits of broken concrete foundation and strips of wood fallen from the paint-flaked walls. Little more than a shotgun shack, occasional cracks in the wall spoke of the lack of insulation; Joanne saw right into some of the rooms through the walls. Flowery wallpaper hung loose from the inner walls, sagging over tables of jumbled auto parts, taxidermy animals, and fishing gear.

A low door and window set into the foundation led under the house. Live things moved inside. The stench of too many dogs. *Dogs!* she thought. For fear of alerting the dogs and giving away her presence, she made a wide swing away from the door then back to the side of the house on the other side.

An old stump sat near the back door to the house. Fresh blood painted the top crimson. Rust-colored blood crusted the rest like some Aztec sacrificial altar. Moab stood over it. He held a kicking rabbit by the scruff, struggling to push it down onto the stump and hold it there. The rabbit's eyes were wide, rolling, searching for a place to run.

Joanne hid behind a large oak. A lean-to against the tree covered three gas cans stacked upon each other. Crouching behind the cans, she readied her camera and took a couple pictures. The heady fumes of gasoline assaulted her nostrils.

"It's cleanin' time!" Moab announced. He held the rabbit by the neck and brandished the saw.

The back door burst open. A screen clanged. Steps creaked.

"What the hell are you doin', you little bastard?" James Tate bellowed. "I was willin' to forget the first un, but now you'll be payin'!" Moab dropped the saw and backed away. The rabbit darted off the block and disappeared into the bushes. "What, by merciful God, have I told you!"

Joanne sank behind the cans. The man rounded the corner of the house. The top of his overalls hung down past his waist revealing a white tee-shirt clinging tightly to his muscles. A three-foot willow switch extended from his fist. He swept it through the air with a whoosh, slapped it against the house. Paint chips flew.

"You're gettin' your lickins now, boy!"

Damsel ran out, nearly tripping on the steps in her long, plain nightgown. *She'll stop the madness*, Joanne thought. The housewife knelt on the ground, head down, weeping, hands clutched at her forehead in prayer.

"Oh precious lord!" Damsel prayed. "Give us the strength to teach your lessons! Your light shineth upon us!"

Tate pointed to the block. "Get yer butt over here, boy!"

Moab complied, shuffling to the bloody block. Tate immediately grabbed Moab by the back of the head and pushed him down, rubbing his face in the clotted blood and scraps of flesh. "Bad!" Tate yelled. "Bad!"

Joanne gasped and grabbed her chest. *Oh God!*

"Pull down yer britches!" Tate commanded. Moab bent over the block and did as told. His bare buttocks were scabbed, lined, scarred. Red whelps crisscrossed wounds both new and old. Infections ravaged his skin. Tate pushed the boy's face back into the blood. Shaking, Joanne snapped a couple more pictures.

"'But truly I am full of power by the spirit of the Lord,'" Damsel recited, "'and of judgment, and of might, to declare unto Jacob his transgression, and to Israel his sin.'"

Joanne's stomach turned and the taste of bile filled her mouth. She looked away, searching the best route of escape. Then she heard the air split, skin slap. She turned back. The whip flew in the air, rhythmic, landing again and again against the boy's raw skin.

No! Joanne wanted to yell. Burst forth. Stop the violence. But fright froze her to the spot. Ripped the breath from her.

Moab grimaced with each whip but remained silent, eyes steady, detached. He didn't flinch when branch met flesh.

Damsel chanted, eyes closed, head down. "'For whereas my father put a heavy yoke upon you, I will put more to

68

your yoke: my father chastised you with whips, but I will chastise you with scorpions.'"

The switch flew back and forth, red at the tip. Tate heaved, muscles bulging. He breathed heavy, eyes narrow, mouth open, striking with a fist clenched upon the stick.

Joanne raised the camera and snapped more pictures. *I've got you, you sick bastard! You're going away for this!*

Pictures taken, Joanne crept from the scene, stepping deliberately, carefully, glad to look away from the horror taking place.

"'And if ye will not yet for all this hearken unto me, then I will punish you seven times more for your sins,'" Damsel chanted.

Joanne knelt for a moment at the foundation door to take a last picture.

But she fell off balance.

She tried to catch herself against the back of the house. Her ankle turned. She fell sidelong into the little door under the foundation. She had hardly knocked the wood with her shoulder when brown hunting hounds assaulted the little window, baying in excitement. The air filled with their howls. The door rattled against the padlock as they sought to push it open.

Damsel stopped chanting. The whoosh of the switch fell silent.

Joanne gasped and looked toward the Tates. James stomped toward Joanne, switch in hand.

"You heathen bitch!" he bellowed. "What the hell are you doin' here? You'll get your lickins, too!"

Joanne screamed and sprinted toward the trail, back the way she'd come. She didn't dare look back. The camera swung with each frantic stride.

"You stop, woman! I'm gonna whip you good!" Tate's voice was low and resonant, like a bomb exploding. "My property! By the Lord's sweet justice, I will stand my ground against you, Jezebel! You're lucky I didn't fetch my shotgun!"

"Git 'er, Husband!" Damsel yelled, "Give 'er justice!"

Joanne raced up the hill through the hutches and passed the shed. Her breaths came quick and shallow. Her sides ached. She burst into the underbrush and slammed through the brambles and thorns. "Help!" she screamed. "Help me!" But she knew no one would hear.

Tate crashed through as well, tripping and catching himself in the vines where she had slipped through. "You run, woman! You run! Ain't no hidin' from the eyes of the Lord! Ain't no forgivin'!"

A breathless glance behind her showed the man wallowing in the undergrowth, the trail disappearing before him. The bramble came alive and curled around his limbs, thorns cutting through the flesh like knives. His face contorted, eyes wide and focused, burning into her.

But the more he struggled, the more the greenbrier wrapped around his ankles and wrists.

Joanne cleared the brush and leapt the fence, falling and rolling on the other side into the pasture, then she dashed toward her house and climbed her fence. Finally on her own property.

From behind she heard cursing and the angry chittering of birds. She stopped and looked back.

Blue jays and sparrows dive-bombed Tate, a good dozen of them, circling his head, crashing against him to circle again. He swept at them with switch and hand. Bayed like the hounds. Knocked a couple out of the air. Still they came, drawing blood. Their chirps and twitters came out bitter and angry, the cry of protecting nestlings.

The vines were losing their grip.

Joanne put her hand to her mouth, unmoving, as she watched the commotion. Nature had turned against him. *How?*

Tate stopped attacking the birds and looked toward her. He stared, intent. Dark eyes radiated a burning hatred.

Joanne stared back, chest heaving, backing away from the fence. Then she ran again, turning to look only when she was next to her house.

Tate ripped his hands and legs free from the vines. Turned. Walked away, still fighting the birds. His scalp bled from a dozen talon and beak wounds.

Joanne sprinted up to her house and locked the front door behind her. She checked to make sure Skip was still sleeping, then she stepped to the phone. Pausing to catch her breath, she dialed those all-too-familiar three digits on her cell phone.

"Hello. I'd like to report a case of child abuse and animal cruelty...."

SEVEN

"Daddy!" Joanne opened wide her front door. Her father stood on the porch, his old, faded John Deere hat in his one hand and a large Walmart bag in the other. Moths fluttered around him seeking the comfort of the porch light, banging their heads against the lamp casing.

"Hi, Muffin."

Joanne blinked several times before she caught herself. He hadn't called her that since she was nine years old. "Come in, Daddy."

Charlie flashed a tight smile and walked across the threshold, looking around the living room. The bag swung at his side.

Joanne shut the door and locked it, glancing at the shadows in the yard out of habit. She caught the mixed scents of Old Spice and pine shavings. "What do you think of the place?"

"Could use some new paint out there. And you'll be needin' to strip off that worn linoleum sometime."

"Grandpa!" Skip hollered, running from the kitchen.

"Hey, my boy!" Charlie got on his knees and hugged the boy tightly. "You been a good boy for your momma?"

Skip nodded vigorously, wincing a moment as his face rubbed against his grandfather's stubbly jawline.

"Well," Charlie continued, releasing the boy, "good boys deserve toys, don't they?" He handed the shopping bag to Skip.

Skip smiled and looked up at his mother.

"Go on, son. Open it!" Charlie beckoned.

Skip pulled out a box decorated with pictures of a large, red barn and farm animals. He blinked and cocked his head.

"It's your own farm!" Charlie said. "Now you can be a country boy, just like your grandpa!"

"Thanks, Grandpa." Skip stood, holding the box, staring down at it with a look of both happiness and bewilderment. Joanne knew what he was thinking. It wasn't anything like the game system he'd been begging for.

"Now go set it up in your room. I'll be there in a few minutes to show you how the tractor works."

"Okay!" Skip ran off down a hallway.

Charlie's smile lingered. "He's a good boy. You've done good raisin' him, Joanne."

"Thanks, Daddy," Joanne replied, blinking. She stepped up, took his hat, and set it on the coffee table. "Why are you being so friendly?"

Charlie winced. "Hon, I really came by to tell you.... Hell, I'm proud of you for doing what you did. It was the right thing, though I sure as hell woulda gone about it differently!"

Joanne smiled weakly. "Thanks, I guess."

"And ... maybe I've been a bit unforgiving." Charlie wrung his hands and looking away. "After all, you moved down here to be nearer to me. Finding out you were in danger somehow brought it home."

Joanne stepped forward and held him tightly, closing her eyes, surprised at her father's strong back muscles hidden in his thin frame.

Joanne released her father and stood back. Charlie smiled but swayed in embarrassment.

"If it were daytime, I'd show you the yard and garden," Joanne said, "but I'll at least show you around the house."

"Joanne, I think I'd rather you tell me what's been going on around here, huh? Have they caught the boy, yet?"

Joanne sighed again. A cigarette smoldered in an ashtray on the table, an open pack of Marlboro Lights next to it. It had been a decade since she stopped smoking, but the urge overtook her and she'd started again.

"Moab's still out there, somewhere," she explained. "The detective said they thought they spotted him out by Pitcher Lake. They have a deputy drive by here every few hours, though, just in case. He's slippery. Jumped right out of their hands and ran to the woods."

"I read the paper today at the sawmill. They've got that sonofabitch father of his locked up in Masith Jail."

"Yeah. The photos I took were helpful. They say I may be called to testify in a couple months." Joanne walked over to the table and sat in a chair with a thump. She grabbed the cigarette and took a drag, closing her eyes. "Bastard's tried twice to get out. Claims God showed him the way to escape. The paper said his wife's at the county jail."

Charlie sat in the other chair. "When'd you start smokin'?"

Joanne took another drag. Embers glowed at the base of unflicked ashes. She tapped them into the ashtray. "I quit before Skip came along. Just felt like starting again, I guess."

Charlie cleared his throat and hacked. He pulled out a handkerchief, raised it to his mouth, and deposited phlegm with his tongue. He shoved the cloth back into his pocket. Joanne didn't miss the irony that she'd just taken up cigarettes again but was sitting across from a man who was suffering from their effects.

"Humane Society came a couple days after and took the rabbits and dogs away," Joanne continued. "The paper said there were over two hundred bunnies crammed back there! A lot of them are so diseased they'll have to be put down. And there were a dozen hounds under that house."

"Grandpa! I'm ready!" Skip yelled from his room.

"Comin', Skip!" Charlie stood up. His knees and back popped.

"I'm glad you came by, Daddy."

Charlie flashed a smile and winked. "Ain't nothin', Muffin." He turned and walked down the hallway. "Rev up the tractor, my boy!"

Ain't nothin', Muffin. She smiled. She'd forgotten how he used to say that.

Grandson and Grandpa, their voices carried down the hall. Memories of her youth trickled back to her, long hidden beneath teenage arguments and years of separation. Suddenly she was eight again, and a little yellow pup was placed in her hands. "We'll call 'im Silver," her daddy had said, "'cause he cost me a silver dollar." She could still smell the new puppy. And then there was that old green Schwinn he'd bought and fixed up for her. Christmas morning of her tenth year, it was bright and shiny, like new, with promises of wind through her hair and summer rides along tree-lined roads.

Something moved to her left.

Joanne turned. There was only the window and the raven blackness beyond. Water dripped in the kitchen. Toys clinked in Skip's room.

She stood and flipped off the light. It took a moment for her eyes to adjust, but she could see outside. An azalea bush rustled with a breeze. The moonlight glowed a ghostly white on the lawn.

A twig snapped just outside the window. Then came a hollow, thumping sound, like water chugging out of a gallon jug.

Joanne backed away. "Daddy?" she called.

"Yes, Jo Ann?" His words echoed down the hallway, jovial. It was the first time she'd heard true happiness in his voice in decades. She didn't want to ruin the mood, didn't want to end his moment of joy. But the hollow sound came again, farther away, toward the porch.

"Daddy? I think someone's outside."

Charlie came back to the dining room. "Why are the lights off?"

"Shh," Joanne cautioned. They stood there listening for a moment. The breeze rustled the azaleas again. Water dripped.

Then there was a whoosh of air. The front door shuddered. Orange and blue flames leapt outside the living and dining room windows.

"Oh my God!" Joanne gasped.

"Shit!" Charlie exclaimed. "I'll get Skip. You call 911."

Joanne rushed to her cell phone as Charlie hurried down the hall. She dialed the all-too-familiar digits, watching with growing horror as the blue and yellow flames grew larger, obscuring her view of the porch.

"Hello?" Joanne cried, "I'm Joanne Crowley. I...."

A rock shattered the front window. Glass shards flew through the living room, glittering orange and red. Joanne screamed and dropped the phone.

"Leave it, son. We gotta go, now." Charlie dragged Skip by the arm. Skip grasped a red barn in his arms. Plastic cows and chickens fell out as he was pulled through the room.

Joanne bent and picked the phone back up. "Hellohello? We've got a fire. Someone's outside. We...."

A red plastic gas can flew end over end through the dining room window. Glass pelted Joanne's body. Gasoline splattered on the walls and floor. The flames grew closer.

"Shit!" Joanne yelled. She followed her father and son through the kitchen toward the back of the house.

"Mommy!" Skip cried. He sniffled, his eyes wide.

"It's okay, son," Charlie said in a rush, pushing the boy and Joanne. "We'll be okay."

Joanne felt a deep vibration pound her back as hot air blew past her head. She glanced over her shoulder. The dining room was a wall of flame -- a glowing, hellish blue.

They arrived at the back door.

"Daddy, someone's out there. What can we do?"

"Well we sure as hell can't stay here." Charlie reached out and grabbed a couple knives from the knife block. He handed her a filet knife and kept a butcher's knife for himself. "Okay, here we go."

Charlie unbolted the back door and flung it open. He stepped out.

A board slammed into the old man's chest with a crack. Charlie fell back onto Skip. The butcher's knife clattered to the floor. Plastic animals scattered.

Joanne screamed and pulled Skip away from the door. Charlie huffed, trying to catch his breath. With a shaking hand, he reached and grabbed the knife by the handle.

She looked outside. A figure stood there, just out of the light, facing them, two-by-four board in hand. Thick, black smoke bellowed over their heads and out the door, growing deeper by the minute. They were all coughing.

Joanne took a step out the doorway. "Moab? You're not going to get away with this!" Her heart pounded. Her breath caught in her throat. Her words sounded weak to her, empty.

The figure stepped back into the shadows and disappeared.

Charlie held his chest, but he had struggled to his knees. Skip scrambled to gather his toys, crying.

"We've got to get out of here," Joanne said to her father, talking through a covered mouth. "Are you all right?"

"I'm fair enough," Charlie said. But he winced as he straightened, grabbing his ribs. He coughed. Crimson showed on his lips. "Let's get to your car."

"Shit!" she cried. "My keys were in the living room."

"We'll take mine."

The smoke had grown too thick. The three were forced to leave, coughing and sputtering. Stepping outside, Joanne saw her home in flames. The hundred-year-old wood succumbed all too easily. Fire leapt high above the porch, catching the trees. The yard glowed and flickered in the fire's light, yellow and orange, with vast, dark clouds of smoke rushing over it. There was no sign of the teen. There seemed a hundred shadowy places to hide between the back door and Charlie's car.

Joanne led Skip and Charlie around a lilac bush, the burning house to her left. Glass shattered. Wood crackled. She pulled them through a patch of irises, tromping the well-tended flowerbed. The car was just ahead behind a couple pine trees.

Charlie doubled over, grabbing his chest. His knife fell, point first, sticking into the ground.

"Momma! Grandpa's hurt!"

"I know, kiddo." She tried to sound calm, to control her breath. "Can you make it, Dad?"

Charlie nodded, but he only took a step.

Joanne turned. A figure rushed toward her. A board slammed her side and splintered, knocked her back. Joanne screamed and swiped her knife, missing.

Moab stood in the angry light, heaving. His shirt was torn. His teeth shone orange and glistened in the flames. "Flushed you out!" he growled. "It's cleanin' time!" He dropped the shattered board and pulled a hatchet from his belt.

She stepped back, circled around toward Charlie. Charlie brandished his knife and steadied himself, pulled Skip behind him with the other hand. Skip watched, wide-eyed, and held the toy barn close to his chest.

"Moab. Put down the hatchet," Joanne urged. "It's over now. It's time to give up."

Moab leered, head down, a bull ready to charge. "You took my rabbits," he drawled. "You took 'em *all*! And you took my ma and pa. Now you'll pay." He raised the hand hatchet. "I'll cut you good. Then I'll clean that boy of yours. He'll scream *real loud*!"

Charlie reached out and slashed the teen's shoulder. Moab cried, turned, and swept the hatchet through the air. The rusty blade cut deep into Charlie's arm. The old man gasped and dropped his knife. Skip yelped and fell backward.

"Hey, you bastard!" Joanne screamed.

Moab turned and got Joanne's foot in his chest. The boy stumbled backward, caught himself, glared up at her.

Joanne backed off. Moab followed and raised his hatchet.

She looked past the teenager. Charlie had gotten to his feet, his shoulder glistening. He gazed at Joanne while herding his grandson toward the car.

She read the look in her father's eyes. There was sorrow there. And sacrifice. And the urge to protect. She understood completely.

"Come on, then, you little bastard!" she goaded. She took several more steps back. Moab stepped forward, matching her. "Yeah. I took your damned rabbits!" she continued. "I took 'em all! You'll never hear their screams! They're mine now! All mine!"

Moab shrieked and rushed at Joanne. Hatchet raised. Eyes wide and fixed. Face painted by flames.

Joanne swung out. The filet knife arced through the air and missed the boy by inches.

Moab brought the hatchet down. It nicked Joanne's cheek and cut into her left shoulder, hitting bone. She screamed as the pain seared through her.

The teen knocked her to the ground and put his bare foot to her throat. She reached up with her knife, but he grabbed her arm as she grabbed his with the other. The two struggled for control, each with a hand on the other's weapon.

Joanne feared she'd pass out. She gasped for breath against Moab's foot. Lights popped in and out of her vision.

She pulled loose from Moab's grip, but the boy brought the hatchet down again. The blade sliced into her left hip, instantly painting her jeans with blood. The pain pushed her into momentary unconsciousness before she swam back to reality.

Moab grabbed Joanne's knife with his free hand and backed off. She kicked him in the knee with her good leg. He yelped then fell back to the edge of the shadows, limping.

She struggled to her feet, wincing each time she leaned toward her wounded hip. The house was an inferno. The heat pulled sweat from her brow. She glanced toward the car. Skip was in the passenger seat, eyes wide and hands on the window, but Charlie had collapsed against the hood, gasping, on his way around to the driver's side. Smoke blocked her from seeing any more.

Help's coming, Joanne thought. *Gotta stall. Gotta stall.*

The house exploded, knocking her to the ground with a blast of hot air. *The gas line!* she thought. Flames shot through the roof where the kitchen had been. Shingles fluttered away from the fireball.

Joanne backed toward the rear of the house, leading Moab away from the car, away from Skip, away from Charlie. "Come on, you bastard!"

Moab gritted his teeth and brandished his weapons. "Here bunny bunny bunny!"

She turned and ran, half-limping, around the house. Blood dribbled across her left breast from her shoulder. Even more ran down her leg into her sock, squishing with each step. She winced as she pressed against her hip wound, trying to staunch the flow.

Moab screamed in delight and followed. They ran around the back of the house and across the west lawn toward the Tate house, farther from Skip. Farther from the burning house. Into the shadows. Joanne went as fast as she could, looking frantically for anything she could use as a weapon.

"You ain't gettin' nowheres, woman!" Moab screamed. "I'm gonna cut you good! I'm gonna hear you *scream!*"

She ran under the pecan and through the Wiccan ritual circle, blood dribbling onto the cleared soil and one of the stones. Moab came running after, but then stumbled on a stone and thumped to the ground. It gave Joanne a few more precious seconds.

Tears came unbidden to her eyes and rolled fat and slow down her cheeks. She struggled for each breath. Crashed through wisteria. Climbed over the fence to the Tate property, falling onto the other side. She landed on her bad hip and cried out.

Moab was only feet away, silhouetted like a warrior by the flaming wreckage of Joanne's house, hatchet and knife raised.

She turned and pushed her way through blackberries and greenbrier. Thorns sliced through her clothes, stung her cheeks, ripped her arms. She broke through the other side, directly facing the chopping block. It shone blue with the light of the moon. Flashes of infernal red painted the parts facing her property.

She heard the fence twang as Moab climbed over. The thud of him landing. The cutting and ripping as he slashed through the greenbrier and blackberries.

She remembered how the bramble had come alive, capturing Tate. How the birds attacked. She remembered the vines at the compost. The ladybugs. And all the other weird natural happenings. Without quite understanding why, she cried out, "Help me! Spirits of the wild. Wiccan gods." She turned in a circle. "Whatever you are. Please! Please help me!"

"I hear you, little bunny!" Moab followed her path through the undergrowth. "Ain't no hidin' from the eyes of the Lord! Ain't no forgivin'!"

Joanne stumbled into the shadows behind the Tate house and crouched. She struggled to quiet her breathing as she leaned against the house to take the weight off her hip. Her left leg had gone numb.

The bushes rustled as Moab emerged. He stood at the edge of the bramble, turning his head back and forth. Eyes wide with excitement. Weapons raised.

Then the night went quiet. The breeze stilled. The sounds of the fire went muted.

Then the brambles came to life, pulling in toward the boy like a constricting pupil, tightening, curling and intertwining around his arms and legs.

"Fuckin' vines!" Moab cursed. "I'm gonna get you, whore! Jezebel!"

Joanne backed up, disbelieving what she saw. Light glinted off a blade. Metal slashed through plants.

A battle ensued between the vines and Moab, one wrapping and the other slashing. He seemed swallowed by the bushes, and the cracking of the limbs was like chewing. The vines pulled in again, dragging the screaming teenager into their darkness, but the blade ripped through them, glistening with their juices. The boy emerged, gasping and bleeding, a dark shadow from an open wound.

He met her eyes. "There you are, bunny!"

Joanne turned and ran again. She passed the empty lean-to where the gas cans had been. Likely the same ones used to burn her house.

She passed the door under the house. Looked to open and hide. It was padlocked.

Joanne hobbled up the path on the hill and hid behind a rabbit hutch. Her breaths came in gasps. Adrenaline rushed through her heart and body. Her clothes were ripped and drenched with blood and sweat. Every moment was a battle to keep from passing out.

There was a rumble, like thunder, as the roof of her house collapsed. The fire whistled and crackled, roaring through the still night, the sound of dreams burning. But she couldn't hear Moab. Didn't know where he was.

She leaned against the hutch and stared into the shadows. Moab hadn't followed her up the pathway. Nothing moved. Her hands ground into lichen and rough wood. The acrid smell of rabbit shit assaulted her nose, invaded her mouth, crept down her throat.

Leaves rustled. Joanne turned just in time to jump aside. The hatchet hit the hutch, splitting the wood. Rotten splinters flew as Moab pulled it out.

Joanne sliced the boy's face with the knife. He fell back and shrieked in pain as she turned to run. But the flat of the hatchet blade slammed against the side of her head. She fell against another cage, knocking it over. It fell to the ground and broke into pieces.

The world swirled as if she were drunk. Then focus returned as Moab poised above her, covered in bloody scratches and ripped clothing.

Her knife was gone from her hand. She felt around for it in vain.

"'I am full of power by the spirit of the Lord!'" Moab chanted and raised the hatchet.

She held her breath and closed her eyes.

A wind brushed her face. She gasped. Moab screamed. Joanne opened her eyes. Moab stumbled backward, his face a fluttering mass of dun-colored feathers flecked with white. The great horned owl shrieked. It grasped the boy's neck and gouged at his face, its wings flapping in a maddened rage.

Joanne turned and pulled herself to a crouch, clutching a moldy board from the broken hutch. Shaking her head, she managed to stand and stumble down the trail away from the Tate house. Moab screamed behind her, fighting the owl, but she didn't look back. She could barely focus to find the path.

Delirious with pain, lightheaded, Joanne reached the shed at the top of the hill, passing the window with the bloody handprints.

"Oh! You're gonna get your lickins, woman!" the boy bellowed, his voice growing stronger as he climbed the path. "Pa said you're a witch. That you conjured up the devil's nature against him. The Good Book says, *Thou shalt not suffer a witch to live.* So I'm gonna clean you slow!"

The ground seemed to lean and rotate. Joanne fell through the doorway of the shed. Her hands and face hit the floor, ground into the remains of dead rabbits. Fetid bones. Matted hair. Leathery skin. The room buzzed with disturbed insects. The decaying flesh of hundreds of rabbits sent waves of gas into the air. But she pulled herself through it all toward the back, trying to hide in the shadows. It was her only hope. Tried not to vomit. Fought unconsciousness.

"Here bunny bunny bunny!" Moab called, just outside the door.

Joanne sat against the back wall and slipped down. Her hands fell into bones and damp flesh. The bones ground against each other. Putrefied meat squeezed between her fingers. She stifled a cry, then wrapped her hands around the board like a baseball bat, waiting to make her last stand. The distant, light of her burning home dimly illuminated the room through the window of the shed. The bloody handprints were black against orange, wavering firelight. Then Moab's shadow passed across them.

The teen appeared in the doorway. He brandished the knife in one hand and hatchet in the other, hunched, heaving with each breath. "That's a good bunny," he whispered, just loud enough to hear. "I *see* you."

"Go away!" Joanne shouted. In a fit of pique, she threw a handful the rabbit remains. They hit the boy's chest and bounced harmlessly to the floor. Moab chuckled and stepped inside.

Joanne braced herself against the wall. Gripped the board. Fought for focus.

The floor vibrated. The shed shook.

She cried out as the body parts beneath her came alive, wiggling, inching forward from under her like so many rotting caterpillars.

Moab stepped closer. Almost striking range. "It's cleanin' time," he growled.

The remains rose from the floor. Flung toward the boy. Formed in a mass behind him, preventing his escape.

Moab stopped his attack and gasped.

From all around them came a rising scream, the voice of hundreds of rabbits, full of torment and pain, wailing higher and higher, crying out as one.

The mass coalesced. Bone met bone. Rotting flesh pulled together into muscle and sinew.

The cry increased, focused behind Moab, rose in pitch until it rang in Joanne's ears and she had to cover them. The form behind the boy took on a shape of its own, horrible, with nails and a gaping jaw. An elongated head developed. Powerful legs bulged with rotted muscle. Long ears. A massive, lumpy, rotting rabbit shambled toward him.

Moab shrieked and tried to push past the beast, but his cry was drowned out. The beast swept at the boy, ripped into his chest. It lunged at Moab, ripping and shredding, screaming as it opened its constructed face. Fangs and claws made of rib bones sliced through Moab's flesh. The boy writhed in pain, wailing at the top of his lungs.

"Help me, Jesus!" he cried. "Help me! Jesus! Jesus!" His scream grew animalistic, high-pitched, as the beast skinned him alive.

"Stop it!" Joanne yelled, "Stop it!" She shut her eyes, sobbing, shaking her head. "Stop it!"

The rabbit cries lowered. The ripping stopped. The jabbering of the beast faded away.

Joanne's breath rushed in and out without making it to her lungs. She dared to open her eyes.

The door was clear. Moab lay groaning, half-buried in bones and decrepit flesh. His face was a mass of bloody tissue. His chest gaped. But he was alive. For now.

And so was Joanne.

Sirens wailed through the night, growing stronger and nearer. Still fighting unconsciousness, Joanne stumbled out of the shed and lumbered in a daze back toward her property. This time the bramble moved out of the way. No thorn touched her. She didn't even stop to think about the oddness of it as she shambled to the fence and then struggled over it.

The night around her settled into silence. The darkness swallowed the living. Joanne spiraled into an empty void and passed out on the other side of the fence.

EIGHT

"Thank you, Baby," Lashanda said, and handed her dirty plate to one of her daughters. Destiny flashed a shy smile to Joanne, took her plate as well, and turned into Charlie's kitchen.

Her father could just be seen through the doorway as he took the plates from the girl.

Joanne flicked her lighter and lit a Camel, drawing deep to get the cigarette started. She released a cloud of smoke and turned to watch Skip set up his toy farm on the dining room floor. He had played a lot with his grandfather's gift in the two months since the fire, the only remnant of their previous possessions other than her car. Behind Joanne sat a table covered with the remains of Thanksgiving dinner. Half a turkey sat cold, abandoned by the others, but they had had their fill of cornbread stuffing, collard greens, hominy, and candied yams.

Joanne hadn't touched the turkey. She was vegetarian before ... before that night, but she was even more so now. The sight of meat repulsed her to the point of nausea. And dead things, like roadkill, conjured horrifying memories that chased her in her dreams.

And the screams. The hideous screams. The cries of the rabbits. The screams of Moab. The wailing of the beast. She shivered and took another long drag. Every night, it all came back to her in nightmares that left her sheets wet with sweat. Even when she managed to doze, often it was broken by Skip screaming in his sleep and needing to be soothed back to less troubling dreams.

The smell of sweet potato pie wafted from the oven. But it couldn't dispel her disgust.

"Joanne, honey, you've already got a cigarette started." Lashanda pointed to an ashtray Joanne had put on the table only moments before.

"Oh," Joanne simply stated, and kept smoking. Her eyes were still focused on the turkey remains -- an oil-glistened pile of bones and ripped flesh. She had to look away.

"Is that boy, Moab, out of the hospital yet?" Lashanda asked. "I hear they're going to put him away at the mental hospital up in Little Rock."

Joanne shuddered and remained silent.

"When's the Tates' sentencing?" Lashanda continued, hesitant. "Next Friday, right?"

"I don't want to talk about it."

"Lashanda," Charlie called from the kitchen. "That was some o'the best yams I've had since I was your girls' age!"

"Thank you, Charlie!"

"You'd melt if you were half as sweet as your dish!" Charlie added, chuckling. But he suddenly stopped laughing and coughed deeply. Painful to hear, the coughs came from deep in his lungs, wracking, bending him over. The chest contusion from being hit by Moab, and the heart attack it induced, didn't kill him, but his wounds still hadn't completely healed.

Neither had Joanne's. She rubbed her hip, still feeling stitches removed a few weeks before. Her shoulder ached constantly from the deep wound that had badly healed and scarred over.

Lashanda's smile faded. "Joanne, honey," she said, voice low, "you just aren't yourself these days. You've lost your job. The strain of livin' with your father is takin' a toll. And I know how hard it must be for you to get past what happened." She placed a hand on Joanne's knee. Her jingling bracelets fell silent against the blue jeans.

How could you know? she wanted to say. *How the hell could you know?* She took another drag. "What happened? Huh? What happened? Even you don't believe me."

Lashanda sighed. "You were delirious, Joanne. Lost a lot of blood. Anything coulda happened. But you defended yourself and got away. That's what matters." She gave Joanne's knee a pat and took her hand off. "I know a therapist," Lashanda continued. "He helped me cope after my miscarriage, then again after the divorce. He's good. I think he could help."

"Okay, girls. I think I can get it from here," Joanne heard her father say in the kitchen. Plates clanked against each other.

The twins came in and stood in front of their mother. Matching outfits and matching, sweet smiles. "We're all done, Mommy," Kayla said. Destiny nodded.

"I think maybe you should play with Skip," Lashanda suggested.

"Yes," Joanne said to the girls. "You three kids go play together."

"Yes, ma'am," Destiny said, glancing over her shoulder toward Skip.

Joanne took another drag. "Well, Lashanda, one thing is certain. I managed to get rid of my neighbors, but they got rid of me, too. I'm selling the place."

"Have heart, girl. It's a new start. A chance to leave the past behind."

Joanne raised her head and breathed deeply. "I thought I left my troubles behind when I moved here from Newark! But you're right. It's almost behind us now. Then we can get on. Then we can get on." She turned and watched the kids play.

Skip had lined up all his plastic animals in front of the barn door. Red horses and pink pigs stood side by side as if formed up for roll call. Two yellow bunnies sat facing them.

"Can we play?" Kayla asked him.

Skip ignored her, moving a cow toward the bunnies in slow motion.

"Skip," Joanne said. "Be nice to Kayla."

Skip stopped and turned his head to the girl. His eyes were glassy. His face was blank. He stared at her several seconds before speaking.

"Wanna see my rabbits?" he drawled.

The Way to Hell

Dag leaned over his own corpse, laughing between shocked gasps for air. "You fools!" he yelled at the two cops who had shot him. They stood only ten feet from him, but they didn't seem to see or hear him. "You played right into my god-damned hands!" Death-by-cop had been the plan.

He looked around the darkened alley at the impenetrable shadows behind dumpsters and along every edge and urine-soaked corner. Now that he was dead, the colors were muted, the sounds muffled, and a mist seemed to play along every surface.

Any moment now! Dag thought, and watched for a change in the darkness to show the gate to hell. He got on his knees right in the midst of the blood oozing from his corpse. He raised his hands and eyes to Los Angeles's luminescent nighttime smog and prayed.

"Oh, my Dark Lord. Hear my demands! Open your gates and take me now to Hell! Send your demons to burn my soul. I am your loyal minion, a demon in waiting to do your deeds!"

He waited a moment, then dropped his eyes back to the shadows. The darkness didn't shift. The demons had not come. The sounds of the city moved around him no different than before.

The cops had since lowered their weapons and stepped toward Dag's corpse. One passed him and shone his flashlight behind a dumpster, securing the scene. The other leaned over the body, illuminated by the patrol car's headlights at the end of the alley. "Hal," the cop said, "I think you're right. He matches the description of the Sunset Slasher."

"Damned straight, pig," Dag said, and pushed the cop. The policeman fell to the slimy pavement and cursed. The other cop stepped back to his partner, holstering his gun.

Dag looked at his translucent, spiritual hands. "I'll be damned!" He grinned and recalled all the ceremonial sacrifices for immortality and strength he had performed. "Fucking black magic worked."

Dag tried to grab the partner's revolver and yank it from its holster, but he could not grasp it. His fingers passed right through the Glock's grip. The desire to move the gun, however, seemed enough to lift it out of the holster and send it sliding over to Dag's body.

Amazed at this power of levitation, he *willed* his corpse to sit up. The body's head wobbled about, arms slack at the side.

"Watch out!" the fallen cop shouted and shot another four rounds into Dag's corpse. The body wrenched away from Dag's willpower as its flesh ripped apart with each shot, holes pounding through the faded Metallica tee-shirt.

Dag howled with laughter, bent over with the hilarity of it as the policemen carefully examined his body. He was more than an ordinary ghost. But he was no demon. He figured from his experience with black magic that his powers were fleeting and could disappear in time. How long, he didn't know.

He focused his attention back on the revolver and levitated it upward. The gun flew about on Dag's unsteady will, bouncing in the air as if on marionette lines. The cops stood back, eyes wide. "Are you seein' this?" one cop said to the other.

Then Dag focused harder. The trigger twitched, then finally it pulled back all the way and a shot hit the brick wall, showering one of the cops with bits of clay.

Dag laughed and did it again and again, shooting madly and randomly, ricocheting off a fire escape and blasting chips out of brick walls. The cops ran for cover behind their patrol car, making frantic calls for backup again. Sirens wailed in the distance and grew louder. When the bullets were used up, Dag dropped the revolver and did the same thing with the semi-automatic he had fired at them before he died. The shots shattered the patrol car's windshield and perforated the hood.

But Dag had already tired of the pranks. Where were the demons? The gates of Hell? Satan's irresistible call? He kicked his own corpse, then frantically paced the alley, slamming his hands against the hood of the patrol car while at the same time "pushing" with his mind, denting it, and then smashed a headlight.

"Where are you, my dark lord?" he yelled. "Have I not pleased you? I've killed five virgins, one for each point in the pentagram. Slashed their fucking throats. Drank their blood and sacrificed them to you? Haven't I done enough to be by your side?"

No answer. No gaping maw of flame. No invitation to Hell.

"This is bullshit!" Dag said and stormed out of the alley directly past the two nervous policemen and out into the street. There he used his willpower to break storefront windows and dent in car doors until, almost a block away, he sat on the stoop of an apartment building and tried to regain his composure.

Dag thought back over his life, now ended. He felt the pain of ears boxed by aggressive teachers. They busted his butt with a paddle that had holes drilled through it "for better sting value," as one had put it. And then there was his fat stepmother, home all the time as his father worked three jobs. She burned his skin with cigarettes, just to get a laugh. "You need punishing for your disrespect, you little shit," she would scream.

He got his revenge against her, though. Oh yes. Beat the living shit out of her as a 16th birthday present to himself.

And into adulthood, still he struggled against The Man, be they over-demanding bosses, pushers, or ball-busting cops. He had been powerless, always powerless. But he had done his duty, made the killings, and now he would be powerless no more. If only Hell would show itself and Satan would reach out for him, he would be a demon and change the world as *he* saw fit. He'd burn them all!

Dag looked back toward the alley. More police cars had gathered there, but he didn't care. Nothing down there concerned him anymore.

He turned and looked the other way down the street. A Catholic church was in the final stages of remodeling after the big quake last year. The Cathedral of Our Lady of the Angels. Piles of building materials and crated statuary were stacked in the shadows outside its looming structure. He sure wasn't going to find the gates of Hell *there*. But he'd had fun spray-painting pentagrams on it in the past.

All the books on black magic had described what to do while alive; they didn't mention what to do *after* you died in order to get a special place in Hell. "Okay. Think." Dag remembered back to all the rituals he had learned from books of black magic, like *The Grand Grimoire*, the *Key of Solomon*, and the *Grimorium Verum*.

Suddenly he raised his head. "Ah! One last ritual! That's what I need. I'm sure of it! A summoning." He jumped up and rushed down the road toward the dilapidated warehouse where he performed his rituals.

"We have to meet face to face. I'll summon you, Dark Lord! Fucking blood will spill. Then you'll see I'm worthy. Then you'll take me to your side."

* * *

It took all night for Dag to fumble with the pentagram as he got used to his powers of physical manipulation. Actually holding objects was too difficult, but levitating them became easier with practice. Luckily, all of his ritual paraphernalia was still hidden away. He set up the silver vessels. He arranged the sacrificial knife. Using the lighter on the candles had been the hardest part.

Time was running short; dawn would soon come and he still didn't have a victim. Virgins were in short supply in the wee hours of the night in downtown, after all. The only person Dag managed to find was an old bum behind the warehouse. The drunken beggar woke up after enough kicking, then, guided by blows to his sides and back, stumbled into the warehouse. There Dag punched him until he heard bones break and the old man collapsed in a moaning heap. With intense effort, he levitated the victim into the pentagram to make the final cut to the neck.

"Oh, my dark and unholy liege," Dag recited over a goblet of the bum's blood, "receive from your servant this sacrifice to you. Grant me a place at your side! Come and make my soul yours to do your bidding! Open the gates of Hell!"

Dag levitated the goblet and tipped it to his lips. The blood poured through him to splash onto the painted pentagram and the victim's body. But Dag tasted something nonetheless. The salty iron of blood lingered in his mouth.

The candles blew out. Dag dropped the goblet, splashing more blood over the floor and its symbols as a blazing red swirl of energy formed in the air in front of him. It grew to a tempest, ringing the pentagram around him with a hurricane of flame.

Dag screamed in pain from the heat, at once in agony and ecstasy, like when he had hung from cables by hooks through his skin, or when he took part in bloodletting and scarification rituals. "Yes!" he screamed over the growing noise of the fire, arms out. "Take me, Satan. I am yours!"

The fire shifted, changed colors from red to blue and then red again. The two colors swirled together, as if fighting for control, maddeningly flashing until, all of sudden, the blue flames overtook the red and filled Dag's vision.

The blue wall of fire parted as a beast stepped through, passing into the magic circle despite its protective powers. Dag gasped and scooted back. Nude and masculine, the demon was broader and taller than any human and was covered in bulging, seeping wounds. Its bull-like head was smashed in on one side, with bones shattered and sticking through the pus and flesh beneath massive steer horns. It stank of rot, shit, and burned hair. "I am Moloch," it growled with a voice so low and gravelly that it was hard to understand.

Dag regained his composure and knelt to the demon. "Take me! Take me to Satan's side."

Moloch laughed, deep and hearty, and kicked Dag's face so hard it threw Dag over, nose barely an inch from the flames. "Think you worthy?" Moloch said. "You are a bastard of the light."

Dag threw himself to the demon's feet and tightened his jaw. "I am Satan's servant. I did all the rituals. I sacrificed five virgins to him and drank their blood. And I have called you here with one more victim."

Moloch sneered. "I am no willing minion of Satan, and I would stop you from joining him if I could." The demon looked down. The bum's body had caught fire. "This is not a virgin. You are not worthy of Satan. But you may serve *me* if you wish."

Dag blinked. *This is a test of loyalty*, he thought. "It would be rewarding to serve a demon of your power, but I am faithful only to Satan. What can I do to gain a seat at his side that I haven't done yet? Isn't a life of sin enough?"

The demon snorted. "Think you the only sinner? Innocents are murdered every day. It takes more to make a demon." Moloch placed a meaty hand upon Dag's head. Ethereal blood and pus coursed down the demon's arm and continued down Dag's face. The beast giggled -- exactly the same giggle that had been uttered by Dag's second victim, an eight-year-old girl, as he had lured her into his van with a puppy and kidnapped her. Dag shivered with dread, then with excitement, as he remembered the ecstasy of that kill. Those reed-pipe screams. The slice of delicate skin. It had been the best one.

"There *is* a way to Hell for you, Bastard of the Light -- a corner of it, at least. And there you may serve Satan to the best of your ability."

"Only a *corner* of Hell?"

The demon frowned. "Rather you wander this world forever? Powerless? A ghost?" Moloch's rumbling voice vibrated deep in Dag's chest. "It is the best that *you* could hope for. This is your only chance! Take it or leave it."

"Fine! Name your price!"

"You must summon an angel."

Dag blinked in surprise. *Was mortal death not enough, or the murder of innocents?* "H...How?"

Moloch grinned. Coagulated blood and ripped flesh moved with the muscles. "Demons come to exceeding evil. Angels come to exceeding good."

"So I must do something ... very *good*?" The thought was repulsive. But he couldn't remember any rituals to summon *angels*. He had never even been inside churches except to vandalize them.

"And when you attract one," Moloch continued, "you must kill it."

Dag coughed and stood, forgetting himself, and looked into Moloch's eyes. The demon lashed out with a roar and grabbed Dag's hand. Moloch's image shifted in the heat of the fire. The cloth of a dingy bathrobe folded over fat, pale flesh. Rolled dirty blond hair grew out of the beast's head, and suddenly Dag was staring in horror at the visage of his stepmother.

"You need punishing for your disrespect!" the stepmother said and pulled his hand into the flames. Dag screamed in agony and pulled his hand back into the circle. The fire had dissolved his spectral fingers to knobs. Even as he fought unconsciousness, the sweet sensation of pain coursing through his nerves, firing deep pleasures that sent shivers up his back and pulsed blood into his growing male organ. Spirit or not, the mechanism seemed delightfully the same.

Dag shook his head and tried to concentrate. He returned to a submissive posture, careful to avert his eyes from the beast, or his stepmother, again. "Even if I summon an angel, Dark One, how do I kill it?"

Moloch laughed, the cackling laugh of the stepmother twisting into the deep and loud bellow of the demon as he shifted back to his first form. "Angels cry when their morals die," Moloch said. "Tempt him to submission."

Dag puzzled over this as Moloch turned to reenter the flames. "Wait," Dag said. "You mean I have to tempt the angel to do something immoral?"

"Even the *desire* to deny God's will is enough, and the angel will fall! You have three days to do this or you wander as a ghost forever."

Moloch stepped through the portal. The flames and heat abruptly disappeared with the demon, leaving Dag breathless. The bloody, blackened pentagram glowed orange in the dying light of the bum's burning body.

* * *

"Summon an angel," Dag mumbled to himself. "Tempt him to submission."

Dag had spent the last two days wandering L.A., struggling to find good deeds worthy of attracting angels. He put out a leaf fire that had spread to the side of a house. He tripped a thief as he ran from the police. He scared off a construction worker before a load of rafters could fall on him. But after each incident, there was still no sign of any angels.

And his hand, while not painful, was still only a burnt stump.

Now he sat atop a phone booth on Sunset Boulevard watching the morning rush hour pedestrians flow around him. They were ignorant of his ghostly presence, though every now and then a person would look his way and cock their head, then move on with a puzzled expression.

Pointing with a finger of his good hand, Dag popped the hat off a man twenty feet away. He had practiced his spiritual skills a lot in the past days. The man yelped in surprise and turned to pick it up. As he bent down, Dag kicked his foot out and sent a force to knock the man to the concrete. Normally Dag would have laughed at such light amusement, but he didn't even crack a smile.

"Summon an angel," he repeated. "Tempt him to submission! My ass! And today's the last day or I stay like this forever."

He eyed a squat, concrete gargoyle at the top of a law office. Concentrating, he reached out and sent his force up there. He felt the gargoyle's rough texture, felt its base give. With a massive effort he pulled back, and the gargoyle tumbled off its perch toward the sidewalk below.

But just as quickly he yelped and sent his force out again, this time to catch the statue. As much as he would love to see the people below it squashed, he slowed the progress and gently set the gargoyle on the ground. People stopped to stare in awe at the floating statue as it touched down, looking up to see if anything else was falling.

Dag looked around for any sign of angels or demons. But there were no unexplained lights, fires, or shadows. No bellowing roar nor the strum of harps carried by the wind.

Suddenly Dag jumped off the booth into the crowd, using his powers to throw people around like dolls. They screamed and slammed into each other as if in a giant mosh pit. "What do you want, my Dark Lord?" he screamed, mindless of the chaos he caused around him. "Satan! Take me! Or give me the knowledge to do this task! I'm lost!" He stopped his attack and dropped to the ground, holding his head. "I'm fucking lost."

Around him lay a dozen injured pedestrians trying to recover themselves and make sense of what happened. One woman held a crying baby tight to her breast, her forehead red and turning blue from a knock against a stone wall. "My God," she prayed. "Help me."

"Your god can't help you now, bitch," Dag muttered. "Your soul is as useless to him as mine is to Lucifer."

Dag dropped his hands to the concrete and stared into space. He no longer paid attention to the injured around him or the people helping them. "Your soul!" he said. "That's it! That's how you attract *angels*! Save *souls*, not lives!"

He leaped up and started walking, not sure where he was heading. "Yes," he mumbled. "Save souls. How do you save souls?" He snapped the fingers of his good hand. "You need a god-damned miracle!" With that he ran back toward the side of town where he had died.

* * *

Dag arrived at the Cathedral of Our Lady of the Angels. The tall, angular bell tower had just had its bells replaced that day. The copper roof blazed in the sun, as did the monstrous brass doors. Workmen busied themselves around the building's base as small groups of tourists walked around the perimeter of the site.

Dag headed directly to the south side below the cathedral's massive cross. Around him, carefully separated from the other construction materials, statuary sat in crates ready to be lifted to their places for display to the world.

Concentrating, he levitated himself up five stories to the roof of the cathedral. Once on top he rested a moment and watched the crowds below. When there seemed to be a peak in the number of passersby, he said, "This ought to get an angel's attention!"

He pointed at the bell tower and pulled with all his spiritual might. The four massive bells swung, soundless at first, then tolling loudly.

All eyes turned to the roof.

Dag turned his attention to the statuary below, exerted all of his energy into it. Slowly the crate containing the statue of the Virgin Mary levitated up a wall over the main entrance. The boards rattled and fell away, followed by packing material. Soon the statue itself, devoid of cover, rose majestically to the top with the sound of the bells.

The workmen and tourists stopped what they were doing and pointed up at the spectacle. Cell phones were aimed at the statue.

Dag's energy waned. He focused harder. Grunted from the effort. Felt as if he were being wrenched apart. If the statue dropped, the plan would fail. He stretched out his hands to aid the levitation. It was then that he realized he was visible to the crowds, glowing bright white with the release of his energy.

And another thing was happening. Dag noticed an intense light at eye level to him, about fifty yards in front of him in the air. The crowd hadn't seemed to notice it, but, like a portal, it was slowly opening with the progression of the statue.

The statue's progress suddenly faltered, and Dag reached harder to keep his grasp on it. It stopped its course and lowered slightly. The portal, too, seemed to mimic the action by closing a bit. Dag gritted his teeth and groaned with the effort, and the statue continued slowly up the wall. The portal opened as well, and through it Dag saw a luminescent figure just inside.

By the time the statue of the Virgin Mary rose to the top of the entry and sat serenely on its pedestal in front of a golden backdrop, pedestrians had stopped along the sidewalk to gawk. A traffic jam had formed. Dag stopped his exertions and leaned heavily against the statue. The bells slowly stopped their tolling.

The portal opened completely. Dag's eyes lit up, and the spiritual equivalent of adrenaline pulsing through him. *Yes*, he thought. *Come on, you fucking angel. I've got your attention now*!

A handsome man appeared from the light, perfectly proportioned, clothed in glowing robes and sporting a huge pair of powerful, white wings. His long, golden hair whipped around hypnotic, azure eyes. He moved over to Dag in one smooth motion to stand next to him on the roof.

Dag looked away and allowed his exhaustion to show.

"Dagwood," the angel said in a deep and flowing voice, "what have you done?"

Dag shuddered inwardly at the pronunciation of his full name. It conjured old memories of schoolyard taunts. But he forced a smile. "It is my gift to humanity," Dag faked. "I ... I think I'm dead. I had to do something to atone for my sins."

The angel placed a light hand upon Dag's shoulder. Dag had a passing desire to push him off the roof, but he knew it wouldn't do any good.

"This is an honorable thing," the angel said, "but it is not for me to judge what is proper atonement."

Time for temptation, Dag thought. *Get him to submit. Let's try some jealousy*. "I bet you wish you could have done that," he said, wiping his brow.

The angel just looked down to the masses. "No, Dagwood. I am not a miracle worker. But I can compliment you on your attempt."

Scratch jealousy, Dag thought. *How about lying?* "You know, *you* could appear to them and they would think you did this. I wouldn't mind, you know."

The angel smiled at him. "I am content, Dagwood. Crowds are gathering, and soon the whole world will share in the event. Many hundreds of souls will be drawn to this cathedral and saved in the next few months because of you."

The angel's words stung, but Dag tried not to show it. *How about tempting the angel with vanity?* "Yes, but don't you think you could save more souls if they saw a *real* angel up here instead of me? You're so magnificent!" Dag tried hard not to let his hope show through, averting his eyes.

The angel laughed, smoothly, almost chillingly. "Why, Dagwood, they have already seen an angel up here, and it isn't me!"

Dag cocked his head in confusion. With a start of realization, he turned his head to look over his shoulder. A set of broad white wings fluttered in the breeze. *His* wings.

"No!" he screamed. He grabbed the angel's robes and shook him. "No, god-damn it! I'm not a shit-eating angel, do you hear? I'm not!" He released the angel and stood back, arms out. "Hail Satan!"

But the bells rang again, drowning him out.

"Sorry," the angel said, his voice growing raspier, "but you've now done too much *good* to be Satan's minion. And you're a weak soul. You'll spend eternity in Heaven, but bound in a gilded cage, forever watching the bliss around you without interaction. There's no pain in heaven, child, and you will be powerless to God's will."

Dag lifted into the air, glowing brilliantly, much to the crowd's excitement. "No! Fuck all! Let me down! I deserve Hell! I'm a minion of Satan! Of *Satan!*" The crowd didn't seem to hear him.

As Dag rose to his Heavenly portal in the clouds, he saw the angel below melt away. Robes rotted and fell off. The vast, white wings shriveled, replaced by the tortured, pustular body and bull's head of Moloch.

"Remember," the demon growled, "I am no *willing* minion of Satan. He shall not receive a demon servant today, but instead face many more saved souls, and *I* am stronger for it. Satan won't find you in *this* far corner."

Dag screamed again. "You shithead! You tricked me!"

The demon threw back his head and bellowed as Dag disappeared into the glowing portal. "Welcome to *your* Hell, Bastard of the Light!"

Fatty

"You're too god-damned fat!" Jeremy's father said. "Too much fat will kill you, you know."

Jeremy sat leaning over the kitchen table, eyes closed, gritting his teeth, wishing the school bus would come sooner. But then, school wasn't much better.

His father sat across from him eating cereal. He took another spoonful, then continued talking with food in his mouth. "At your age I was the pride of my school. Quarterback. Getting pussy in the back seat of my Mustang almost every night. And I had *muscle*, boy, not flab!"

Jeremy predicted his father's words so well he mouthed them as they were said. But they were true. He was the fattest boy he had ever known, 290 pounds at age 17.

A small radio with a crooked antenna sat on the linoleum counter, a morning news break blaring from its battered speaker.

Two boys were found dead at Northridge High School late last night, leading to cancellation of school today ....

Jeremy sighed and looked up. His father stared back at him, dribbling milk on his dingy, sleeveless tee-shirt. His eyes were hard, dark, and accusing. These were beating eyes, but this time Jeremy wasn't afraid.

"I'm not you," Jeremy said quietly.

His father's eyes gleamed as he painted on a cynical smile. "You sure as hell ain't!" He splashed his spoon into his corn flakes and pointed a rough finger at Jeremy. "If I had the money for it I'd put you into military school. There you'd learn *discipline*. You'd learn *honor*." He started eating again. "Hell, even if I had the money, they wouldn't accept a fat slob like you who's afraid of girls." He paused a moment, then added wryly, "Don't ask don't tell."

.... School administrators say the boys were known to have bullied a number of other kids in recent years ....

Jeremy rose from his chair. His belly pulled at the seams of his red and blue-striped shirt. His pale skin spilled out from under it to touch the tabletop.

His father's brow tightened. "Sit down. I haven't excused you yet."

"I think you'd better start treating me with respect," Jeremy said, voice calm. He sensed a growing warmth through him, but he fought it off.

His father rose from his seat, jaw flexing, eyes closing to vicious slits cut into his face. "What did you say to me, boy?"

"And you'd better apologize for all the things you've said to me."

His father took a step around the table. He unbuckled his belt and slid it out of its loops. "Oh, you're asking for it, you little shit! Drop and give me twenty."

Jeremy felt a thin smile form on his face as he held his ground. The heat was getting stronger now, pulsing through his body. He let it build ever so slowly.

.... *Like the other deaths, they were found to have asphyxiated on a yellow, organic substance that has investigators baffled* ....

Jeremy shook his head. The smile disappeared. "I'm not doing anything else for you, Father. This is your last chance. Better say you'll change."

"Or what? You think you can take me on?" The father doubled the belt and snapped it as loud as a whip. "Bring it on, you obese slug!" He swung the belt over his shoulder and slapped it hard across Jeremy's face.

Jeremy took a step to the side, face turned and burning. His eyes watered from the sting.

"How do you like that, fatty?"

Hot energy rushed through Jeremy's bones and organs into his belly. He lifted his shirt and smiled madly at his father.

The man stepped back. "What the hell?"

Jeremy screamed in pain as the skin at his navel split open. Fat rushed out of him in a continuous stream, collapsing his belly. It splashed against his father and rolling over him, coating his body and clothing.

His father tried to wipe it off, grunting, seeking escape. But the fat held him tight. Jeremy sensed it seeking openings, sliding down his father's throat, clogging ears and eyes. He felt the pressure of air in his father's lungs as it pushed against the fat in a vain effort to escape. The man fell to the ground, head and chest covered in yellow, sloshing sludge. With his mouth working soundlessly, Jeremy's father lay still and went limp.

Jeremy withdrew his fat, felt it slide in and redistribute through his belly as the tear healed. His father lay in a fetal position, eyes and mouth open and filled with fatty residue, hands at his throat, unmoving.

.... Though symptoms at first seemed medical in nature, the police now fear some sort of bizarre homicide.

"Watch out, Father," Jeremy said as he pulled down his shirt and walked out of the kitchen. "Too much fat will kill you, you know."

Anger Not the Gods of
Rake and Mower

Wielding a leaf rake, Wesley Stark slammed shut the door to the shop and stomped into the front yard. "Damned neighborhood covenants!"

"Wesley!" his wife, Katie Marie, called to him through a window. "Are you going to mow today? The covenant says we have to keep the grass lower than two inches, you know!"

Wes stopped and shuddered. He felt like saying, *Why the hell don't you come out and measure it yourself!* Instead, he pasted on a smile and hollered back, "No, dearest, our lawnmower is broken down again."

Through the window he heard dramatic music from Katie Marie's crime drama. "Well, you can at least rake the lawn, can't you?"

Wes gritted his teeth. "That's why I have the freakin' rake."

"Good. The covenant says we have to pick up the leaves in a timely fashion."

He muttered under his breath, "I'll give you a god-damned covenant!"

The "neighborhood covenant" governed everything outside their home. All exterior fixtures, porches, and awnings had to be white. The garbage can had to be plastic, spill-proof, and wheeled. No outdoor pets. No folding outdoor furniture. No lawn ornaments. The lawn couldn't be too weedy. And not a speck of trash or debris was tolerated. He couldn't even change his '68 Chevy pickup's oil in his own damned driveway.

He and Katie Marie had moved to Elmwood Heights only a few months before. The neighborhood looked so tranquil, so orderly, with neatly trimmed green lawns, clean sidewalks, and well-kept houses. Now he realized this was all because of the intrusive restrictions, something he'd skimmed through in the paperwork.

All his neighbors were old, rich, and reclusive. They didn't care to speak to him on the sidewalk, but they were quick to point out any little thing that went against the neighborhood covenant he signed, ratting him out to the Covenant Committee, who left passive-aggressive messages on his voicemail. Those old fogies had time in their retirement to follow all the guidelines. God, how he wanted to piss them off! If only he could plant a bright pink flamingo in the middle of Katie Marie's landscaped flowerbed.

Despite his disgruntlement, he honestly *did* care about his yard, even if he wasn't in the mood at the moment. He had this little ritual – silly, really – where, before each mowing or raking or trimming, he lowered to his knee at the edge of the lawn and ran his hand over the grass. His palm would graze the surface of the blades, feeling their squared-off edge from the last time he had mowed. Then he would brush away some leaves if there were any. Finally, he would move his eyes across the patch in front of him searching for weeds and pull each weed out by the roots.

But he simply wasn't in the mood today. All he really wanted to do was go in and watch the ballgame with a cold one in his hand and a big bowl of popcorn. He smiled to himself and muttered, "The lawn gods can go without their ritual today."

Wes walked under the big oak in the yard and lowered his rake. There were an awful lot of leaves. "If there were a leaf god, I'd sacrifice my left nut so I wouldn't have to do this."

The musical tinkling of the metal rake prongs struck a lyrical chord. The rustle of the leaves provided an underlying rhythm. The wind sang melody. Before Wes realized what was happening, the wind whipped up in front of him. Leaves danced in a whirlwind and coalesced into a human shape.

Wes found himself eye-to-eye with a woman, her skin dry, cracking and brown, hair interwoven with twigs and leaf bits, a tunic made of brilliantly colored oak leaves, and acorn earrings. Her eyes flared with bright yellows, oranges, and reds.

"What the hell?" Eyes wide and mouth open, Wes didn't know whether to run or to rake her out to the road.

"I am Autumna, Goddess of Fallen Leaves." Her voice was as dry as she looked and sounded like she needed to clear her throat.

"You're not going to take my left nut, are you?"

She seemed unfazed. "You will not touch these leaves," she said.

"Sorry, leaf lady, but I've got a nagging wife on my back and a neighborhood covenant to follow." He pulled on his rake again.

Autumna threw out her hands. Instantly leaves, acorns, and sticks fell on Wes from the tree above.

"Hey!" he yelled.

"You will not rake these leaves, mortal, for you disrupt the natural balance. Leaves must lie where they fall and fertilize the earth."

He paused a moment, registering what an excellent suggestion that was. "Fine!" He feigned annoyance. "I'd rather be watching the game, anyhow."

But the earth shook before he could throw down the rake. The grass at his feet suddenly grew at an astonishing rate, the blades wrapping and weaving to form a humanoid form, as tall as Wes with a gaping hole for a mouth and empty sockets for eyes.

Verdant and smelling of a freshly mowed lawn, the figure spoke. "Behold! I am Lolium, God of Lawns, and you *shall* remove the leaves, for I need light!"

Wes sighed. "I don't take commands from plants, bub!"

Autumna seemed quite distressed by the lawn god's appearance. Leaves rustled as she shook with rage. "Do my leaves not fertilize your roots, Lolium? Be gone."

"My subjects provide me with fertilizer, O brittle one!" Lolium replied. "I owe nothing to you. And the sunlight is of greater necessity in this time of waning days."

"Give me a break," Wes said. "It's too much freakin' work to rake all this. I say go with Leafy."

Wes turned to go. But he was stopped when something grabbed his ankle. A third figure formed, green like Lolium, but with broad leaves and thorns. Dandelion flowers graced its humanoid body here and there, and thin, thorny tendrils had shot out of it to grab Wes's leg and ankle.

"Oh gimme a break!" Wes said. "What are you, god of crabgrass or something?"

"I am Taraxacum, God of the natural plants you spurn for a monospecies lawn!"

"Be gone, Weed!" the grass god spat. "You are not welcome in my lawn!" Lolium's grassy arms grew forth to cover Taraxacum, but the weed god was unimpressed. Without a flinch, he sent tendrils to clog the grass god's roots and began suffocating him. The leaf goddess laughed at their struggle.

"I shall spare you this time, Lolium," Taraxacum said, removing his tendrils. "Thou knowest mine power is greater, but we share a common cause this day!" Taraxacum turned his clover eyes to Wes. "Lolium and I demand that thou rake thy own yard, for we needeth the rays of the sun. If thou rejectest our demand, I shall sprout weeds tenfold across thy lawn." He reached out a hawkweed arm and made a fist. Below him sprouted clover, dandelions, and chickweed. "How wouldst thou like thistles in thy flower beds?"

"Fine, fine!" Wes said. "I'll rake the stupid lawn. Just don't make any more damned weeds!"

"No!" Autumna said. Then the leaf goddess turned her head to the sky and cried, "Oh Crapolleus, come to my aid and I shall be in your debt!"

The wind gusted again, and trash came with it. Newspapers, tin cans, and plastic debris of all sorts rolled and flew to a spot next to the goddess, glomming together into the rough figure of a pot-bellied man. "Watta yous want? I'm busy, here!" it said.

"Just when I thought things couldn't get weirder!" Wes said. He was surrounded on each side. He looked around to see if anyone was watching, but no neighbors were in sight.

"I am in need of allies, Crapolleus," the leaf goddess said, "and the tree goddess is working a clear-cut up in Washington. I will be raked if I do not get help."

"Hmff." Crapolleus turned his double chins to face Wes. "I don't give a rat's ass if you rake these leaves," Crapolleus said, loudly, ignoring Autumna's sudden gasp, then pointed a finger at Wes. "But if you pile them to be hauled to the dump, I'm comin' back, you see, and I'm gonna bust ya good. I ain't got room for yard debris. You'll be pickin' so much trash outta your yard that it might as well be a landfill!"

"Great!" Wes said. "Let's recap. If I rake the leaves and pile them by the road, I'll get trash in my yard and have Leafy mad at me. If I don't rake the leaves, I'll get weeds growing everywhere and incur the wrath of Grass-Guy. Is that about it?"

"So which is it?" Lolium asked, the grass in his body writhing like snakes.

"To rake or not to rake?" Autumna rasped.

Taraxacum pointed to the ground as quackgrass sprouted there. "Maketh thy choice, mortal!"

Wes opened his mouth to answer, but his wife yelled from the house again, head only half turned away from the TV. "Are you raking, honey? Remember the covenant."

"That's it!" Wes threw down the rake and pulled car keys out of his pocket.

"all right already! So what's your choice?" Crapolleus asked, his voice a menagerie of crinkling plastic and banging cans.

"Wait here. I'll be back in a moment with my decision."

And with that, Wes got in his old truck and drove away to the nearby hardware store.

Minutes later he returned with a new lawnmower in the back, a gas can, and a very large brown shopping bag.

The gods were still waiting where he had left them.

"We have grown impatient," Autumna said, leaves whirling around her. "We demand your choice now, mortal!"

"Fine!" Wes pulled down the tailgate and hefted the mower to the ground. "This is a god-damned mulching lawnmower. Fully fueled and ready to go." He shifted his head from god to god as he spoke. "It mulches the leaves, so there will be no raking. The lawn will be fertilized this way *and* the light will get to the grass and the stupid weeds. And I won't have to pile leaves to be hauled away to the landfill. Will that make all you *freaks* happy?"

The gods nodded.

"I do accede," Autumna rasped.

"Thy agreement is acceptable," Taraxacum said, new dandelions blooming out of his chest.

"But here's the catch," Wes continued. "I'll do this for you, but you have to do something for me, too. If any of these fussy old neighbors complain about my yard, I want you to make their yards worse than mine."

"It shall be so," Lolium replied. The others gave nods of approval.

"Then it's a deal," Wes said. "Thank you."

"Fuggedaboutit," Crapolleus said.

Wes yanked on the mower cord and smiled as the gas engine roared to life. "Now, get the hell outta here, you two-bit deities."

Taraxacum and Lolium sank back into the lawn. Autumna fell into a pile of leaves and scattered with the breeze. And Crapolleus blew away like so much debris in a windstorm, leaving candy wrappers and molding newspapers in his wake.

"Finally!" Wes started pushing the mower across the leaf-strewn lawn but stopped abruptly. "Oh! Almost forgot!"

Leaving the mower running, Wes walked to his truck and retrieved the large shopping bag. With a flourish he pulled out a giant pink flamingo and triumphantly planted it smack in the middle of Katie Marie's flowerbeds. It stood there on its aluminum pole, its long neck gracefully swooping to its down-turned bill, for all the neighborhood to view and admire.

Wes went back to the mower and smiled as he ran over the leaves, mulching as he went. "Ah! Now that's the way to *rake*!"

The Children of Magnolia House

JULY

"**H**oney, I'm in love with it already!"

Maggy gawked as the house loomed before them, growing taller in the windshield as the car moved closer. Two stories and an attic with more gables than necessary, Magnolia House was like a gingerbread dream. It surpassed Maggy Bentley's greatest expectations. That queer feeling of childish curiosity crept into her heart for the first time in many years. Eyes wide, she craned her head to look up at the fine woodwork along the eaves.

The realtor, Paula, drove them down a long, straight driveway lined by eight massive magnolia trees on each side that gave the house its name. Still in bloom, they sported bright white blossoms as big as Maggy's hands if she splayed her fingers out.

"Jim, this is magnificent!" Maggy turned to face the back seat. Her husband, Jim Bentley, appeared less excited. He shrugged and pulled out a notepad. The view from the back seat wasn't quite the same, she figured; he peered off to the side through the magnolias to the wide lawn and adjoining grove of pines.

"Just wait 'til you see the insides, Maggy," Paula said. "There's a great staircase leadin' up to a landing with a huge grandfather clock, then the staircase splits off to either side of the house." Paula pulled the Cadillac up to the entrance of the mansion. "I needn't tell you that this is the gem of Calhoon County." She shut off the engine and opened her door. "And it's Gentry Realty's shinin' star," she continued once outside the car.

Stepping out, Maggy immediately felt the difference between the car's air-conditioned interior and the oppressive humidity of July in central Mississippi. It certainly wasn't Seattle, where air conditioners were rarely needed.

Jim looked up the stairs to the double oak doors hidden in the shade of the veranda. "Looks like it needs a fresh coat of paint," he said, his baritone voice rolling low enough not to be overheard by the realtor, "and Lord knows we'd need the shade of that porch."

Maggy shook him off and gazed again at the expanse of the veranda. She envisioned the kids running across it, late for the bus, and lemonades served at the porch swing in the corner.

Paula joined them at the foot of the stairs. The heat had already pulled droplets of sweat onto her forehead, sparkling against her brown skin. "It's got a lot of history, this old place," Paula said. "Opal Evers was the last one to live here, with her husband, Joe, who passed away back in the 80's. It's been in her family since the Civil War. I hear she was a sweet old lady, but she passed up at

Calhoun Oaks a couple months ago -- about the time I came here from Atlanta."

Maggy creased her brow. "So now the Evers are selling it?"

"Not exactly, honey," Paula answered. "She didn't have any more family left. It's all handled by her estate. It was all arranged, you see. She was very clear in her will about how things should be handled...." Paula motioned to move up onto the veranda. Things were cooler there. "The money her estate earns from this property will be given to charity, along with all the other assets. She had a lot of stock in Louisiana oil. Seems the only relatives she had were very distant."

"So what kind of charity are we talking about?" Jim asked, scratching at the paint on the railing. He flipped open his notepad and started jotting notes. Maggy saw him write "Lead paint?".

"She never had children, but she donated everything to kids' organizations: Boy Scouts, Girl Scouts, Big Brother, Big Sister, YMCA, YWCA, private schools, anti-child abuse agencies, orphanages, you name it. Every little bit helps."

Paula pulled at her collar and dabbed a handkerchief across her brow. "Poor old lady must've been sweet, but I don't think she was all there. Just before she died in the senior home she called for her lawyers. When one of them came, she's said to have taken him by the hand and pulled him down to her mouth." Paula leaned toward the Bentleys and spoke in a hushed tone. "Then she whispers, 'Make sure they take good care o'my children. They love a good story, an' they're such good boys an' girls.'" She chuckled. "But she never had children, like I said. Eerie, huh? The only thing anyone can figure is that she was talkin' about the kids she looked after in her younger years, when she ran a daycare here in the house."

"How sad," Maggy said.

Paula pulled out a huge ring of keys and tried one at the front door. "Ah ha! First try. Whatta you know?" The huge oak doors opened and revealed a large entry resplendent in mahogany woodwork and hardwood floors. Paula motioned for the couple to enter, then she closed the doors behind them. A flick of a switch later and the stately crystal chandelier illuminated the room. An expansive, classical ceiling medallion with a floral motif over the chandelier. Oak entry table. A tall mirror with a vase of roses.

"This is gorgeous!" Maggy cried as she turned toward her husband. "Jim, look at this room!"

Jim smiled at her without looking around. He was only three years older than her, but the wrinkles in his face made him look a decade her elder. Such was the life of a medical administrator.

Maggy thought back to their recent conversations. He had taken this job more to please her than himself, though he wouldn't say as much. The house they would choose, too, would be for her. After all, she had followed him around the country as he got one degree and then another. Always she was the faithful housewife, then mother. The job in Washington State was fine, but he knew she longed for a place away from the hustle and bustle of urban life. Sure, he passed up better positions: Minneapolis, Phoenix, St. Louis. There he would have been groomed for bigger steps up the ladder. The little town of Gentry wasn't much, but the hospital was new, at least, and he would be near the top. The pay was just "okay," but who cares? Costs weren't too high here. "We'll probably live like kings compared to the country bumpkins of the deep South," he had said. Maggy had grown up in a small Southern town – a country bumpkin herself. Her artistic pursuits would flourish in the peace of the countryside.

"Well, honey?" Maggy asked again.

"Yeah, Mag. Gorgeous. Look, there's the grandfather clock."

"Oh, it's a beaut, isn't it?" Paula asked. "The clock, like most of the interior, is as it was back in the 1800's. The Evers family renovated the place in the '50's, and then again in the '80's, especially when it came to electricity and plumbing, then they worked on the foundations and the exterior. It's all been kept up. There's central heat and air, too, but more could probably be done to insulate the house. The windows aren't the double-paned type, for instance." Paula opened a couple of coat closets for them to look into. "As you could feel out there, it gets pretty hot in the summertime, but these high ceilings were designed to help keep the house cool. Winter almost never brings any snow here in Mississippi, but we have our share of ice storms. Some houses in this part of the country can have bug problems, but there's been no termite problems with this house, and roaches and other vermin have been monitored...."

"Roaches!" Jim exclaimed. He flashed his eyes to the dark corners of the room. Roaches weren't common in Seattle.

"Don't you worry none," Paula assured, her hands gesturing with open palms. "It's all been on contract with the bug folks. They've been comin' around twice a year and tell me there hasn't been a problem in years. Just be cautious and don't leave food around or anything, and you'll be all right. Seal up your bags and jars. Sweep up crumbs. Common sense'll be enough."

"And they updated the appliances?" Maggy asked, sniffing at the roses on the entry table.

"The Evers were careful to maintain the appliances and keep the place clean. You'll love the kitchen. But let me show you the living room first." Paula led the Bentleys through the doorway to the left, one of four leaving the entry on the first floor. "The Evers family had a long tradition of caring for children, going way back in generations. I'm told this grand old mansion has served as a private school or daycare for as long as Gentry has been a town. It even served as an orphanage for a number of years during the last of the Civil War and the decade followin' it."

"Was there much fighting around here during the Civil War?"

Paula shrugged. "I'm from Atlanta, so I don't know much about it, but from what I've heard there weren't any major battles 'round here. You'd have to go south to Vicksburg or west along the Mississippi River, I think, to find old battlegrounds."

"Where's the basement access?" Jim asked, opening a coat closet.

"There's no basement in Magnolia House, like most homes in these parts, and an old root cellar was filled in years ago. B'sides, I find basements a bit creepy, don't you? Besides, if any ghosts care to hide out, I guess it'd be there." Paula gave a silly wink, and both she and Maggy chuckled.

Jim looked up and gave a quick smile. Superstition had no home with him, or herself for that matter, she thought. He was every bit as agnostic as she was. Belief in ghosts was as ridiculous as believing in UFOs, the Luminati, or Big Foot.

The threesome entered the living room. The room was well lit and spacious, and the grand fireplace around the corner was stout with granite stonework and mantle. At the far end, around the corner, another doorway led to a dining room. Except for the fireplace, the only other object in the room was a large, bookshelf cabinet at the far end.

Maggy's mouth fell open. "Jim! Look at the size of this room! You could fit half our apartment in here!"

Jim just nodded. But the quick twitch of his cheek muscles, a quirk that Maggy had learned to love, gave away his hidden excitement.

Paula continued by opening a side closet. She moved her hands carefully, Maggy noted, so as not to break one of her long, painted nails. "You can see that closet space has been added in recent decades. But that hasn't taken much away from the spaciousness of the living room. Imagine, if you will, having a big family gathering or a magnificent holiday party."

"No doubt," Jim said. He stepped up to one of the large windows and looked out onto the west side of the property. Paula had continued describing the house, but Jim interrupted her. "Paula," he asked, "are there many children in this neighborhood?"

"Probably not. It's a pretty low population around here. Used to be more here than now. But, like so many of these little towns, all the young folks have been movin' away and takin' their kids with them. Lately, though...."

"Well, I thought I saw a kid over there in the woods."

Maggy looked out the window as well, putting her arm around Jim's shoulders. She saw the edge of the woods, replete with dogwoods and towering pines. A well-worn, clay soil footpath wound into it. She didn't see anyone. "Probably just some neighborhood boy, Jim," Maggy said, "I hiked around in woods like these as a girl."

Jim nodded. "Well, I guess so," but Maggy noticed him write "Needs better fences and gate" on his notepad. Maggy knew he was thinking about those "punk kids," as Jim had put it – young teens who had spray-painted the side of their apartment in Seattle. The event had been a catalyst for the decision to move. Maggy flashed him a knowing glance, but Jim pretended not to notice.

Paula continued once the Bentleys turned away from the window. "As you can see, the only piece left of the Evers' furniture is this bookcase." She opened its large cabinets to reveal shelf after shelf of thin books. "I've been told it's an antique of fair value. Opal Evers stipulated that the bookcase and all its contents were to be sold with the house, as is. No doubt it's another of her dedications to children."

"What do you mean?" Maggy asked, moving to take a closer look as Jim made some notes.

"These are all children's books, Maggy," Paula answered. "Take a look for yourself. I'd guess there are at least a couple hundred of them. And look at this." Paula opened the lower cabinets. There, revealed in the bright sunlight, were open boxes of children's toys.

"My word!" Maggy exclaimed and bent down to get a closer look. There were toy cars, balls of all colors, dolls, some made of porcelain, with wigs and eyes that closed, and all sorts of doll clothes. There were little fire engines and wagons, horsies and a miniature farmhouse. A little steel submarine rose from the depths of one box, while a plush dolphin dove into another. Whistles and horns and jew's-harps fought for space with crayons, action figures, and airplanes. Modern Star Wars action figures sat crowded next to an early GI Joe figure. There were toys both recent and old, chipped and stained, played with and cherished.

"Some of these things are real treasures, Maggy," Paula said slowly. Her tone did much to show her respect for the playthings. "I remember seein' some of these toys in old pictures my nanna used to show me. Some are surely antiques. I'll bet you could get top dollar for them on Ebay." After a tick, she added, "Though I think Mrs. Evers meant for it all to stay with the house. She wanted the home sold to someone with children of their own."

A warmth spread through Maggy as she looked at those toys, almost as if they radiated energy of their own. *No, she thought, I don't think I could sell them. I'd be selling someone's dreams. Besides, Jarod and Christine would probably like some of them.*

Almost as if reading Maggy's thoughts, Paula asked, "How old are your little boy an' girl?"

"Four and six," Maggy answered, "Jarod's the oldest, though I'd bargain Christine thinks herself more mature! She thinks she can do anything he can do. In fact, she's always wanting to do what the grown-ups do."

"I'm sure you've looked into schools already," Paula said, "but Calhoun City, where your kids would go, has a brand-new elementary school with lots of new tax money funding it."

Maggy closed the cabinet. All three moved on to the rest of the house. The first floor consisted of the living room, dining room, kitchen with a back door, pantry, lavatory, and a sitting room with another, smaller fireplace. Paula walked along with Jim and Maggy explaining some of the details but, for the most part, remaining silent and allowing the Bentleys to explore for themselves.

The house had been prepped for their arrival, aired out, with fresh flowers placed on end tables and counters. But even after close inspection in the cupboards and closets, Maggy hadn't noticed the usual mustiness associated with old homes. She was pleased to see a modern cooktop stove, new dishwasher, and marble countertops.

"Used to be," Paula explained, "the kitchen and pantry were separate from the house and connected by a covered walkway. That way there was less chance of a fire breakin' out. What is now the kitchen and pantry used to be the servants' quarters a century ago." Paula fiddled a bracelet around her wrist as she talked. "Now the old kitchen building is gone. There's a guesthouse about a hundred yards away where the groundskeeper used to live, and the Evers had an old maid from the country come in to do the housework. I met her not long ago. She's a colorful one, for sure, full of crazy stories!"

Soon the three ascended the staircase to the landing. "As you can see," Paula explained at the landing, "the staircase splits at the landing to the right and left. Used to the males went one way and the females went the other way. This was back in the Civil War days, you see. Even husband and wife slept separate. Now there's a hallway back there linking the two sides."

"Does the grandfather clock work?" Jim asked.

"Oh, of course! But it's very old, and it needs to be started and wound each day if you want to keep it working. This clock is unique in that it's built right into the staircase and the wall. It's impossible to take it out without damaging it."

They continued up the few remaining stairs. The upper floor of Magnolia House showed three bedrooms, two bathrooms, an office, and plenty of storage space. The attic, too, was accessible via a thin stairwell, and, at the top of the stairs, showed itself to be spacious enough for a couple generation's-worth of ardent collecting.

Maggy stepped into the smallest of the bedrooms while Jim and Paula talked about the hardwood floors. She pictured in her mind her daughter's little bed sitting in the corner. A window looked out at the spacious back yard and guesthouse. Maggy imagined lace curtains draped across the window. The desk and vanity mirror that had been her grandmother's would go perfectly next to the window.

Maggy heard a muted thump. A rustle came from behind the door to a small, thin closet. *Mice*, she thought. She quietly grabbed the knob and mustered her strength. Holding her breath, she yanked it open. Empty. Nothing scurried. The dim light from the window showed an open pack of crayons on the floor of the closet. Some were still rolling. *No mouse holes or droppings*, she thought. She looked up. Scrawled in a child's handwriting on the peeling wallpaper were the words

Opul gone

in crimson-colored wax.

"Hey, Paula?" Maggy called. Jim and Paula stepped into the room from the hallway. Maggy pointed into the closet. "What is this? I thought you said Opal Evers didn't have children."

Paula's face flushed, her eyes widened, and she drew in a quick breath. The look vanished as quickly as it had come, though, and Paula resumed her previous, jovial appearance. "Oh, that must be from those children Opal used to take care of." Paula reached over and shut the door. "Guess we missed that spot. It'll be cleaned up right away." She smiled and motioned toward the window. "Care to see the back yard?"

There better not be mice, Maggy thought. The three of them made their way back to the staircase.

"So there aren't any necessary repairs?" Jim asked at the landing.

"None that I'm aware of," Paula answered. "The roof is gettin' a little old and will probably need re-shingled in a few years, but there aren't any leaks. Of course, you'll probably want to have a home inspector take a look at it. And there's lots of landscapin' I'm sure you'd like to do."

Jim scribbled something into the notebook.

Maggy stopped at the foot of the stairs to look again at the entry before they walked out of the house. Jim and Paula were talking, but she paid no attention. *Grand*, she thought, *and it could all be ours. Just like in the movies. The kids would have so much room to play.* She ran her hand over a mahogany baluster and looked up at the gleaming chandelier. It made her feel rich just to stand in the room, to be some Southern belle like Scarlet O'Hara from *Gone with the Wind.*

With a sigh, Maggy followed the others out of the house onto the veranda. Once again, the heat slapped her in the face and wet her forehead. She squinted her eyes against the white-hot glare of the sun.

"And there haven't been any crimes or vandalism?" Jim continued.

"Jim," Maggy scolded, "we aren't in Seattle anymore. There aren't gangs or vandals or carjackings! No one's going to spray paint anything around here." Maggy smiled and put her hands on her hips. "Just a bunch of neighbors, right Paula?"

"That's right," Paula answered, re-locking the front door. "Not much to worry about 'round here. Heck, not many people even bother to lock their cars or doors. Folks all know each other."

Jim still looked concerned, so Paula gave a more direct answer. "No, there have been no crimes reported involving this property that I'm aware of." Paula resumed her soft smile and said, "Would you like to take a look around the grounds?"

"Absolutely!" Maggy said, perhaps over-eagerly.

"I'd like to take a look at the foundation," Jim said.

The threesome returned to the Cadillac briefly to drink from water bottles before embarking on a quick tour of the grounds. Magnolia House sat on about eight acres of land, most of which was reclaimed fields and pine. In front of and behind the house spread lawns of well-tended grass. On either side were pine forests edged with mimosa and dogwood trees with a scattering of wild shrubs, thorny tangles of greenbrier, honeysuckle, and fruit trees.

Near the end of the back lawn, toward the northeastern corner, sat the small outbuilding. Its simple design spoke of long but good care, though it offered little room on the inside. A quick inspection of the interior showed it to have a living room/dining room with a fireplace, a tiny kitchen, and a small bedroom with adjoining bathroom and closet space. But the wallpaper was peeling, the rooms smelled musty and moldy, and the fixtures were old and tarnished. The avocado shag carpet was stained and worn.

Oddly, a little red tricycle stood in the corner. The paint was marred by years of heavy use. Maggy went over to it and pushed it back and forth. It squeaked for want of lubrication.

"Definitely need some serious work in here," Jim said, scribbling away on his pad.

Paula nodded. "True, true. It seems Opal didn't use this space for a long time, and they didn't invest as much in this outbuilding. But I think you can agree there's a lot that can be done here. You could think of it as a guesthouse, or a mother-in-law apartment."

"Strange to have a tricycle here," Maggy said. The others didn't answer.

Stepping back outside, she saw attached to this building was an open shed area for storing riding lawnmowers and landscaping tools. Off toward the northwestern corner of the back lawn lay a good-sized garden radiating around a cherubic fountain. The fountain wasn't running, and the garden was crowded with waist-high weeds and renegade tree seedlings.

The entire tour had lasted a couple hours, and they were all panting and wiping their brows. "So," Paula said upon returning to the Cadillac, "have you seen everything that you would like to?"

"Yeah," Maggy and Jim said simultaneously. Then, frowning, Jim continued. "I think we've seen enough. This place is bound to be over our price range." He closed his notebook with a flip. "There's a lot of work that needs done, particularly with that back building and the landscaping, and taking care of the property would be expensive. Plus, I'm not convinced we need so much land."

Maggy sighed at this last statement. She looked again at the old stone foundation, the vast porch, the stately appearance of the house and its quaint detailing. She had already started picking out curtains in her head. But Jim was right. How could they ever afford this place and its upkeep? But the look in Jim's eye seemed to suggest he was playing hardball with the realtor.

Paula shrugged. "I'm sure there are some good financing options for you, but I can bring your concerns about the price to the seller." Jim remained silent and looked around, seemingly uninterested. "Well then," Paula said, "there's a fine, new two-story brick house on the east side of Gentry we can go to. And there are some more modern homes down in Calhoun City we can look at."

A moment of silence passed between the three of them, broken only by the drone of grasshoppers and the soft whisper of the warm summer breeze through the pine trees.

"Maggy," Jim said, interrupting his wife's thoughts. He started to say more, but he shut his mouth and gazed at his wife.

Maggy raised her eyebrows in regret. "Are we moving on?"

Jim sighed, but Maggy recognized his willingness to please her in the raise of his eyebrow and the smile in his eyes. "Well, let's see if the seller will negotiate the price," he said.

Maggy clapped her hands together and felt her eyes go wide. She threw her arms around Jim and, turning her head, took another look at their future home.

SEPTEMBER

"Mommy," Jarod asked, tugging lightly on his mother's sleeve, "why does Chrisy get to have the room closer to you?"

Maggy looked up from the box she was unpacking. It was one of the last and least important, holding nothing more than a few knickknacks to go on some shelves in the master bedroom. Pulling out a porcelain figurine, she smiled and looked into her son's hazel eyes. "I thought you would like the bigger room."

Jarod looked down for a moment and shifted his feet.

"You're such a big boy now that you don't need your Mommy as much as your little sister does, right? Besides, your room has more windows. Why, you can see all the back yard like your sister's, but you can look out to the woods on the other side, too. You like that, don't you?"

"Yeah. I guess I like my room okay."

Maggy tussled Jarod's hair, then she raised the figurine to eye level. About five inches high, it was a little boy in overalls running next to a frisky yellow puppy. She smiled. Jarod had given it to her last Mother's Day, with a bit of help from Dad.

"Mommy?" Jarod continued, stepping to the box and pulling out a jade trinket chest.

"Hmm?" Maggy put the figurine in its place next to a porcelain bunny from Christine.

"Why does Chrisy get up at night?"

Maggy exhaled in surprise and raised an eyebrow at her son. "What do you mean?"

Jarod shrugged. "I hear her outside my door at night, rolling a ball or something. She thinks it's funny. Sometimes she talks to someone, too."

Maggy forced herself to breath and soften the lines on her face. *Don't want to scare him,* she thought. *Probably just sleepwalking.* "I don't think you need to worry about it, honey. I'll talk to her and get it worked out."

"Okay," he said. "I'm going to go outside and ride my bike."

Maggy nodded. "Just stay in the driveway, son." She watched as Jarod skipped out the room and went down the stairs.

Maggy walked over to one of the large windows overlooking the back yard. Magnolia House was perfect. No one could ask for a more romantic place to live. The place was spacious. The yard beautiful. The area serene. Outside, the few deciduous trees were beginning to change color, autumn hues highlighted by the morning light. *Christine's new behavior must be a result of the move,* she thought. *Jim would know what to do about it.*

The move had been a pain, with Jim driving that outrageously large rental van all the way from Seattle with the Jeep in tow. He simply refused to listen to reason and hire someone, stating, "It's all a matter of money, Mag, think of the money we're saving." So she and the kids drove all the way behind him in the Prius. It was horrible. But at least it was over with. Friends had helped load in Seattle, and, luckily, their agent, Paula, had arranged for help with unloading in Gentry. Then came the unpacking. Since Jim was already getting into his job, she of course had to do most of the unpacking and arranging. Her painting had to wait. *Oh well,* she thought, *not much more to do.*

Maggy turned and looked at the rest of the boxes sitting on the bed. *Bother,* she thought, *I need to shower.* She had been too busy that morning with fixing breakfast and seeing Jim off to work to do it earlier.

Maggy turned the corner into the hallway. She would have to use the hall bathroom rather than the master bathroom since, despite what Paula had said, everything was not working perfectly. Jim had discovered the water had been turned off, so he turned it back on and tried to run the shower in there and wound up getting water all over the floor and into the bedroom. A vital piece of the plumbing had been removed for repair at some point and never replaced. Neither of them knew anything about plumbing, so it would remain unused for a few days until the only plumbing company in Gentry could get out there to fix it. Well, one bathroom was enough, really.

Christine was at the bathroom playing with the door. "Look, Mommy," she said, and pressed the button that locked the door.

Great, Maggy thought sarcastically to herself. "Honey, you mustn't do that."

Christine looked blankly at her mother and locked and unlocked the door with her index finger.

"Christine, honey," Maggy continued, taking Christine's hand away from the door, "if you play with that and lock yourself in there, we won't be able to help you if you need it. And if you lock it and close the door and no one is in there, then we'll all be locked out. That's bad, you see?"

Her daughter only looked confused. "So why is there a lock on it?"

Maggy shook her head. How do you explain privacy to a four-year old? "You see, honey, grown-ups don't like to be bothered when they're in the bathroom, so they lock the door to keep people from entering."

Christine was still confused.

"Never mind. I need to ask you a very important question."

"Okay."

"Honey, have you been sleeping all right at night? Jarod says he hears you up at night."

Christine blinked and played with an oversized, green button on her pajamas. "I sleep fine, Mommy." Then she smiled broadly. "Snug as a bug!"

Maggy grinned. "Snug as a bug!" She grabbed Christine by the waist and tossed her lightly in the air. Christine giggled as she flew, then laughed riotously as Maggy tickled her upon landing. "Snug as a bug!" Maggy repeated. "Why are you still in your jammies? You go get dressed. Mommy will be in the shower, okay?"

"Okay, Mommy." Christine giggled again before she skipped into her bedroom next door.

I've got to get that lock disconnected or something, Maggy thought, and entered the bathroom, closing the door behind her.

The shower was refreshing. One great thing about Magnolia House was its extra-large water heater. No cold showers anymore. No more waiting an hour after the clothes were done.

Maggy was rinsing out the shampoo when she heard the toilet flush, followed by a sudden change in shower temperature. She grimaced and tried to protect herself against the steaming water. She moved the curtain aside to look toward the toilet, but shampoo washed down into her eye. Her eyes were blurry and painful, but she could see a boy standing at the toilet.

"Jarod," Maggy said, "Mommy's taking a shower. Next time use the lavatory downstairs when someone's in here, okay?"

The only answer she got was a boyish giggle. When she looked out again, he was gone.

Maggy soon finished and dried off. *This water's a little hard*, Maggy thought. *Took too much to rinse it off. And the glasses! They all have spots. We'll have to treat it*

134

somehow. Maggy wrapped a towel around her body and another around her hair. *Maybe I'll ask the plumber when he comes. But isn't there something I could buy. I guess I'll....*

Maggy stopped cold. A shiver ran up her spine. The door lock was pushed in. She reached out and tried turning it, confirming it was locked. *Had Christine locked it before I stopped her?* She wondered. *No, of course not. Jarod wouldn't have been able to get in. Jarod must have locked it before he left. That's why he giggled like that.* Maggy smiled and shook her head. *Ha ha,* she thought, *This big old house is getting to me!*

But when she stepped out of the bathroom and looked for him, Jarod wasn't in the house. Looking out a back window, she saw him on his bike way down at the back of the property past the guesthouse.

* * *

Jim got home at five-thirty. Maggy heard the front door open and close with a click. "Ah!" Jim exclaimed. "Lasagna. My favorite!" Jim continued through the living room and into the dining room. "Maggy! You've really outdone yourself!"

The lights were off to allow the candles to work their magic. There on the table sat a meal fit for a king. Lasagna sat in a casserole dish in the center surrounded by a basket of croissants, a large bowl of peas, a dish of asparagus with cheddar cheese, and a nice red wine chilling in a bucket. The tangy smell of marinara sauce mixed with the intoxicating scent of the buttery croissants.

"What's the occasion, Mag?"

"I finished unpacking today. I guess it feels like we're finally moved it," she said from the kitchen. She walked into the dining room. Her red dress highlighted the necklace around her neck. "And it's our one-month anniversary in Magnolia House."

She turned toward the stairs. "Kids, time to eat!"

Jim shook his head and smiled. "Well, I won't bother to get into something more comfortable." He put his arms around Maggy, kissed her lightly on the lips, and winked. "What's for dessert?"

Just then the kids came running past them, dressed in their formal clothes.

"Chocolate mousse," Maggy answered, and winked back.

Dinner went well, with the kids even trying everything. "So I've told you about my day, Mag, how was yours?" Jim asked.

"Other than finishing unpacking, I finally got around to mopping the floors. Trust me when I tell you we should hire a maid! The plumbers called, too. Said they would have to push us back another day. Seems someone's kitchen turned into an ever-flowing fountain. I told them about the hard water problem we have. They said they'd 'be sure to take it into consideration.' That surely means another eighty bucks or so."

"Daddy," Jarod said, quick to turn the topic to him, "there are trails all over the woods." Jim looked up, concerned. "There are lots of toys and stuff back there, too."

"Son," Jim replied, "you really shouldn't go back in there without us."

"Oh, relax," Maggy said. "Let him have his fun. I don't think there are any vagrant gang members running around back there. If anything, there are a few neighborhood kids. He needs to find friends."

"Have you met any other boys back there, Jarod?" Jim asked.

"Yeah," he said, surprising both parents, "I've seen several. Most of them ran away, but I met a couple of them. One's named Nat. The other's Jeremiah. They're friends. Nat's my favorite. He showed me a game today called leapfrog."

Maggy chuckled. Had she never mentioned leapfrog to the kids?

"Where does Nat live, son?" Jim asked.

"I don't know," he answered and shrugged his shoulders.

"Well," Maggy said, smiling. "You see, Jim? He's made friends already." She turned toward her son. "Next time you see them, Jarod, you bring them to the house so I can meet them, and we'll make some lemonade, okay?"

"Okay."

"I don't like lemonade," Christine said, screwing up her face and sticking out her tongue. "Ick!"

"Then your friends can have hot cocoa," Maggy said. "How's that?" Christine nodded vigorously.

Maggy turned her attention back to Jim. "Jarod gave me a start this morning."

"Oh?"

"Yeah. I was taking a shower when he decided to come in and go pee pee, isn't that right, dear?" Maggy winked at her son.

"No, Mommy, I didn't do that."

Maggy's face went blank. "Of course you did, honey, I saw you standing at the toilet."

"Honest, Mommy, I didn't do it."

"I didn't do it either, Mommy!" Christine chimed.

"Yes honey, I'm sure you didn't."

"Well maybe it was one of his friends," Jim offered. "They probably didn't know any better."

"Is that true, Jarod?" Maggy asked. "Did one of your friends come in to use the bathroom?"

Jarod shrugged. "I don't know, Mommy. Not that I know of."

"Well, son, next time you see them you tell them it's very bad manners to go in a bathroom that someone is using."

Jim and Maggy exchanged a look of puzzlement but didn't say anything more about the issue. Soon the kids were allowed to go put their dishes in the sink and go play.

"It seems Christine may be sleepwalking," Maggy said after they left. Jim looked up, concerned, but remained silent. "Jarod said he hears her up at night playing in the hallway and talking to herself. But she says she doesn't wake up. I'm afraid she may fall down the stairs or something."

Jim nodded and put his wine glass down. "It's probably just the stress of moving away from the only home she's known. It's a busy time, and we're often too distracted to devote enough time to her."

Maggy looked down and thought, *You mean* you *are too distracted*, but she kept the thought to herself.

"I'll ask for advice from one of the child psyches at work," he finished.

* * *

The weekend found Maggy stripping the old wallpaper in the musty guesthouse. It was a messy job, and she had just begun. Much of the wallpaper was hanging loose from the walls, and the design was horrid. It reminded her of some of Jim's ties. But the wallpaper was only the beginning. The carpet would have to be replaced. The bathroom mirror was cracked. In addition, she discovered that a family of mice had made themselves a home in the bedroom using yellowing newspapers as nesting material.

Maggy had just stopped to take a drink when she heard laughter in the yard. She stepped into the living room and looked through the little window in the door, parting yellow corduroy curtains. The cloth smelled of mildew. Jarod and Christine were running around the yard near the garden and tossing a red rubber ball with a star on it. But they weren't alone. Two boys and a girl were running around them. One boy, surely no older than seven, had dark black skin and a ragged puff of nappy hair. Barefoot, he was dressed in shabby clothes that seemed to be made of burlap. The other children were very pale and over-dressed, though they looked like children from an old daguerreotype photo. The boy wore light blue overalls and a starched white button-down shirt with his hair parted in the middle and oiled. *Oiled! People have such strange customs down here*, Maggy thought. The girl, on the other hand, was dressed in a white dress and ribbons as if she were going to church.

Maggy decided she would meet the new friends. She shut the curtains and opened the door, spilling her glass of water. By the time she picked up the glass and stepped outside, the only children she saw were her own.

"Jarod. Christine," she called, and her kids came running to her, breathless. "Who were those children?"

"That was Nat and Jeremiah and Pearl, Mommy," Jarod said. "We've had the best time. We went and played catch and I taught them how to play Frisbee. Nat says that when he lived here he would go fishing just down the road with...."

"Wait a minute, Son. Slow down. Where did they go?"

Jarod seemed dumbfounded. "I don't know. They had to go."

She thought, *Did he say, 'when he lived here?'*

All three looked out over the lawn. Nothing moved there save a handful of oak leaves blown by the wind. The ball lay in the grass, weathered by years of neglect.

* * *

"It's been a heck of a week, Mag," Jim complained as he lay limp in the recliner. "The nurses' union is giving us grief about the new benefits package and hanging all over us to get new employees. They just don't appreciate how far in the red we've gone."

It was nighttime, and the glow of corner halogen lamps gave a warmth to the living room. Jarod played with Legos on the floor over by the fireplace.

"The restaurant options here are the pits, Honey," Maggy said, ignoring Jim's complaints about work. "It's all burgers or pit barbecue joints, unless you count the Mexican place down Highway 9." While she talked, she mindlessly flipped through cable channels and thought about her oil paintings. She had spent several days working on a view of the front lawn through the sitting room window, but she had made little progress. There were simply too many little things that needed addressing.

"I guess there's no such thing as fresh salmon here, huh?" Jim asked. "Or sushi? If only we could go back to Pike Place for some off-the boat fish!"

"Yeah! And - oh! - I'd kill for a good cup of coffee!"

"Amen!" Jim added. Maggy joined him in a good laugh, then they both sighed as one, missing the Northwest.

"What's Christine up to tonight?" Jim asked.

"Last I knew she was up in her room having a tea party with her dolls."

"We shouldn't keep them up much later."

Maggy watched Jarod dreamily. "They've grown too fast. He starts first grade tomorrow, and she's already in pre-school."

"Yeah, but at least we didn't have to get on a waiting list like back in the city!"

Jarod hummed softly to himself. His attempts at creating the objects of his imagination were bearing more fruit lately, as evidenced by his father's growing ability to identify them.

"Mommy, will you read to me tonight?" he said without looking up.

"Of course, Honey. How about Berenstain Bears?"

"Umm," Jarod answered, still building a little house, "I think I'd rather read one from over here." He turned and pointed toward the closed bookcase.

Maggy looked at the bookcase as well. "Well, okay. They're mostly books about Christmas and other holidays, but if you want...."

"Not all of them are on Christmas," Jarod interrupted. "Sara told me about a Dr. Seuss book about a furry guy who doesn't like stumps. She said it's her favorite."

"Sara?" Jim asked.

"Yeah, and she said her second favorite is about a boy, but that one fell behind the bookcase and she can't reach it." Jarod struggled to break apart two stubborn Legos, resorting to using his teeth. "She said she likes the cover cuz it's green."

Maggy and Jim were speechless for a moment, then Maggy broke the silence. "Honey? I told you to introduce your friends to us. We should meet them and their parents before you start inviting them in like that." She got up and went over to the bookcase. Glancing around, she found it was too dark to see into the crack behind it.

"Jim," she asked, "where did we put the flashlight?"

"There should be one hanging in the closet there."

Maggy opened a closet door and found the flashlight hanging there. Looking closely, she found that Jarod had been correct. A tattered book was wedged down into the space with a wad of dust bunnies. It looked pretty fragile, but she figured it would hold together well enough if she got a clothes hanger and pulled it out.

Just then Jim's cell phone chimed. "Hi, this is Jim Bentley." There was a moment of silence. "Okay." He waited for a minute before talking again. "Hi, John. What's up? Oh!" His eyes went wide. "Well, what.... Uh, huh. Is it out? Okay, I'll be right there. Did you notify the insurance.... Okay, I'll come right in. Bye."

Jim stood up and went to the entry. Maggy heard the jingle of keys as Jim turned the corner back into the living room. "Mag, there's been a little electrical fire in one of the personnel rooms near Pathology. It isn't much, but I really ought to be there to get things in order." He walked over to Maggy and gave her a kiss, then he lightly pinched Jarod on the cheek. "Hopefully I'll be back in an hour or two. Please tell Chrisy I'll be back soon."

"Okay, honey. Take care." Maggy walked him to the door and watched as he started up his Jeep and rolled quickly down the driveway.

Returning to the living room, she turned her attention back to the book. With a couple well-place pushes against the heavy cabinet to inch it forward, and the help of the coat hanger, she managed to pull the book out. The cover was olive green, with a picture of a boy in ragged clothes and wide-brimmed hat standing in front of a yellow fence. On the cover was written "Adventures of Huckleberry Finn (Tom Sawyer's Comrade) by Mark Twain" with the H and F, and the author's name, in yellow. Gently opening the front cover, she found to her great surprise that it was a first edition print. Handwritten on the cover page in faded, flowing script was "To the children of Magnolia House, Christmas 1885. - Iler Mae Evers."

Maggy turned her attention back to Jarod and went to sit on the ground next to him. "Jarod, honey," she asked, "how did your friend Sara know about this book? Did Opal Evers read to her before we came?"

Jarod barely looked up from his Legos and, still humming, shrugged his shoulders.

OCTOBER

The windows were open to allow a pleasant breeze to come in from the "Indian summer" outside.

"Is someone there?" Maggy asked, looking around the door frame into the entry.

She had been in the sitting room working on a landscape when she heard the distinct sound of a ball bouncing on hardwood. When she stood up, the sound stopped. The kids were both at school, and Jim was at work.

"Hello?" she said, looking up toward the second level, but no one answered. The house was silent.

Suddenly she jumped as the clock bonged. She caught her breath and let out a halting laugh. "One o'clock," she said nervously.

"Hickory dickory dock!" a little girl chanted. Maggy wheeled and caught sight of a white skirt and a black dress shoe as the child disappeared around the corner to the kitchen.

Maggy gasped, heart pounding. She found it in herself to step around the corner and peer into the kitchen. A counter, white tiles, fruit basket. Nothing out of place. She took another step.

"The mouse ran up the clock," the girl continued. Her shrill voice echoed off the kitchen tiles. Once again Maggy turned too late and saw the flash of a white dress.

"Sara?" Maggy guessed, thinking about the girl that Jarod had mentioned a week or so before.

The girl giggled, then Maggy heard the shoes run across the tile and onto the hardwood of the dining room. "You're it!" the girl yelled.

Maggy jogged after her through the kitchen, the dining room, the living room. She looked behind the curtains and under tables, listened for doors opening, for the pounding of girl's shoes on the floor. But the house was silent.

"Little girl?" Maggy called out from the entry, "Sara?" But her voice came back distant and hollow.

* * *

Jim came home at the usual time, seven o'clock, and the four of them sat down for supper.

Maggy sat quietly, stabbing at her thawed and boiled ravioli.

"And then the fire alarm rang, and we all walked outside!" Jarod said, eyes wide and beaming. "Mrs. Foster said it was a drill, but Pete said no. I told him he was dumb."

Maggy glanced up and put on a smile, half listening. "That's nice dear. Then what?" She looked back at her ravioli, but she caught a glance from Jim.

"He was looking for smoke. I told him he needed glasses, and I was right! There was no smoke!" Jarod burst out with laughter. "Poop head!"

Christine and Jarod both laughed hilariously, mouths open, bits of ravioli falling to their plates.

Jim smirked and glanced over to Maggy. His eyes suddenly lost their smile.

144

Once the kids settled down, Jim asked with a worried tone, "How was your day, honey?"

"Fine." She broke a piece of garlic bread and flashed a tight smile.

"Can I go get more?" Jarod asked.

"Me too!" Christine shouted. Maggy nodded, so both kids ran off to the kitchen with their plates.

"I'm sorry I'm late again," Jim said when the kids were gone. "It's just...."

Maggy held up her hand. "It's me. I think I'm losing my mind a bit."

Jim sat back. His shoulders loosened and brow relaxed.

Maggy grimaced. "Maybe I'm alone too much." Jim looked down but remained silent. She continued. "This afternoon...." How could she say it? *Honey, I think there's a ghost child running around the house chanting nursery rhymes?* "I just get these strange ... feelings, like I'm being watched. Like I'm not alone."

Jim nodded. That little renegade strand of brown hair fell onto his brow. It was the only cute thing left of the college boy that she had fallen in love with. "It's a big house, Mag," he said, "and we're still settling in. Maybe you should go out some. Join a painting club or something, like you did back in Seattle. Or, I've been thinking: maybe we could get a dog for this big place. You could use the company."

"I do get a tad lonely." Maggy looked him in the eyes. "Do you think we could eat lunch together?"

Jim frowned and looked back to his plate. "I'm awful busy, Mag. Maybe I could fit it in once in a while, but it would be late. Sometimes not 'til two o'clock."

Hickory dickory dock, she thought. "Whatever. Give me a call when you can."

The kids returned and dug into their dinner again. For several minutes the only sound was the scraping of forks and a distant groan as the house settled.

"Daddy, I made a picture for you!" Christine chimed suddenly, making Maggy jump.

"I know, Chrisy," Jim answered. "Mommy showed me when I got home. It looks very pretty. It's a picture of a tree, isn't it?"

Maggy recalled the barely recognizable rendering of an orange collection of vertical lines with lime-green circles over it.

"Uh huh," Christine said, nodding vigorously. "I go there every day after school to see Sara."

Maggy choked on her pasta, taking a moment to frantically catch her breath.

"Nuh uh," Jarod said, glaring at his sister.

"Do too!"

"No you don't anymore!" Jarod argued. "Not after last week!"

"Okay. Okay," Jim said. "That's enough. Jarod, why do you say this? What happened last week?"

Both the kids were quiet as Maggy and Jim looked on.

"They had a fight," Jarod finally said.

"Shut up!" Christine chastised.

"Sara said she lives in Magnolia House," Jarod spouted toward Christine, lips pursed and looking down his nose at her. "When Chrisy and I told her no, they got into an argument."

Jim put down his fork. "That's enough, Jarod. Chrisy, next time someone says something like that, just be quiet and walk away. It's a foolish thing for your friend to say. *We* live in Magnolia House. Now you should go and make friends with her again, and if she says that again just ignore her."

"Okay," Chrisy said, playing with her food. "But I'm not letting her have tea with me anymore."

Maggy coughed again. Not fully recovered, she asked, "You mean to say that Sara has been in the house having a tea party with you?"

Chrisy nodded slowly. "I'm sorry, Mommy. I've told them you wanted to see them first, but they say they don't want to be seen by the grown-ups yet."

"*Them?*" Maggy asked, too loudly. Her meal was long forgotten, the room immaterial. Her total attention was on her daughter.

Christine's eyes widened, swelled with moisture, burst forth into a rain of tears. "I'm sorry, Mommy!" she sobbed.

Jim got up and put his arm around the girl. "There, there. Mommy isn't blaming you." He threw a severe look at Maggy.

Maggy sighed and slumped her shoulders. Hand over her eyes, she excused herself and walked out to the living room, the wet apologies of her daughter following her out.

* * *

Noon, the next day, and a light rain was falling. Maggy made her way around the house watering plants. The stereo in the living room was belting out Pavarotti's version of D'Anzi's aria, *Malinconia D'Amore*, and the tenor's clear voice echoed through the house. She had first learned the aria in Italian class at Rhodes, but the song had lost its charm.

Malinconia d'amor. / L'amavo tanto, / l'amavo d'un amor sincero e puro; The melancholy of love. / I loved her so, / with a love sincere and pure.

Maggy stepped slowly from the master bedroom to the upstairs hallway, watering can in hand. Her eyes began to water. She feared to look around each corner, afraid to see a flash of skirt or hear a childish giggle.

Io l'adoravo come un fiore raro / ma il giuramento suo non era vero; I loved her like a rare flower, / but the vows she spoke were untrue.

She turned to go into Jarod's room ... and suddenly stopped dead in her tracks with a loud exhale, the watering can dropping to the floor with a loud clatter and splash of water. Standing in the middle of the room was a small boy about Jarod's age. He wore light blue overalls and a starched white button-down shirt with his hair parted in the middle and oiled. He was one of the boys that Jarod and Christine had played with outside the guesthouse.

"Hello! I'm Jeremiah," the little boy chimed, and waved quickly. "Where's Opal?"

Maggy felt the blood drain from her face. She couldn't breathe. Finally she put her hand on her chest and took a deep breath. Just a child. Just a flesh and blood little boy ... who came in unannounced ... on a school day.

"Opal doesn't live here anymore," Maggy said.

"Oh." Jeremiah was already bending down and playing with one of Jarod's toy cars. "Isn't it just fine?" he asked. The last word was drawn out with a rare, genteel, Southern accent. "Never have I seen a carriage this color!" He pronounced it like *cuh-luh.*

"Um," Maggy said, "you scared me. Shouldn't you be in school, Jeremiah?"

Jeremiah ignored Maggy, preferring instead to drive the blue convertible car around a circular throw rug.

"Jeremiah," Maggy said, taking a step closer, "you shouldn't come in without knocking, you know. It's not nice."

He stood up, his eyes wide. "But I live here!"

Maggy blinked. Flesh and blood, she thought. Just a boy who came in unannounced. "Jeremiah, what is your phone number? I think I need to talk to your mother."

Jeremiah stared blankly at Maggy. Then, without a sound, he disappeared, the car falling to the floor with a clatter.

Maggy yelped and put a shaking hand to her mouth. Her eyes darted around the room in the hopes of seeing him, but Jeremiah was nowhere to be found. There was no place for him to hide.

"Oh!" Maggy said quickly and backed out of the doorway. "Oh, God!" Maggy's hand was still at her mouth in shock. She stood, dumbfounded, in the hallway for a couple minutes trying to rationalize the situation. But she couldn't deny what she had seen. She had been blocking the doorway, so the little boy couldn't have run out.

Maggy turned and ran down the hallway, down the staircase, and out the front doors to stand, breathless, under the veranda. She sat hard upon a wicker chair by the front door and stared out into the rain-soaked driveway.

Oh, God! she thought to herself. *What just happened? What just happened?*

* * *

Maggy sat on the veranda for the better part of an hour before she got the courage to go back in for the car keys. Retrieving them in a heartbeat, she left the house again, started the Prius, and headed off the property. Fifteen minutes later she pulled into the parking lot of Calhoun Memorial Hospital and jogged inside, heading straight to the administrative suite.

"Mrs. Bentley!" the secretary said, a smile plastered across her face. "What a surprise to see you. How are y'all doing out there?"

"I need to see Jim right away," Maggy said, fighting to appear emotionless.

"Well, he's in a meeting right now, Mrs. Bentley. Would you like me to tell him you stopped by?"

"It's important, Thelma," Maggy said with a touch of urgency in her voice.

"All right," Thelma said, her brow creased. "Please wait here while I tell him." Thelma stood up and walked briskly down a neighboring hallway.

Maggy paced nervously for several minutes. Finally, Jim emerged with Thelma in tow.

"Maggy," Jim said, taking Maggy's hand. "What's wrong? You're ashen. Are you okay?"

Maggy pulled Jim away from the reception desk. "Jim," she whispered, barely audible, "something very strange just happened at home."

Jim blinked and waited patiently while Maggy struggled for the words.

"I ... I was in the house, watering plants," Maggy whispered, "when I went into Jarod's room.... Jim, there was a little boy in there. He said his name was Jeremiah."

"What's so strange about that?" Jim asked, frowning. "So he came in without asking...."

"No, Jim, let me finish." She looked over her shoulder to see how close Thelma was. "I ... I was talking with him ... and he just ... disappeared."

Jim blinked again. "Disappeared," he repeated, incredulous, a little too loudly.

"Yes," she whispered. "*Disappeared.* One moment he was there, playing with a toy car. The next ... he vanished!"

Jim rubbed Maggy's hands, his face perplexed. He was about to speak, but Maggy interrupted him. "I know, I know. It sounds strange, but I know what I saw. And he didn't, like, leave the room without me seeing. I was blocking the door, and I was watching him the whole time. I even saw the car he was holding drop to the floor."

"Look," Jim said, "I have to get back to the meeting. I have union leaders in there. We'll talk about this when I get home. Meanwhile, why don't you go and get the children out of school early and take them to get ice cream at King Kone or something. And calm down, okay?"

Maggy huffed. She wanted to scream. *Does he think I'm lying?* But she nodded, forcing calmness. "Okay," she said, "I'll do that." *What else could I say?* she thought. *Maybe I imagined it. Maybe I'm going insane. Ghosts don't exist, right?*

They looked each other in the eyes. An intercom in the hallway outside announced that a doctor was needed somewhere. Thelma sharpened a pencil. Jim tapped his fingers on his thigh.

"Okay then," Jim said haltingly. "I have to get back."

She nodded. He gave her a peck on the lips and they went their separate ways.

Maggy did pick up the kids early to get ice cream, returning to Magnolia House later than usual. Jim arrived a little early, but neither of them brought up the subject of Jeremiah. Instead, they stayed together that night in the living room watching a documentary and went to sleep early. Maggy lay awake for hours, dreading that at any moment she might hear childish laughter over Jim's snoring.

* * *

The next morning came. Jim took the kids to school as usual, leaving Maggy alone with an unpleasant feeling in her gut. The house was empty, now, and she wondered what spirits lurked in the halls. Yet she was determined that she had imagined the whole thing. She spent the day painting, in defiance, attempting in vain to forget. But the paintings were as dark as her thoughts, the brush strokes fast and swept like the tight breaths she took.

And nothing odd happened, that day or the next.

Two days later, Maggy was sewing in the office when she heard a clatter from downstairs. Instantly her stomach dropped and her heart raced. She gasped, and the sewing machine stopped its drumming to idle expectantly. Then she heard the clatter again. It was the sound of someone throwing things to the floor. Then two children laughed.

Maggy stood up on shaking legs and walked to the stairs. The clomping of her shoes against the creaky, wooden floor sounded impossibly loud to her. She stopped at the top of the stairs and stood listening. All was silent again.

Gathering her strength, Maggy quickly went down the stairs to the entry and stopped again. She started the search with the living room. Turning the corner, she stopped in the doorway. The toy cabinet had been thrown wide open. The toys themselves had been pulled out and were now spread across the floor; the boxes in which they had been contained were overturned. A Tonka truck still rolled toward her doorway.

She looked nervously around the rest of the house, but no one was to be seen, and the doors were locked.

* * *

"Jim, this house is haunted," Maggy said that night, her voice more solid than she had expected. Jim lay with his back to her, but she knew he was faking sleep; his breath was too light, too irregular. "Did you hear me?" Maggy asked.

"Yes," he said.

Outside, leaves hit the window. A wind was rising. She smelled rain in the air.

"Do you know what I mean?" she asked.

"Yes," he answered. He didn't elaborate, as if trying to avoid the subject. But Maggy pushed forward.

"It's the children," she added. "Not ours. Jarod and Chrisy's 'friends.'"

Jim sighed heavily.

She hesitated, unable to say what she was thinking. "I mean, it's like the other day -- that incident with Jeremiah. Then this morning I heard a clatter and went downstairs to find that all the toys in that cabinet had been strewn across the living room floor."

Maggy let what she had said sink in before she continued. "But that was nothing ... *nothing* compared to what happened this afternoon. I was washing dishes and I heard laughter in the sitting room. The kids were still at school...." Maggy choked slightly. "I finally found the nerve to put the dishes down and look in there. But no one was there." Tears welled up in Maggy's eyes. Jim finally turned, but his face was in shadow. "I walked into the room and saw my paintings sitting there, leaning against the wall where I left them. And, on one canvas, there was a little stick figure painted in red right in the middle. I touched it. The paint was fresh!" Maggy's breathing was much harder now.

Jim reached out and touched Maggy's shoulder, but Maggy jumped in surprise.

"Shh," Jim reassured, and Maggy moved closer. "It's all right."

"It's not all right," Maggy whispered, too softly. "I'm afraid to be here alone anymore for fear of hearing someone in the halls or catching a glimpse of some child sitting in the other room. I can't even look outside anymore. I've seen them playing in the yard!" Her voice was rising. "Jim, what are we going to do?"

"What are you suggesting, Mag? That they're ghosts? Do you seriously think we're being haunted?"

"That's what I said, damn it!" Maggy was shaking enough to make the mattress jiggle. "What the hell else could it be?"

"I don't know. I'm sure it's all innocent. Maybe it's a couple little kids playing a prank on you. You know?"

The windowpane rattled with a sudden gust.

"God damn it, Jim," she yelled with surprised anger, sitting half out of bed. "Don't you think I know the difference? Can't you just believe me?" Tears sprang forth again. Jim recoiled as if punched. "You're always gone! You never see them! I just sit around this god damned house while you work away our marriage. And you never see them!"

"So what do you want?" Jim yelled back. "Huh? Do you want me to quit my freakin' job? Is that what you want? Because I can't cut back! It's a new hospital and there are a million things that need done and I'm the one they load it all on! We've got a huge mortgage to pay off. You're the one who wanted this place!"

Mouth hanging open, Maggy was too shocked to cry. But she wanted to. She wanted to so badly.

Jim caught his breath. "And now you tell me about ghost kids running around the halls? Well what the hell are we supposed to do about it? Move again? Get a witch doctor?"

Maggy did start to cry then. "I don't know," she sobbed, burying her head in the pillow. "I don't know." The sobs wracked her lungs, exploded in loud gasps and wetted the cloth under her face. "I'm going insane."

She felt Jim's hand stroke her shoulder, tentative, wary. But she rolled over and pulled him close to her, her face in his chest. She cried herself to sleep that way, nestled in his arms, dreaming fitfully.

NOVEMBER

Maggy had taken to leaving the house after Jim and the kids left in the mornings. The house wasn't getting cleaned, but she found a certain solace by taking her canvas, easel, and painting supplies with her to one of several beautiful areas around the county. Her mind eased a bit, and she allowed herself to return to the painter's way of thinking from the right side of the brain. Magnolia House seemed far away when she outlined the form of an oak tree, its barren branches crooked and gray and radiating away from the trunk in ever-diverging forms. The air had a chill to it, yet she didn't allow that to take away from the joy of painting landscapes.

She usually found herself returning to one location in particular. Recently renovated by the local Elks lodge, the covered bridge over Johnson's Creek was a beautiful example of 1920's engineering. Spanning forty feet, the wooden structure sat firmly against each shore, merging into a gray rock face on one side and gently resting on soil on the other side. The wood was painted a barn red on the outside, and the shingled roof was a light green -- a color combination that, on any other structure, would look ridiculous. The bridge with its accompanying creek and forest made for a very bucolic setting.

But she always had to return to Magnolia House. Each afternoon Maggy would have to pack her canvas and equipment into the Prius, go pick up the children, and return to the house. There was always some sign of the other inhabitants. Toys were taken out and left lying around the house or yard. Scribbled drawings made on the walls. Footprints left in the driveway. And, every now and then, she would catch the flick of a dress out of the corner of her eye or hear muted laughter from the other room. Sometimes she'd even hear one playing or whispering in the hallway at night. She often found herself waking from nightmares, and every night she would sneak into the children's rooms to make sure everything was all right.

* * *

The next Saturday, Maggy once again found herself working in the guesthouse, this time ripping out carpet. It was violent work, fit for her mood, and it kept her mind off of the ghosts. Christine was with her, despite the dust and sweat. Maggy wanted her close. There had been no sign of the ghost children all morning. It was as if they had avoided her, which was just fine with her. But Christine kept looking through the window and doors for her "friends."

Maggy had just pulled up the carpet from one corner of the room when she heard a child call out, "Chrisy! Come play with us!"

Before Maggy could stop her, Christine ran out the door, laughing. Maggy ran to the door to call her back but stopped cold.

The back yard teemed with children!

Where the lawn had been empty moments earlier, there were now dozens of children, some black and some white, ranging in ages from around five to about ten, dressed in a myriad of clothing styles and eras. There was even a Native American boy in moccasins and a red loincloth. Where before there had only been the soothing whisper of wind through the pines there was now the joyous merriment of children running and playing, completely ignoring her. One boy in faded overalls went zooming past her door on the little red tricycle.

"Chrisy," Maggy mouthed, but little more than a hoarse croak issued. Christine was now playing chase with two little girls who looked to be straight out of old black-and-white photos of Civil War-era children.

"Chrisy!" she repeated more urgently and stepped with increasing speed toward her daughter. "Chrisy, honey, we need to go inside right now." Maggy dodged two boys as one chased the other with a wooden revolver.

Christine stopped the chase for a moment to look at her mother, allowing one of the girls to catch her. "Got you!" the girl yelled, tagging Christine's arm with her palm.

"No fair!" Christine said to the girl.

Maggy grabbed Christine's hand and started to drag her toward the house.

"But, Mommy, Nan and me and Hester are playing!"

Maggy didn't answer.

"Mommy, why don't you like my friends?" Christine asked as she pulled against her mother.

Maggy rushed into the back door of Magnolia House and called out for Jim. Turning into the entry, she stopped dead at the foot of the stairs watching four little girls playing with dolls on the steps. One of the girls looked up and saw them standing there.

"Hi, Chrisy!" the girl said, her lithe voice chiming. "When Sara gets here do you want to play tea in your room?"

"Sure," Chrisy replied, ignoring her mother's tight grip on her shoulder.

"Maggy!" It was Jim at the top of the left flight of stairs next to the office. "Can you believe this?" Jim's eyes were wide, and he held Jarod's hand as the boy strained to go down the stairs.

"Jim," Maggy said, "we've got to go."

Jim nodded, his face slack and eyes darting. He pulled Jarod with him down the stairs and around the girls. Soon the family was in the Jeep driving off the property.

* * *

"Daddy, why did we leave?" Jarod asked. The four of them were sitting on a picnic table in the Gentry Town Park huddled against a chill breeze.

Christine started to cry again. "You told me to make friends with Sara again, Mommy! Did I do it wrong?"

Maggy didn't know how to answer.

"I ... I'm speechless," Jim said. "One moment the house was empty. The next.... I think it's painfully obvious that our house is haunted." Jim turned to Maggy and put his hand on hers, "You were right."

Maggy nodded.

Jim continued, "A boy materialized right next to me in the office. Scared me to death! He said his name was Sid, and he wanted to know where Opal was. When I backed away, the boy just pointed at the window, then he disappeared! I looked out the window, and one minute the back yard was empty, the next all these kids were running about. I went to get Jarod, and three other kids were in his room with him!

"I'm sorry I didn't believe you." He paused a moment, then continued, "So what do we do? We certainly can't go on like this! Should we get a priest? A psychic?"

"What's a psychic?" Jarod asked.

Maggy didn't know how to answer her son. She just shook her head and stared at two girls swinging in the playground. She couldn't help but wonder if maybe *they* were ghosts, too.

"Jim, it's not like they're harming us. But I ... I'm scared to death."

"Daddy, can Chrisy and me go play on the slide?"

"No, son, you two just sit here for a while, okay?"

"Jim!" Maggy said abruptly. "Didn't our real estate agent ... Paula ... didn't she say that Opal Evers had a maid?"

Jim thought for a moment. "Yes, I believe she did. I think she said 'An old maid from the countryside.'"

"Well, don't you think the maid would have seen all this? I think we should find out who she is and get some information."

Jim nodded, and soon the family was off to visit Gentry Realty to question Paula.

* * *

Night had fallen by the time they drove up to the old wooden shack and pulled into a dirt driveway. It had taken hours to find the place in the rural roads around Gentry, following Paula's directions. The GPS was hopeless on the winding, dirt roads, when they could actually even get a signal. But the result seemed promising. Lights streamed through the little windows of a home that matched Paula's description.

Jim and Maggy walked up to the screen door and knocked, rattling the flimsy mesh and plywood.

"I'm comin'," a voice called out, wavering with age. Soon the inner door creaked open to reveal an aged black lady, her white hair frazzled and unkempt. "Who are you?" she demanded, eyes narrowing behind thick glasses.

"I'm sorry to disturb you," Jim said. "Are you Delilah Curry?"

The woman's tired eyes looked at Jim suspiciously. "Yes. Why? My Jerome done gone and broke the law again?"

Jim was confused a moment. "Um, no. I'm not a policeman or anything. You used to be a maid for Opal Evers at Magnolia House, right?"

Delilah softened for a moment. "Yes, I was. Heard she passed away a little while ago, God rest her soul."

"Mrs. Curry, I and my family," Jim motioned to the Jeep, where the kids had crawled into the front seat, "live in Magnolia House now, and we need to ask you a couple urgent questions."

Delilah cackled a little, her eyes sparkling. "I 'spect you're here to ask me about them ghost children, aren't you?" Her smile broadened at the look on Maggy's face. "Maybe you and the family had better come in. It's cold out tonight, and I still have some warm cornbread and chitlins on the table from my supper."

* * *

The five of them were seated comfortably in the cramped living room of Delilah Curry. The room's walls were wallpapered with faded green stripes and covered with family photographs in cheap frames. An old iron stove sat at the far end giving the room warmth. The linoleum in front of it showed burn marks from a hundred embers that had jumped out over the decades. The house smelled of bacon from the chitlins, but there was a homey undertone that can only come from decades of home-cooked meals, old clothes, and old woman.

Delilah Curry was a fragile-looking old lady with skin stretched tight across most of her bones, but she moved as if she were in her sixties. "Now don't you be alarmed or nothin' about them ghost children," Delilah said, a smile across her face. "I was wonderin' how that realtor would break the news to the new people movin' into Magnolia House. Seems they didn't, huh? Musta thought it was some silly tale I told 'em." Delilah cackled quietly. "Opal always loved them children like they was her own. She never had none, you know. Barren. But she didn't care. Them children were like her own."

"What did you think when you first found out?" Maggy asked.

"Oh, well, Opal says to me, 'Now, Delilah, you gotta know somethin' strange that's happenin' 'round here. There are ghosts in this home.' Well I was always real scared-like of ghosts and such, bein' a religious woman. So when she tells me this, I turned to leave. But then I stopped myself. I had a family to raise, you know? I had five children at that time and a no-good drunk of a husband, so I couldn't go leavin' good money. So I turned back 'round and told Opal I was takin' the job, ghosts or no ghosts.

"Now, I don't know what I was expectin'. Maybe I thought some devil would be jumpin' at me 'round each corner or some white man I could see through would be shakin' chains or somethin'. Or maybe things would go flyin' through the air. But I never saw nothin' like that. I saw children playin' 'round the house and yard, and sometimes somethin' strange would happen, or they'd all come and go sudden-like, but I thought they was all Opal's kids and their friends. They was shy 'round me for a while, but they seemed real normal 'cept for how old-fashioned they seemed. So about a week after I started workin' for Opal I says to her, 'Ms. Evers, how come you said this house is haunted? I ain't seen no ghosts.' Opal then looks at me and smiles. Then she grabs my shoulder and turns me 'round to face some little children playin' on the front steps of the house and says, 'You're lookin' at 'em.'

"Now, I thought maybe Opal was pullin' my leg. 'They ain't ghosts,' I said to her. 'They're just kids like any other.' Then Opal calls out to the children and says, "Nat. Anna. Call Jeremiah here. I need him right now.' Then the kids say, 'Okay,' close their eyes and then ... poof! ... there appears right before my eyes this third little child! Just like that. I didn't take it too well. I ran off and didn't come back for a couple days. But I eventually had to go back 'cause I couldn't find a job anywhere."

The room was silent for a moment.

"So, Delilah, you're saying we shouldn't be afraid of these ghost children?" Maggy asked.

"Afraid? Heavens no! These little children are as sweet as can be. Just like kids anywhere. Maybe just like they'd been when they were alive. You get used to them."

"But, Delilah," Jim said, "we're a little uneasy having ... ghosts in our home." Jim glanced nervously at Chrisy and Jarod. The two were on the floor coloring an ancient-looking coloring book with crayons so old they were brittle.

"I understand that," Delilah replied, "but *you* got to understand somethin'. Magnolia House is *their* home, too. As rightly as I can tell, them ghosts are the souls of people who lived there as children, goin' *way* back. Heck, I'd occasion'ly see Indian children playin' out there! I guess there's just somethin' about Magnolia House that makes them want to have a vacation there from Heaven or somethin'." She rubbed her arthritic knuckles and stopped to think for a moment before continuing. "Now, there are some things I should tell you 'bout the children. The number of 'em grows more and more toward the end of the year. They really love Christmas, you see. Though they love holidays of all sorts. It was always Opal's thing to read stories to 'em at Christmas time. They would all expect it and would file into the living room and sit on the floor, all crowded together. Then Opal would read to them about Jesus from the Bible and tell them all about the story of Christ's birth. Then she would read other stories to them about Christmas. Opal always loved to read to the children, but Christmas was her favorite."

Maggy grimaced a little. She was agnostic. Lately though....

Delilah continued, "Now don't be thinkin' they're just goin' to be runnin' wild and takin' over your life and all. You gotta give 'em room, but they ain't goin' to bother you at night. They don't need to eat, but sometimes they'll go through the motions when it suits them, usually when it's cookies or pie or when they have some little prank to pull. But they're real good children and usually do as told. They'll even stay away, usually, when you have guests over or somethin' and tell them ahead of time. Jus' like with living kids, you have to set rules and bound'ries. Even bedtime!"

"But how do we get rid of them?" Jim whispered, glancing at his own children with guilt.

"Now, Jim," Delilah scolded, raising her finger, "I just told you that Magnolia House is their home, too. You can't be gettin' rid of the children without gettin' rid of the house, too. So I suggest you either get used to them or move out!"

* * *

The rest of the month was tense at Magnolia House. Every day Jim and Maggy would discover another new child or two. There were children around the house and yard at every daylight hour, now, and sometimes into the early evening. Groups of them would be jumping rope in the driveway, digging in the garden, or playing cowboys and Indians in the woods, sometimes including real Indian children. Their footsteps and laughter echoed through Magnolia House as they chased each other up and down the stairs, and there were always finger marks where a child had tasted the frosting of a baked dessert or licked the bowl. Furthermore, the ghost children were staying inside more often now. "It's too cold outside," some would say.

Jim and Maggy refused to trust the ghost children. Christine and Jarod were never allowed out of their parents' sight, and they were forbidden to play with the ghosts. Naturally Christine and Jarod were appalled at the new regulations. "They're our only friends!" Jarod lamented, but Maggy only replied, "You'll know why, someday. Just do as you're told."

Jim was more adamant. Maggy, at times, would ignore it when the ghost children and her children would talk to each other, but Jim would always scold her for that. With Jim around, any attempt by Jarod or Christine to interact with the ghosts would be reason for a quick scolding and separation. Most of the daytime hours were spent at work or school, taking time after school for "drives in the country." Weekends were likewise spent away from the house, though the Bentleys quickly ran out of new places to go, and it was too cold for outdoor activities.

DECEMBER

The constant strain of avoidance was taking its toll. The house was a mess and the yard had grown unkempt. Jarod was constantly angry with his parents. Christine cried all the time. And Maggy and Jim were cross and stressed.

"This has got to stop," Maggy said. She and Jim were sitting in the dining room around nine o'clock at night after the kids had gone to sleep and the ghosts had left. A fire crackled in the living room fireplace.

Wind whipped against the window of the dining room, and Maggy felt a slight draft prick at the arm nearest the windowsill. Jim lowered a glass of wine from his mouth. The surface of the red liquid rippled from a slight shaking. He nodded.

"I think it would be a good idea if we had Delilah Curry come work here again," Maggy continued.

Jim looked up, perplexed. "Why?" he asked.

"Jim, this house is in shambles. We're so busy keeping the kids from seeing the ghosts that we haven't had time to do anything else. We need someone to watch over Jarod and Chrisy and maybe help with the cleaning."

"Maggy, she's so old. I'd swear she'd snap in two if she tripped. She'd probably break her hip or something. She's surely too old to do all the work around the house. And what if the kids got in trouble? Do you really think she'd know what to do?"

"I'm not necessarily suggesting we leave her here alone with them. But at least she would be here to watch Jarod and Chrisy while we do some of the things that need done."

"Why not get another maid? Someone else."

"And who are we gonna get? How do you think the average person would take a house full of ghost children? Delilah already knows about them. What's more, she's *used* to them. She may even help *us* get used to them."

Jim had started to raise his glass again, but he slammed it down, sloshing the wine onto the table. "Dang it, Maggy! No one's going to just get used to them. Either they go or we go. Besides, I called a Catholic priest today in Jackson. I read he performed an exorcism a couple years ago in Alabama. It took forever to find him, but he said he would be happy to come next month. All we have to do is keep the kids away from them one more month and it'll all be taken care of."

"What?" Maggy said, tensing. "Why the hell didn't you ask me about this? You hired a priest without asking me? No priests! Do you hear me? No chants or rituals."

The only sound was the wind again as the two stared at each other across the table.

"You sound as if you don't want them gone," Jim said under his breath.

Silence again as Maggy stared at the tabletop.

"Well?" Jim asked. "What is it? Are we in agreement or not?"

"I'm seeing it differently, Jim. I mean, the ghosts never caused much problem. It's like last week. You had that heart doctor and his wife over for dinner and it all went well. It was still early enough to see the ghosts, yet they weren't around. They didn't bother us. They play with Jarod and Chrisy, and Delilah swears they never do anything bad. What do we have to fear?"

Jim glowered at Maggy for several minutes. "*Fine,*" he spat. "We can hire Delilah Curry, if she's willing. But the ghosts have to go. The priest is coming, like it or not!"

* * *

Two weeks had passed after they hired Delilah. Maggy had to get away from Magnolia House and the role of mother. She needed some time to clear her head and left for the covered bridge, purposely leaving her cell phone by the door. Maggy knew Jim wouldn't approve, but the stress had become too much. Besides, she hadn't painted -- seriously painted -- in over a month. Things had been too strange. The easel in front of her had upon its surface a large canvas with the covered bridge half-painted upon it. She was really too cold for comfort, and there had been an ice storm only a week before, but the action of sweeping the brush across the canvas surface and the soft gurgling of Johnson Creek melted away some of the tension in Maggy's shoulders.

It was a Saturday, but Jim was at work sorting out some of the economic concerns of the hospital. Or so he said, anyhow. Maggy suspected that he was doing the same thing she was – running away. She left the kids in the care of Delilah. The old woman was proving to be a godsend for the Bentleys. She had been given explicit instructions not to allow Jarod and Christine to interact with the ghost children, even though the little ghosts knew Delilah well. It had been half a decade since Delilah had stepped foot in Magnolia House, but the ghost children had greeted her as if it had only been yesterday. Delilah, in return, had given every single one of them a giant hug, much to Jim's disapproval. Delilah's sheer joy at seeing the children of Magnolia House again and treating them as if they were her own lost children only added to Jarod and Chrisy's confusion and anger at being kept apart from them. Seeing this, Delilah was quick to act in accordance with Jim's rules. "It's okay," Delilah had said. "I ain't gonna mess around against your wishes. I'm just happy to get to see my children again." The old woman had shone like the rising sun that day.

Yes, Delilah was very respectful of Jim's rules. But Maggy wondered if Jarod and Chrisy were playing with the ghosts right now with Delilah's approval.

A part of her wished it so.

Maggy knew that Jim wouldn't be in until suppertime, so she continued painting. The wind started picking up around three o'clock, so she packed up the canvas and supplies and aimed the Prius toward Magnolia House. An hour later she drove up the driveway and stopped at the veranda.

Maggy closed the door and went to the rear of the car. She started to open the hatch but stopped. Something was wrong.

Maggy straightened with a start and turned quickly toward the veranda. Lined up on the veranda were at least thirty ghost children. Gone were their smiles. They just stood there, faces slack, arms at their side, watching her. A chill ran up her spine, and she took a step back in fear. The overcast sky only deepened the shadows on their faces, and the wind and rustling leaves eerily blew past, magnifying the ghosts' eerie appearance.

"Go to the hospital!" shouted one child near the front doors. It was Nat. He took a step forward.

"Chrisy's been hurt!" shouted Sara.

"Go to the hospital!" yelled another.

"Chrisy fell and hurt her head!"

"Go see Chrisy!"

"Delilah's there!" Jeremiah said.

"Go see her!"

Maggy ran to the front of the car and leaped into the driver's seat. Breathless, she roared out of the driveway and down Highway 9 to Calhoun City.

* * *

"Oh, Mrs. Bentley, I'm so glad you're here!" Delilah cried, eyes and arms open wide, when she saw Maggy step into the waiting area.

"What happened?" Maggy asked as she stepped down the hall, frantically looked for room 2023. "Where's Chrisy?"

"Mrs. Bentley. I didn't know what to do," Delilah cried as she did her best to keep up with Maggy. "She ... she locked herself in the bathroom and I couldn't get in. I didn't know what to do!"

Maggy found the room and turned through the open door.

"Chrisy, honey!" she cried, putting her hand on Christine's arm. Christine's head was bandaged, and the area under her eyes was becoming dark and bruised. Chrisy murmured, "Mommy."

Maggy looked up and saw Jim standing on the other side of the hospital bed. Jarod was sitting in a chair next to him somberly playing with an action figure on the bedside table.

"Someone tell me what happened!" Maggy demanded.

"Get her out of here!" Jim said, pointing at Delilah.

"But Mr. Bentley, I didn't do anythin' you didn't want me to!"

"That old woman went against our instructions, and look what's happened!"

"What are you talking about?" Maggy demanded of Jim. "Tell me what happened!"

"Christine fell in the bathroom and hit her head on the tub. She got a concussion and a few stitches. She'll be all right. But she was trapped in the bathroom when it was locked from the inside! Those ghosts are to blame. I know it! And this sad excuse for a maid should have been there! I told you we shouldn't have hired her! And didn't I tell you not to leave her alone with the kids?"

"Mrs. Bentley, I swear I didn't do anythin' I wasn't s'posed to!" Delilah said in her defense.

Maggy sighed and put her hand to her head.

"Get out!" Jim said to Delilah and started toward the old woman.

"Jim, stop," Maggy said. The sudden calmness of her voice was enough to stop her husband. "Delilah," she continued, "were you the only one there when it happened?"

"Yes, ma'am, except for Jarod and a couple of the children."

"Why don't you tell me what happened."

"Yes, ma'am." She took a deep breath. "Jarod and Chrisy and me were playin' when she needed to go potty. So we went up to the bathroom. Next thing I know I hear the little one fall and hit her head and start cryin'. I tried to open the door, but it was locked. I tried so hard to open it, but it wouldn't move. I called to her to unlock it, but the poor thing just cried. I didn't know what to do. Jarod started cryin', so I kicked at the door, but I just wasn't strong enough."

"It's true, Mommy!" Jarod added. "Delilah was kicking and hitting that door like a pro wrestler, but it wasn't budging!"

Delilah continued. "Just then Nat walks up to me and pulls on my apron. 'Mrs. Curry,' he says to me, 'I can help.' I was all in tears, and past any help, so I says to him, 'Okay, Nat, you go in and unlock the door.' I know it was against your wishes and Mr. Bentley's wishes, ma'am, but I didn't know what else to do. So Nat walks through the door and unlocks it from the other side. I was able to go in, then, and see to the little girl. I bandaged her head right away and stopped the bleedin'. I called 911 for an ambulance, then I called Mr. Bentley." Tears streamed down Delilah's face as she turned and looked down at Christine.

Maggy looked down at Christine, too. "Chrisy, honey, did you lock the door to the bathroom?"

Christine nodded slowly.

"Why did you do that? Didn't I tell you not to?"

"I'm sorry, Mommy. I just wanted to be like a grown-up 'cause that's what you said grown-ups do."

Maggy brushed the back of her hand across Chrisy's cheek.

"You mean *Chrisy* locked the door?" Jim asked Maggy.

Maggy nodded. "I caught her playing with the lock some time ago. I guess she remembered and tried it again."

Some moments of silence passed. Then Maggy looked her husband in the eye. "You see, Jim? I guess the ghosts aren't to blame after all. Looks like they were the heroes here. Without them our little girl would have been a lot worse off."

Jim nodded and remained silent, staring at the bedstead.

* * *

Christmas day arrived, two weeks later, and Christine was back to her normal self. A great multitude of children milled and played in Magnolia House on Christmas Day, the air redolent with scent of cloves and cinnamon. Every corner had holiday decorations. A massive tree stood in the corner of the living room, and another graced the sitting room. Maggy waded through the throng toward the living room followed by a dozen children demanding a story to be read. There were so many children that she couldn't remember all their names.

She smiled as she hung the last of the decorations in the entry. "Okay, okay. Go into the living room and I'll read you the best one of all." The children yelled out a *hurrah!* and ran into the living room. All the furniture had been moved out of the living room to make room for everyone except for the bookcase and a large recliner next to it. Soon all the children were skipping and running into the normally spacious room and finding places on the floor until there was hardly space to walk without stepping over them.

"Cookies, anyone?" Delilah called out from the kitchen, and soon platters of brightly decorated and cleverly cut cookies were passed around the room. Maggy moved toward the chair as carefully as she could, escorted by her two children. Christine smiled up at her mother as Maggy sat down in the recliner and Jarod took a seat on the floor.

After Chrissy's accident, Jim had softened, and within a week they finally gave their approval for Chrisy and Jarod to play with the kids again. All was forgiven, and the priest was told not to come.

"Okay. Quiet now!" Maggy called out over the din. "Quiet and I'll read you all another story."

The noise settled, and soon there was hardly a peep from the children. Maggy smiled and grabbed a large, black-bound volume from the bookcase. But she had just started to open it when someone tugged on her shoulder. Turning, Maggy saw Sara standing with a little girl Maggy had never seen before. The new girl was probably about eleven years old with long, straight, brown hair and a wide smile exposing a gap in her teeth and a slight overbite.

"Who do we have here, Sara? Another new arrival?" Turning toward the new girl, Maggy said, "You were almost too late to make the story hour."

"Mrs. Bentley," Sara said, "this is Opal. She'll be joining us for awhile."

Delilah, who was standing at the entry to the dining room, dropped her jaw and leaned forward.

"Opal?" Maggy asked.

"Yes, ma'am," Opal said. "Glad to make your acquaintance."

"Opal Evers?" Delilah asked and moved forward.

Opal turned and hugged Delilah around the waist. "It's me, Delilah! I've missed you so much!"

Delilah shook her head in astonishment and hugged her back, eyes welling up. "Well! God be good! I was wonderin' if you'd be comin' around."

Maggy could hardly believe it. She remembered to close her mouth, then blinked and composed herself. "Incredible. It's so good to meet you, Opal!" She wondered how many of these children had been prior owners of the house. *Will I be in the crowd here, one day?*

"Okay, you two, take a seat." She smiled at them, then opened the book in her lap.

Maggy paused a moment before reading to look up at her audience. Jim stood in the doorway of the entry, leaning against the frame and smiling. Standing next to him, Nat took Jim's hand in his.

The lights of the Christmas tree in the entry reflected off the nearby window and defied the coldness of flurries falling in the dim light outside. The children all stared at Maggy expectantly and grew quiet. So, after a quick glance at her own children at her sides, she began reading:

> And so it was, that while Mary and Joseph were in Jerusalem, the days were accomplished that she should be delivered.
>
> And she brought forth her firstborn son, and wrapped him in swaddling clothes, and laid him in a manger; because there was no room for them in the inn....

Mommy

"I can't tell you what it means to have you look after our little girl. We just need a break, is all. Just a ... a break," said Mrs. Langston, the last added with a waver.

"It's no problem, Mrs. Langston," said Kaylee. "You guys have been neighbors for so long, it's a wonder I haven't babysat for you before." She hefted her schoolbooks from one arm to the other and smiled.

Mrs. Langston rummaged through her purse, light pouring out of the half-open doorway behind her. Bulging black leather blended into the woman's evening gown as lipstick cases rattled against pens and coins. Mr. Langston stood beside her, his eyes darting back to the open front door, down at his wife's jostling purse, up to Kaylee, and again into the house. The car keys jingled as his beefy hand shook.

Kaylee remembered when *she* had been a little girl, and the Langstons' daughter, Jenny, had just been born. Mr.

and Mrs. Langston had looked so different then. Happy. Relaxed. They used to come to her dad's barbecues. Now she never saw them anymore, and Jenny didn't play in the back yard like she used to. The swing set Jenny got on her third birthday lay covered with vines and half-hidden by tall grass.

Mrs. Langston finally found what she was looking for, a scrap of paper, and handed it to Kaylee. "Now, honey, if anything happens, you call us at once." She made eye contact, and Kaylee saw a thick paste of makeup over badly hidden lines around the woman's eyes. A sliver of brown-dyed hair cascaded over her left cheek, betraying silver roots. She didn't seem like she should be that old. "You should read it as soon as you get into the living room, where there's light. There's plenty of light there."

"Sure, Mrs. Langston," Kaylee replied. She looked at the paper. In the wan light of a yellow porch lamp, she could make out a scribbled phone number. "But you don't need to worry. I've done this lots of times."

Mrs. Langston glanced toward her husband, wide-eyed, before pasting on a smile. "Good. Good." She looked back to the open door and her eyes become unfocused. Then she came to as if remembering something of vital importance. She pointed a jagged fingernail at the teenager. "And don't try to take Jenny outside, do you understand?"

"Yes. Sure," Kaylee exclaimed. "Why would I? It's dark."

"Right." Mrs. Langston shook her head. "Of course you wouldn't. Remember it.... And make sure to keep the light on."

Mr. Langston grabbed his wife's arm and tugged her toward the car, but Kaylee stopped them. "You haven't told me when Jenny's bedtime is. Or is she asleep already?"

The woman let out a quick, uncontrolled twitter of laughter, her eyes flashing and teeth showing, before suddenly getting control of herself. "She's probably asleep already, but ... sometimes we let her up when she wants."

Kaylee blinked in surprise. She'd never heard of such a loose bedtime schedule for a six-year-old.

Mrs. Langston rummaged through her purse again. "Here," she said. With shaking hands, she shoved a fifty-dollar bill into Kaylee's hand.

The couple quickly stepped to their sedan, leaving Kaylee puzzled at the door. Mr. Langston opened the passenger door for his wife, practically ran around to the other side, and all but threw himself into the driver's seat. Mrs. Langston stood at her door, looking toward the house with wide eyes, before joining her husband in the car.

Kaylee turned as the car pulled out of the drive. She was briefly blinded by the light of the living room, then she gasped. Her books fell to the steps.

A little girl stood in the middle of the entry, arms slack at her sides, staring at Kaylee with eyes that burned with accusation.

"Jenny! You startled me!" Kaylee said.

The girl continued to glare, her hands balling into little fists, wadding her Minnie Mouse pajamas with each clench and unclench.

Kaylee bent and retrieved her schoolbooks, then she took a step to enter.

"I wouldn't come in here if I were you," the little girl said.

"Now Jenny, that's not very nice. I'm supposed to babysit you while your mommy and daddy are gone."

"My mommy's not gone."

Kaylee frowned. She looked around the empty room, blinking at the brightness of the place. Every light was on, extraordinarily bright. And there was the overwhelming scent of cheap rose perfume. She stepped inside and closed the front door behind her.

"I told you not to come in!" Jenny screamed in a reed-pipe voice.

They stood in a small entry with stairs behind the girl leading to the second level. To the right was the living room. Odd symbols were scrawled over the doorway. They reminded her of the Viking runes she'd seen in her history textbook, but there were other symbols that looked like her mom's astrology stuff. To the left was the dining room. Kaylee put her books on the entry table and approached the girl. Jenny took a step back.

"Don't come near me or I'm telling Mommy!"

"Honey, I know you miss your mommy, but she'll be back in a few hours. Promise."

"My mommy isn't gone! She's right there!"

Kaylee followed Jenny's pointed finger to the dining room. Beyond the oak dining table was a doorway into the kitchen. Sparkling countertops with yellow cupboards. A gas stove. A knife block. There was a large empty slit where the biggest knife should go.

The kitchen lights went out.

Kaylee caught her breath and stepped back. She glanced down at the child as if to insure it hadn't been her who turned off the lights in there. "Hello?" she called toward the kitchen. No one answered. "Hello?"

The teenager tried to control her breathing. *Just a dead bulb,* she tried to tell herself, but she could almost hear a murderer breathing around the corner.

"Okay," she said more to herself than to Jenny. "Your parents just left. They wouldn't have left without telling me someone was in the house with you. That's why I'm babysitting. You're alone except for me."

"Am not!" Jenny cried. "And *you* have to go *away!*"

"You say your mommy is in there? Then who just left in the car?"

"That was my other mommy."

Another mommy? Kaylee thought. *Stepmom? An aunt, maybe?* "Oh. Can you tell this mommy to come in to see us?"

Jenny nodded her head, blond curls bobbing at her bangs. Then she said matter-of-factly, "Mommy. Come here. I need you."

Kaylee looked toward the kitchen, listening carefully. But there was only the beat of a moth over one of the halogen lamps in the living room.

"She doesn't want to come right now," Jenny said, brow tensed.

Kaylee nodded. She realized her lower lip was quivering, but she made it stop by biting it. She reached into her pocket and withdrew the slip of paper with the phone number. She pulled out her cell phone to call them.

The floor creaked in the other room.

Jenny giggled. It was the light, playful giggle that only a little girl could make, but it sent shivers down Kaylee's spine.

She looked toward the kitchen, but there was only darkness, with a stab of bright light piercing from the dining room.

Kaylee dialed the number from the paper. There was a ring on the other end.

She glanced over to Jenny. Her finger was at her mouth, poking at a devilish grin as if she were privy to something outside of Kaylee's realm. Unnerved, Kaylee turned the scrap of paper over and over in her hands.

"Shit! Come on!" she muttered, listening to the unending ringing.

"Mommy doesn't like cussing!"

Kaylee looked over at the girl, then back to the kitchen. Then she looked down at the piece of paper in her hand. On the other side from the phone number was a scrawled message. It read: *Don't leave the living room. STAY THERE! LIGHTS ON!*

Kaylee gasped. She shot another look to the kitchen. A shadow moved. She was sure of it.

She dropped the phone just as it someone answered on the other end. "Oh fuck!"

"I said Mommy doesn't like cussing!" Jenny screamed, shriller than before.

In a thrust of bravery, Kaylee cried, "You come out now, whoever you are!"

Something heavy and metallic fell to the floor in the kitchen. Kaylee yelped and jumped backward, eyes glued on the kitchen doorway.

The smell of roses assaulted her nose as the shadows in the kitchen took on a life of their own. They shifted, playing on the edges of the doorway and coalescing into a cloud. Jenny giggled in the background as the cloud became humanoid, huge, and opaque black. It became three dimensional, then the figure raised its head. Crimson eyes opened and flashed at her.

Kaylee screamed and grabbed Jenny's arm, pulling her toward the front door. The little girl yelled and fought against the teenager, slapping her, pushing her bare feet against the carpet.

The shadow figure growled.

The ceiling lamp over the dining table popped and went out, throwing that room into darkness.

The figure advanced soundlessly into the dining room.

Kaylee screamed again and grabbed the kicking child by her waist, dragging her toward the front door. "Come on, damn it! Move!"

All the bulbs in the entry's chandelier blew out at once, showering glass shards.

The beast slunk into the entry.

"Mommy's going to spank you!" Jenny cried. "Bad girl! Bad!"

Kaylee reached the door and tried to yank Jenny out.

With a shriek, Jenny pulled a butcher's knife from behind her back and slashed at Kaylee's arm. Kaylee screamed in pain and let go of the girl, arm pumping blood from the wrist. "You little bitch!" she screamed.

Jenny put her other hand at her mouth, cackling, the knife held at an angle away from her. A dribble of Kaylee's blood rolled down the edge to redden the tips of Jenny's little fingers, fingers too small to wrap completely around the knife's handle.

Kaylee wrapped the gash on her wrist with her other hand. Looking up, she screamed and stepped backward.

The figure loomed over her, coldness emanating from it like from dry ice, threatening frostbite at the touch. Before Kaylee could catch her breath, the beast grabbed her hair and pulled her into the dining room toward the kitchen.

Screaming, Kaylee pulled at her hair to try and release the beast's grip.

"You're gonna get a spaan-king!" Jenny chanted, conducting her song with the bloody knife.

"Help!" Kaylee cried, tears streaming down her face. "Oh God! Help!"

"Maybe Mommy will let me cut you again!" Jenny said, waving the knife at Jenny's belly.

Lunging, Kaylee grabbed the knife from the girl's hand and sawed through her own hair. Released from the beast's grip, she dropped the knife and ran as fast as she could back toward the doorway.

Jenny screamed, "Get her, Mommy!"

The figure howled. The remaining lights in the house exploded in a sudden drawing of darkness -- except the living room.

Feeling the figure's chill at her back, Kaylee leapt out the front door and to the foot of the steps. She slammed into the cement at the bottom of the steps, crying and disoriented. In a flash she scrambled up and ran screaming into the night, glancing back.

Jenny stood in the dark doorway, her pajamas colored yellow by the porch light, shaking the knife at Kaylee. Over her head were two bright spheres of flashing red light.

"You're a bad girl!" Jenny yelled after the teenager. "We've got your blood! Now you'll have a mommy, too!"

Jason A. Kilgore

Thicker Than Water

A nicely-painted sign hung in Robert's parlor, just above the marble mantle. *Blood Runs Thicker Than Water*, it said, in red script. His father had placed it there two decades before, much to the disgruntlement of his mother, and it hadn't been moved since. It didn't match the mahogany dining set or the rich, burgundy velvet curtains, but who was there to care anymore? Both of Robert's parents had died years ago, leaving him the house and property as their sole child, and he wasn't one for visitors. Still, he liked to glance at it as he ate his breakfast each morning at precisely five o'clock, before the sun could come up and ruin the darkness in his mind.

He always ate alone, listening to the unending tick-tock of the grandfather clock and the sounds of the old, creaky manse. Over the years, he'd tried to make friends. Invited them over. Even a girl or two. But inevitably he longed for family. He was all that was left of his proud lineage other than distant cousins in far-away states.

His friends never understood. They said he had to move on. Get out of the old house. Live a little.

And, they said (their voices falling low), "Maybe don't obsess so much on occult stuff."

In the end, they all went away, and he was still here.

This morning Robert sensed a change in the atmosphere, a stillness in the air of the old Victorian mansion that had been built by his grandfather's grandfather. He looked up from his soft-boiled eggs, listening, but there was only the shift and creak of the old house as a wind whipped up the fall leaves outside. He turned back to his eggs, smashing one open with his spoon, letting the jaundice-yellow yolk run over the bone china of his plate. But the spoon stopped halfway to his mouth, egg white slipping off the edge.

He heard a dry rasping like the whisper of a veil across dusty floors, so soft that at first Robert thought it was a trick of his mind. Yet the rasp grew steadily louder until he realized it was no trick, no misinterpretation of the whirling tempest outside.

He lowered the fork and scooted his chair back, scraping the oak floorboards in sudden exclamation, and looked down the hallway. The rasping came from down there. Down where the shadows grew darker. Robert raised his cloth napkin to his lips, then dropped it to the table as he stood.

The sound rose and fell, now more like a moan than a whisper, forming syllables he couldn't quite catch. Robert tightened his jaw and took one step, then another, down the hallway.

The moaning came from the first door on his right. The door to the basement.

Robert reached into a pocket of his robe and withdrew a skeleton key, then cautiously placed its gray-black, iron teeth into the keyhole. He turned, and the mechanism inside clunked and unlocked.

He placed his hand on the fluted glass knob, felt the chilled, spiky texture of it, and turned. The latch caught briefly, then the door swung inward.

The moaning grew suddenly louder, its rise and fall now forming clear, sighing syllables. "Free ... us," it said. "Robert. Free ... us."

Old cedar stairs descended into an inky darkness. The wood of the lower steps creaked as something stirred on them.

Robert stood straight and tilted his head. "No," he replied. "Did you expect me to change my mind simply because you haunt me?" He reached out and flicked the light switch on.

Below, at the base of the stairs, lay a skeletal body, its face staring upward. Strips of decomposed skin, as gray as Robert's key, still clung to the corpse's bones. The faded and stained remains of a suit hung crookedly on the body, slipping down to expose a scapula. An arm stretching toward Robert. Its jaw moved, and the words came again. "Free us." The corpse pulled its bony remains another step up the stairs, slipping across the wood with a hollow abrasion.

On the floor behind it, another decomposed corpse in a tattered dress pulled itself toward the stairs. "Free us," it echoed, its voice more feminine. "Robert."

"I'm enjoying the company," Robert said. "Now, if you will excuse me, Father, I have breakfast to finish. Do try to keep it down. You too, Mother." He flicked off the light and shut the door, locking it and putting the key back in his pocket.

Sitting down to his eggs again, Robert smirked as he heard his father say once more, "Free ... us," the words now muted behind the door and merging with the wail of the wind.

"Blood runs thicker than water," Robert said, then finished his meal.

Like Candy, My Sweet

"**Y**ou've been a good boy," the demon whispered, its voice silky and feminine. "All good boys deserve candy."

Allen couldn't keep his hands from shaking. He scratched mindlessly at the frayed cord of his headset and watched the door. He stared hard at the knob. He waited, chest tense, lungs ready to explode for just a breath. Any moment, he thought. Any moment....

"Where is she?" Allen wailed.

"She's coming, buttercup," the demon whispered. Her words were as dry as October leaves, muted and distant through the headphones behind the static. "The wheels are set in motion."

Allen's ears ached. He felt his mouth twist and scowl. Sweat dripped into his eye and stung like chlorine. "Fuck your wheels. Where the hell is she?"

Static. Allen heard only the faint buzz of static. He reached to the old Garrard stereo and adjusted the volume control. The buzzing grew louder. He'd bought the 1970's stereo system because of his love of old records. Paid an insanely high price. He hadn't imagined the spirit that would come with it, hidden in the static of the analog radio.

Allen looked again toward the door. It sat firm in its frame, stout and heavy, windowless.

He turned and gazed into the corner of the room. Darkness. Nothing moved. Only a naked bulb in the kitchen lighted the room and its pitiful, ripped furniture. The hollow light it projected filtered through a shroud of cigarette smoke. But he could make out the slumped body. The limp arms. The legs with one high-heeled shoe still on a foot, the other bare.

"I am here, buttercup," the demon said. Her words boomed through the earphones as Allen yelped in surprise and frantically played with the volume control. "I have been here through it all."

Static again. Allen wiped his brow. Turning to look again at the corner, he remembered Sandy... and the she-devil.

"You said Sandy would be here when I finished the deed. You said she would *be* here."

"She will be, my sweet. You have only one more service to give me."

Allen closed his eyes and sighed, long and deep, as if his soul had escaped in one breath. Months had passed since that first encounter, and every day the demon spoke to him through the stereo, whispering prophecies about his wife. "She will restrict your spending," it would say, "She'll guilt you into not drinking," or "She will stop you from visiting your friend." Always the prophesies were true. The demon taught him. Taught him, patiently, to see how Sandy had grown different. Grown more controlling. Was working toward some secret agenda to control him.

Then it told him why. Last week the demon said, "She is not your wife, Allen. She is a she-devil. She is like me. And she took the real Sandy away. But I am warning you, Allen, for I wish her dead. For you. Kill her when I say, and I shall return your Sandy, the *real* Sandy, to you in the flesh."

"I'm tired," Allen said. His eyes glazed. The bloody knife by his foot blurred into a haze of gray and crimson. The knife he'd performed the ritual on, just like the stereo demon taught him.

Life with the she-devil had been difficult, but Allen held on. Until the command had been given. He had taken the butcher's knife and waited, sitting in the recliner, house dark, cigarettes passing from the pack to his lips to overflow in the tray.

He started to cry. The she-devil had *looked* like Sandy. It was dressed in Sandy's business clothes. It sounded like her. It smiled when it walked in, asked, "How was your day?" And it screamed. Oh God, how it screamed! He still felt the slip of the knife into its flesh. How it had scraped against a rib. How the she-devil had writhed in his grip and grown still.

But Allen knew better. The demon from the earphones told him the truth. The demon from the earphones *always* told him the truth.

"There, there, buttercup. All will be well."

"But it bled. You said it wasn't human, but it bled." Allen looked again toward the corner. He could just see the outline of the she-devil's body, curled into a fetal position. He had dragged its dying body there. His hands had come up wet and red. Its face had looked so real, like Sandy's.

"We demons can be very tricky, my sweet. The blood isn't real."

Allen reached to the ashtray and flicked his cigarette. The ashes fell together, spent and cold, to crumble onto the pile of butts. The blood had *felt* real, he thought. Had been warm. "If I do this last thing for you, do you promise the real Sandy will be at the door?"

Static.

Allen's eyes darted back and forth – to the door, to the corner, to the door again. "Hello? Are you there?"

"I am here."

"Do you promise?"

"Of course. You will get your candy, my sweet."

Allen picked again at the cord with renewed energy. The static grew, but the demon's voice rose above it.

"You must carry this out," the demon said. Its voice grew louder, deeper, growling like when it had commanded to kill. "If you fail ... oblivion."

Allen looked again to the corner. His face went slack. "I haven't failed you yet."

"Then you will submit!"

Allen spasmed as a jolt of electricity surged up his body. He gasped for breath and found himself lying on his side, the frayed and split wire of the headphone still clutched in his hand.

The earphones were quiet. No voice. No static. He threw them aside and pulled the plug from the stereo, turned the volume to high. There was only static from the speakers.

"Demon!" Allen stood and rotated, shouting to the corners. "Demon! What must I do?"

He was breathless now. He ran to the curled body of the she-devil and kicked it. "See?" he yelled. "See? It's dead. You have a bargain to uphold, damn it! The wheels are in motion!"

Someone pounded on the door.

Allen stopped dead and stood silent, staring at the front door, daring himself to breath.

189

The pounding came again.

"Sandy?" he whispered. He took a step toward the door. "Is it really you this time?"

The pounding stopped.

Allen rushed to the door and grabbed the handle. The brass was cold and smooth.

"Allen?" The voice was soft, barely audible through an inch of wood.

Allen flung the door wide. "San...."

The thing was Sandy's height, but skinless, rotted to a black and oily mush. Muddy blond hair clung to the wet and corrupted shoulder muscles. "Hello, my sweet!" it belched, and stepped inside. It grabbed Allen by the neck and shoved him to the floor.

Allen clung at his throat, his hands around the demon's slimy wrists. His head hit something soft and yielding. It was the she-devil.

The demon cackled, moist and phlegmy. It placed Allen's franticly waving hand upon the she-devil's breast. "Enjoy your wife!"

"But ..." Allen croaked, fighting for air. Pops of light announce the coming unconsciousness. "... you said ... she was ... devil." The bones of his neck popped. Pain shot through his skull.

The demon grinned. One tooth dangled by a thread of capillary. "One last thing, buttercup. I take your soul. Then the two of you will be together, forever, in my possession."

Allen's trachea crushed under the demon's grasp. He heaved for breath, but nothing came. As his mind faded to blackness, the demon's rotting, skeletal face inches from his own, it said in a whisper, "There, there, my sweet. All will be well."

The Last Gift of Christmas

"Oooo. It's lovely dear," Kevin's mother said, holding the teal turtleneck sweater up to admire it. The neatly unwrapped box sat serenely upon her lap with green and red ribbons curling down to her ankles. "I was just telling your father the other day how much I wanted a sweater like this."

Kevin could tell she was faking it. She had that I-love-anything-you-give-me voice, and her eyes were open wide as if she were gawking at an eclipse.

Kevin's uncle, Albert, gave a sarcastic chuckle, his movement straining the armchair under his extensive weight.

"I'm glad you like it," Kevin said.

"Your mother's always bitching about how cold she is," Kevin's father grumbled. He gave her leg a pat and half-smiled at her.

"Oh Gary!" Kevin's mother said. She turned back toward Kevin and softened, then glanced outside the window.

Snow was softly falling, and neighborhood boys were throwing snowballs. "It's just that my fingers get a little cold these days. You know.... Bad circulation."

"The boy knows already, Margaret," Gary griped. "Jesus, you'd think you hadn't been complaining about it since he was old enough to crawl!"

Margaret shot Gary an annoyed look.

Everyone jumped as something smashed against house siding.

Gary ran to the window and banged on the pane. "Get outta here, you stupid kids! Stop playin' in my yard!"

The kids squealed in horror and ran away. But as soon as Gary turned and sat down again, Kevin saw them sneak back into the yard.

Kevin turned to look under the Christmas tree and breathed in the heavenly aroma of fir boughs. There hadn't been many presents this year. He remembered when he was a boy and a score of relatives would crowd into their little living room. He was thirty-two now, and it was just the three of them and Uncle Albert. The old folks had died. Everyone else had moved away and scattered across the country. But wasn't that the scourge of contemporary families? The children go off to school and rarely return for good, with better-paying jobs in other states. And the old folks get sent to sterile nursing homes with wheelchair aerobics and hours of sitting in front of picture windows in their last days. The few relatives Kevin had left never called. None of them really liked his dad, anyhow, even though he was only grumpy on the outside.

"I think I see a gift for *me* down here!" Kevin exclaimed, trying to change the atmosphere. He reached for a small, cylindrical package wrapped in blue paper and silver ribbon, the last gift of Christmas. He could tell from the handmade bow and card that his mother had wrapped it. He held it up and shook it gently.

"Oooo. Careful dear," Kevin's mother said.

Uncle Albert chuckled in his throaty, cigar-smoking way. "Must be good and expensive, huh, Kevy-boy?"

Kevin knew from the shape that it was probably canned fruit. His mother didn't actually do any canning, but *her* mother had. So she continued the tradition of giving canned fruit and vegetables, bought in expensive, downtown gourmet shops, in the belief that such things lent a special down-home quality to Christmas.

Kevin made his eyes widen and eyebrows go up. "I wonder what this could be?" he said, adding excitement to his voice. His mother gave a genuine, toothy smile and clapped her hands together.

Kevin tore into the wrapping in the special way that children do. He wasn't a child anymore by anyone's standard – except in his mother's eyes, of course. He unwrapped it that way to please her. Sure enough, he first saw the signature canning lid and decorative canning jar. "Oh," he said, "Canned fru...." The jar glowed with an eerie blue light, pulsing slightly. It seemed empty, but holding it at eye level Kevin found he couldn't see through the blue cloud to the other side. "What is this?"

Kevin's mother moved to the edge of her seat. "Guess," she said, giggling like a child.

"Well, it ain't peaches!" his father grumped.

"Ask it a question," his mother said.

"Sorry?" Kevin said.

"Ask it a question," his mother repeated, gesturing to the jar. "Talk to it."

"Okay," Kevin said. "What do I ask?" The idea seemed silly.

Uncle Albert cleared his throat. "How 'bout you ask it when lunch is."

"Ask it anything you want, dear," Kevin's mother said. "The man at the store told me it knows everything."

Kevin smirked. Then he stared deep into the pale blue light. "Here goes.... Um, *Jar*, what is my name?"

"THY NAME IS KEVIN GERALD MONTGOMERY!" a voice boomed, seeming to come from all around them, and Kevin nearly dropped the jar to the floor.

"Oh, careful dear!" Margaret announced. "You don't want to drop someone's soul!"

"*What?*" Kevin exclaimed, nearly dropping the jar again. "Oh! I get it. You and Uncle Albert are playing some trick on me, aren't you?" He looked for a power switch or battery compartment on it but didn't see one.

"No, dear, honest. Isn't it the neatest?"

Gary guffawed. "Soul in a jar. He was probably a loser before he kicked the bucket."

Kevin looked at the jar again. The designs on the glass looked like astrology symbols. The lid was sealed with black wax. "Mom, maybe you should tell me where you got this."

"Oh, I just picked it up at the thrift shop downtown. It was sitting on a shelf right next to the cutest ceramic duck and a used Parcheesi game. Got it for a steal! Isn't it cute?" Kevin's mother squeaked. "I was headed to that little cooking shop down by Coleman's bookstore when I passed this beauty in a window. I thought it was blueberries, for Pete's sake!"

Kevin and his father both stared at her, one eyebrow cocked.

"The shopkeeper told me the jar was a novelty gift. You know, like fake doggie poo or those cute little eight balls that give you answers. The old tag on it said that if you held it, concentrated, and asked it a question, it would answer. So I brought it home for you."

She waved a hand at him. "Go on, ask it another question."

Still not believing the soul part, Kevin asked, "Whose soul are you?"

"I AM HESPIDUS," the voice boomed again, shaking the ornaments on the tree.

Gary put his hand around Kevin's mom. "That's better than 'Jar'. Why didn't we think to ask it it's name?"

"Sounds Greek or something," Uncle Albert said, moving forward on the couch.

Margaret tilted her head and looked to the floor in apparent guilt. "Now, Kevin dear, I hope you don't mind me using it first, but I got home and was holding it when I realized I had lost my rose-rimmed reading glasses. So I thought out loud, 'Now where on Earth did I leave those glasses?' when all of a sudden this loud voice comes out of nowhere and says 'THOU HAST LEFT THY SECOND EYES BESIDE THY BASIN' or some such thing. Well, now, the jar was so loud that it plumb woke up your father! But there those glasses were, sitting next to the bathroom sink! Can you imagine that?"

"And I haven't gotten a god-damned nap since," Gary complained. "Your mother kept jabbering to that stupid thing 'til last night. 'Jar, where's my good flannel sheets,'" Gary mimicked. "'Jar, where'd I put my Christmas lapel.' 'Jar, when is Kevin getting here?'"

"Amazing!" Kevin said.

Uncle Albert cleared his throat. "Ask it about your future, Kevy," he said, unconsciously rubbing his rotund belly.

"I don't know," Kevin said. "I'm not so sure I care to know that." Turning to the jar, Kevin asked, "Hespidus, how long have you been trapped in there?"

"LIKE THE OUROBOROS, TIME IS BUT A CYCLE!"

"Like the *what*?" Uncle Albert asked.

"What the hell is an aura-bus?" Gary asked.

"Look, Mom, this is a really cool gift, but it's giving me the creeps," said Kevin.

"I'm sorry, dear," she responded, looking honestly hurt. "I just thought it would be interesting... like... like those little birds that dip into water glasses. It's pretty, though, isn't it? Maybe you could put it on the mantle with your high school trophies."

Kevin sighed. The trophies she mentioned were tossed out years ago when he moved to his apartment. "Sure, Mom."

"Ask it another question, Kevy-boy," Uncle Arnold said. "Ask it what we're having for lunch or something."

"Don't you think the questions should be more important than that?" Kevin replied. "I mean, if the jar could answer any question we wish, maybe it could tell us the meaning of life, or how to cure cancer, or maybe how to feed all the hungry people. Don't you think? Maybe those things are a little more important than lunch!"

They were all silent for a moment. The jar continued to glow and pulse in its uncanny manner.

"Well," Kevin finally said. "I'll ask it a *big* question, then." Turning toward the jar, he paused to think, then asked, "Hespidus, how can I bring families together like they used to be?"

"THE JOURNEY'S END IS WHERE IT BEGINS. THE FIRST STEP IS TO...."

But before the spirit could finish, an ice-packed snowball smashed through the window, hitting Kevin's arm. The jar dropped to the floor and shattered into a dozen shards, the lid separating and rolling in ever tighter circles until flat. The light that had glowed from the interior flashed in a brilliant display before blinking out, followed by a disembodied sigh.

Gary jumped out of his recliner and ran to the broken window. *"Damned kids!* You'll pay for this! I'm calling your *parents*!"

Kevin stood breathless. His snow-splattered arms were open wide, his head down, mouth agape, staring at the fractured remnants. "Hespidus?" He looked around blankly. "Are you still here? Hespidus?!"

There was no answer.

"Oh dear!" Kevin's mother whispered, starting to stand and staring at the shards of glass. "Let me get a dustpan for that."

"Dustpan?" Kevin said, as if in a dream. "Dustpan? We nearly knew how to bring together millions of dysfunctional families, and all you can think about is a dustpan?"

Several moments of silence passed. All four of them stared at each other, unsure of what to say.

"Damned kids!" Gary said. "It'll prob'ly cost three hundred dollars to fix this window!"

Albert's stomach growled. "You shoulda asked it what's for lunch."

Devil Seed

Howling echoed through the hallway to the bedroom. Nick lay in bed, stark white light streaming across his naked body, and felt the contrast of the morning sun's warmth on his limp penis and scrotum and the frigidity of the room's shadows on his chest and feet. Fearful paralysis kept him still, eyes wide open and jaw clenched. He wasn't dreaming. He'd been awake for at least half an hour. He and Peggy had tried again to get pregnant, and then she'd gotten up and left the room.

"Peggy!" he yelled again.

His stomach tensed. The howls were deep and throaty, as from a boar on the chase, wet, like with blood, and pregnant with death. They rose and fell, some quick, others protracted like a message to the moon.

"Peggy!" he yelled again.

He wanted to jump up and run down the hall. But he couldn't. He was literally paralyzed, as if hands were holding him down, his heart pounding.

A vision passed through him, a half-dream from the night before. Of candles casting dancing shadows and a vast demon hovering over them, darker than the shadows behind it. Eyes burning a bright red with lightning in them. It had laughed, long and deep, as it reached over them and pulled itself close to Peggy. The demon's power had held him spellbound as something prehensile from its crotch reaching into his wife's gaping mouth and choked off her screams.

"God no!"

At that moment the howl turned gushing, heaving, and fell silent. Then Peggy's choking sobs came muted from down the hallway.

Finally the paralysis lifted. Nick found his legs and crept from the bed, shaking, then made his way down the hallway toward the sound of his wife, hands on the walls to steady himself. The sobs came from the closed bathroom. Nick turned the knob and threw open the door.

"Peggy!" Nick stepped inside and bent down to his wife. She lay against the sink, her legs curled under her nudity, long hair tangled and damp around her face. Her eyes were closed. Her mouth and chin were wet with vomit, as was the floor around her. Red spots of broken capillaries dotted her face. Bruises surrounded her lips.

"Peggy darling...."

Peggy looked up at him, still breathing heavily, and opened her eyes. They were clear and untroubled, blue and unclouded by the trauma she had just experience. "It's okay," she said, peacefully. "Everything will be okay now."

* * *

Peggy hadn't explained what she meant, but merely fallen asleep as Nick cleaned her up and carried her back to bed, where she slept for hours.

Now he sat in the living room, sickened by the vomit he had cleaned up, and worried over Peggy's rather sudden condition. Why hadn't he been able to move when she needed him? *Am I a coward?* he worried. He wiped a hand across his face, feeling suddenly tired. *The nightmare really got to me.*

The room around him was a construction zone. The old, beaten recliner he sat in was the only piece of furniture. Everything else had been removed so he could rip off the walls and remove the highly flammable urethane "low-density" foam insulation from when the place was built. In many places the insulation lay exposed, waiting to be removed. He would then apply sprayed-in, non-flammable cellulose insulation with fire retardant in its place. It was the only room he had worked to re-insulate so far, separated from the dining room by translucent plastic tarp. By next season he will have finished the entire house and insured that their fate wouldn't be that of his parents. It was bad enough to be surrounded by flammable insulation, but because the house was built in the 1930's, the old wood was as good as kindling.

His parents. Nick recalled the horror of that night of his thirteenth year. He had awakened to screaming. Such awful screaming. He had thrown open his bedroom door to find bright red and yellow flames leaping at him from the rest of the house. His parents were burning to death, and there wasn't crap he could do about it but yell for them and hope they heard. Then he was out the window in a cloud of black smoke, then coughing on the wet grass of the lawn as neighbors whose names he never learned crowded around him and offered shocked support. He watched the house collapse moments later, cremating what was left of his parents and his past.

A report later suggested a short in the house's wiring ignited flammable insulation. The fire had spread throughout the walls and attic in minutes. They didn't have a chance.

His uncle said only God or the Devil could have spared him the same fate. Sometimes he wondered which.

But Nick would guarantee that it wouldn't happen here, in his and Peggy's home. Soon this would be the safest room in the house, but he wouldn't rest until all of the insulation had been replaced everywhere. Lack of flammable materials was more valuable than the smoke detectors silently standing guard in every room or the fire extinguisher in the kitchen.

Nick got up and walked to the kitchen. He needed a drink. Opening the cabinet where they kept their liquor, he was greeted by Peggy's unopened bottle of white wine, but he needed something harder. The rum bottle was empty. The only other alcohol they had was the Everclear he used to mix drinks. *A bit stout*, he thought, given that it was 95% pure alcohol, *but a snort of this should do the trick*. Grabbing a shot glass, he walked back to the living room, poured himself a shot, and put the bottle on a step of his ladder. The Everclear burned as it went down.

Nick stepped to the bedroom to check on Peggy. Their cat, Angel, lay outside the door, flicking her tail and laying her ears back.

"What is it, girl?" he asked. He looked inside. Peggy lay as he had left her, sleeping quietly now.

Nick bent down and stroked the cat, but Angel hardly moved, eyes fixed on the foot of the bed. Nick saw nothing under there but shadows and motes of dust.

Peggy moaned lightly and rolled onto her side, then all was quiet again.

* * *

"I threw out all the leftovers," Nick said that afternoon. Peggy sat next to him in the dining room as they shuffled through the month's bills. "In case it was food poisoning."

"Mmm hmm," Peggy answered without looking up.

"How are you feeling now?"

"Hungry." She looked up from the bills and raised an eyebrow. "Be a dear and scramble me up some eggs."

Nick glanced at a clock. "It's only three." He waited for her to say, *Oh, I guess I'll wait.* But the statement never came. Peggy was unfazed, and her brow tensed in that way that told him an argument was coming, so he complied. It wasn't typical for him to cook, but Peggy's recent episode had softened his resolve.

As he cracked the first egg he had a thought: *Pregnant! It must be morning sickness!*

Last night had been one of a number of scheduled "sex nights," and they'd tried again this morning. They had been trying to get pregnant for over a year. Now they were supposed to write down on a chart every damned period and sex episode. Spontaneous sex was out of the question, though this morning had been an act of rebellion. There were all those embarrassing doctors' visits, gynecological exams, and changes of habit, like no more bike riding or tight underwear. Meanwhile, the crib and changing table they bought were gathering dust in a back room.

He thought back. Last night was too soon, certainly, to cause morning sickness or affect her appetite. There had been candles and music and incense, but it wasn't *that* magical. Well, unless you count the stupid black candles that smelled of musk -- the ones that Peggy's sister gave them a week ago and insisted they burn every time they made love. It had astrological symbols and pentagrams carved into the wax. Peggy and her sister were always believing that "new age" mumbo jumbo. A month before, though, conditions had been right. *Maybe she's a month pregnant?*

He cracked the second egg and scrambled them up. His mood lightened. *Embryos. I'm cooking embryos. She's cooking embryos. Serve 'em up!*

Nick cracked a smile as a quick laugh escaped. He quickly suppressed it. *Silly*, he thought. *Morbid.* He let the eggs sizzle and made a mental note to buy a pregnancy tester the next time he went shopping.

Nick heard a groan. He took a step to look around the corner.

Peggy was doubled over, clawing at her stomach and grimacing.

"Honey!" he said and rushed to her. He put his hands around her.

She threw him off. "Go cook, dammit."

He backed away, blinking. She turned, and her flowing seraphim's hair and petite size melted away under the glare of her maddened blue eyes. "I need food now!"

He put up his hands. "Fine, honey, it'll be just a moment. I just thought you weren't feeling so well down there."

He finished the eggs and had hardly put them in front of her when she devoured them and bellowed for more.

"What's wrong with you?"

She grabbed his shirt. "Cook me more now!"

Eight more eggs later she was sated, bits of egg smeared across the tabletop and stuck to her chin and blouse, leaving Nick dumbstruck by her abnormal behavior.

"Thank you dear," Peggy said in the most pleasant voice. Wiping the corners of her mouth, she gently stood and walked past him to her craft room in the back of the house. Moments later Nick heard the sewing machine rattling out its stitches.

He could only stand in shock and play with his mustache, deep in thought. *Are mood swings part of the pregnancy package?* he thought. *Yes, certainly. How the hell am I going to make it through nine months of this?*

He quickly cleaned up the kitchen and went to work on the walls of the living room.

An hour later he was in the middle of removing a light switch cover when howling echoed through the house again. He dropped the switch and screwdriver and backed against the wall. Sudden weakness hit his legs. His stomach tightened. He wanted to run to the back of the house, run to Peggy, but he couldn't move.

He forced himself, one step at a time. Again, it was as if he were pushing against some great force, like a science fiction forcefield.

He reached the sewing room. The door was closed. The rising howl was deafening now, and directly behind the door.

Wanting to scream in fear, he turned the knob and pushed to open the door, but it stopped at only a crack. He saw Peggy's bluejeaned buttocks rising raised in the opening, and she quaked with the next bellow.

"Peggy! Move away so I can get to you!"

Then the howl stopped and she threw up. Liquid splashed onto the floor and swept under the door to Nick's shoes, carrying with it half-digested pieces of egg. He heard something heavy hit the floor with it, then sloshing and slipping, then all was quiet. The stench was overpowering.

Nick backed up and rammed the door. The wood cracked at the hinges. Peggy fell over onto her side, allowing the door to open another foot. It was enough for Nick to reach in and push her aside so he could enter.

"Oh, baby," he said. He knelt and cradled her in his arms. Grabbing a snatch of cloth from her sewing table, he wiped her face clean.

"I'll be all right," she said, then coughed up liquidy phlegm.

"I don't think so, honey. You've got something awful. Some flu or something. Let's get you to bed."

He glanced back down to the floor as he helped her up, and nausea rose in him as well. The floor was awash in putrid waste. A long runnel of it had flowed under a chest of drawers in the corner.

Nick helped her to her feet. "I'm going to call the doctor."

"No," she croaked. "No doctor."

He led her to the bedroom and stripped off her blouse. He laid her on the bed, and moments later she was sleeping. He found a butane lighter by his side of the bed and lit a couple vanilla candles against the reek that now filled the house, then stuck the lighter in a pants pocket.

Resigned, he grabbed the mop, still damp from his prior cleaning, filled a bucket with water and cleaner, and walked back to the sewing room.

The door had closed again. Something skittered behind it, betrayed by its shadow under the door.

He pushed open the door on its broken hinges, expecting to see Angel, but the room was empty. It smelled like a septic tank. All was quiet except for the expectant hum of the sewing machine, which he turned off. Nothing moved.

Searching under the changing table for the cat, he instead found a massive hole gnawed through the wallpaper and drywall. *Rats!* he thought. Nothing else could make a hole that big. He made a mental note to pick up some traps. *Damned cat needs to get to work.*

With a groan, Nick went to work cleaning the floor.

* * *

A day passed, and a bizarre schedule became apparent to Nick. Every few hours around the clock, Peggy would wake up famished, demanding food. She would be normal for an hour or so after she ate. Then, despite Nick's best attempts, she would seal herself up in a room, vomit in that wretched, howling way, and have to be rescued from the room, seemingly half-dead and needing sleep. Always she refused medicine or going to an urgent care clinic. She seemed unable to vomit in the toilet, even when she made it to the bathroom.

And every time the howling came, Nick would be hit with that sudden paralysis and the subsequent guilt for not reacting.

Nick had had enough. He couldn't bear to clean up that stinking mess again, and his worry for Peggy's health couldn't allow this anymore. This was serious, no matter what she thought about it. As soon as the doctor's office opened, he called their general practitioner.

Peggy got up again an hour later. "I'm hungry," she said.

"Honey, we need to talk."

She glared at him, her eyes sparkling with sudden madness, and repeated her demand. "Make me something. Meat. Cook me meat."

He put his hand on her and tried to push her into a chair.

"Move it!" she said and pushed him aside. She tromped into the kitchen and opened the refrigerator. He had never seen her like this.

"Bulimia," he shouted. "You're bulimic, aren't you? I talked to Doctor Mason this morning. He said you have the symptoms."

She ignored him and shoved her hand into the cheese drawer, withdrawing a chunk of feta and shoving it into her mouth. "Don't we have any bacon," she said, crumbles of feta falling from her mouth.

"You have to admit the problem, babe. I've seen it! Look at the way you're eating."

Then something thumped *inside* the kitchen wall.

Both of them looked up at the wall, then Peggy returned to her cheese. Nick continued watching. Something moved behind the fleur-de-lis wallpaper next to the window over the sink, digging in the insulation.

"Rats again!" he said. He looked over to his wife. "Last night I found a rat hole in the wall of the craft room! And two more this morning in the bathroom behind the toilet!"

He listened and watched as the rat went completely across the inside of the wall, pausing at each joist in there and chomping away at the wood.

He turned back to his wife. She had opened a can of mayonnaise and was scooping handfuls of the white slop into her mouth at a time.

"Stop it!" he yelled and threw it out of her hand. The jar bounced across the linoleum floor, throwing globs of mayo to their feet.

Peggy turned and slugged him in the chin.

Nick fell back against the counter and shook his head. He had bitten his tongue. The salty taste of blood filled his mouth. Peggy had already turned her attention to the butter in the refrigerator door.

He was dreaming, he was sure of it. This was a horrible nightmare.

Another rat moved in the walls, but this time Nick heard it exit the wall under the sink. He turned away from Peggy and threw open the cabinet doors.

What greeted him was no rat. It was the size of a small dog or a cat, humanoid, with a squashed face and olive

207

complexion. No fur. It glistened with oil. The beast stared up at him from the hole, beady-eyed and half-shaded, then ran back into the wall with a squeal. Its little ass was baby-like as the thing disappeared up the wall.

Nick screamed "Fuck!" and fell back onto the kitchen floor. He couldn't take his eyes off the ragged hole under the sink trap. He heard the beast rustle through the wall and into the next room entirely.

A moment of shock passed. "Honey?" He wasn't sure if he had put any breath into the word. *Did I really see that?* Finally he turned his head, but Peggy had walked back into the craft room. The sewing machine started back up as if nothing out of the ordinary had happened.

"Peggy!" He got up and went to her, pointing back at the kitchen. "Didn't you *see* that?"

"See what?" Her tone was level and normal. Gone was the panicked hunger, though an open yogurt cup sat at the edge of the table. She looked up at him, puzzled. "What's wrong?"

Nick could only stare down at her in astonishment. He dropped his hand as she went back to work.

"Things are very wrong here!" He grabbed her arm to drag her out of the room, but she resisted.

"You're acting very strange, Nick."

"*I'm* strange?" He pulled her to her feet and dragged her into the kitchen, ignoring the continuing pain from his tongue and the blood in his mouth. He pointed at the hole. "What the hell do you think made that?"

Peggy's eyes grew wide. "Do we have mice?"

"'Mice!" Nick laughed maniacally. "I'm in a fucking nightmare!"

A squeal came from the front of the house, followed by hissing. They looked at each other, then Nick grabbed a broom standing in the corner.

"What are you doing?"

"You'll see. I'm going to kill that so-called *mouse!*"

He ran into the dining room, Peggy at his heels. The cat yowled from inside the tarp-separated living room. It hissed again, followed by sounds of struggle that ended in a sickening crunch as Nick reached out to throw the tarp aside.

The room was dark. But Nick saw movement in the corner. Blood pooled on the floor there, mixing with clumps of insulation and cat hair. The rear half of Angel had been dragged halfway into the wall. Her foot kicked quickly as dying brain still told the muscles there to run.

"Angel!" Nick dropped the broom and picked up a two-foot crowbar.

"No!" Peggy shrieked, then suddenly she was on his back, choking him with an arm around his throat, and her legs wrapped around his waist.

"Peggy. What...." but she choked off anything else he intended to say. He was suffocating, rotating in circles to throw her off. He tripped over his toolbox and fell into the recliner, knocking it over.

Peggy didn't let go, so Nick heaved himself backward, slamming her into the wall. She screamed. Finally she released him and slumped against the wall. Nick was able to step away, coughing and massaging his throat.

He looked again at the hole in the wall, but Angel had been pulled completely up into it. Insulation fell out. The wood thumped as multiple beasts chewed and tugged on their fresh kill.

Wheezing, Nick picked the crowbar back up. With a yell he slammed it into the wall where the beasts had gathered. They squealed in panic and ran through the wall. Blood splattered from the cat's remains. Nick swung again and again where he heard them, then finally one of the beasts fell from the wall, its legs shattered.

Covered in glistening blood, it croaked like a frog and spat at him, multiple rows of tiny, sharp teeth gleaming out of a too-wide mouth. Nick was stunned by how inhuman it seemed, yet perversely baby-like. It had the same proportions as a newborn, with a slit of vagina between its severed legs, but its head was flattened and pug-like. Blood and bits of tissue clung to its half-inch claws.

"What the hell *are* you?" Nick said. The beast rolled over, then lunged for Nick's feet with another squeal. He smashed its skull with the crowbar.

"NO!" Peggy wailed. She climbed to her feet and took a step toward him but fell to her knees.

"What *are* these, Peggy? What's going on?"

"You have to submit too, Nick."

"Submit to what?"

"To the Master."

Nick remembered again the black demon of his dream, its sweeping wings hovering over the entire bed, its head lost in shadow. "I ... I don't know what you're talking about."

"I think you do."

Peggy urgently grabbed at her belly. The skin there bulged, separating her ribcage inside with a snap of tissue. She shrieked in pain and fell to all fours. Arched her back with raised head. Howled like a beast. The cry was deafening, and Nick found himself stepping back and covering his ears. He smelled the stench of her breath. Her eyes glazed over. Mouth agape.

"Peggy!" he tried to yell over it all, but she didn't respond. She only howled louder, lolling her head side to side. Her chest heaved as her lungs expanded with the strength of it, and her belly rolled with life that was not of her own body.

"God!" Nick yelled. "Oh shit!" He couldn't conceive of how to handle the situation. He wanted to run far away from the nightmare of it. He wanted to save his wife. He couldn't move. "Oh shit! Oh shit!" he said and collapsed against the wall across from her. "Peggy!" He cowered, yet could not take his eyes off her.

And the beasts appeared from the wall. In twos and threes. Then a dozen of them, emerging from holes they dug through the insulation. Each of them standing by the wall on their stubby legs and howling with her with bizarre, polyphonic cries.

Again he was paralyzed. The scene was too much to comprehend. Too bizarre to be real.

The howling halted abruptly as her lips expanded like a vagina during childbirth and her jaw dislocated like a snake's. He watched as the bald pate of a head rose from her throat and squeezed through her wide-open lips. The beast spilled from Peggy's mouth onto the floor in a rush of fetid liquid, thumping onto the carpet in an olive lump of flailing limbs. Then she howled again as another beast slipped through with a slap of skin and sudden exhalation from its mother. Vomit pooled around the newborns, but the twins had already stood and slipped across the floor to their siblings along the wall. Severed umbilical cords hung from Peggy's mouth, and she swallowed them back down like spaghetti.

Too horrified to comprehend what he'd seen, bile rose and he vomited too, doubling over and retching uncontrollably.

"No," Nick muttered when he recovered, shaking his head. "No. This can't be. This is wrong. Wrong! This is fucking *wrong*!"

He picked the crowbar back up.

The beasts moved as one, even the newborns, and took a step toward him.

Nick pulled himself up and readied himself, sizing up the little monstrosities.

The beasts snickered quietly, then one squealed, and another, and suddenly they were running toward him on their little legs, claws outstretched.

Nick swung the crowbar, catching one of the beasts in the head. It flew into the wall and fell to the floor in a bloody lump. But the others jumped onto Nick's pants and climbed up his legs. He swung the crowbar again and caught another in its side. But now they were clawing his clothes off his legs, chewing into his knees and ankles.

Nick screamed and flung a couple across the room. It was no use, they were on his back and buttocks, climbing, biting into his neck and hips, his belly, his crotch. The warmth of his blood spilled out across his skin, exciting the beasts in their frenzy. Each time he pulled one from him it took clawfuls of skin with it.

"Peggy!" he screamed. "Peggy!"

She raised her head and stared at him, at first silent as he struggled, then a smile crept across her face. A quiet laugh squeezed from her throat.

"Play, babies," she said, her eyes crazed. "Play and eat up! You're growing boys and girls." She wiped her mouth with the back of her hand. "We've waited *so long* to have you!"

Nick slammed himself against the walls, trying in vain to loose the beasts. He spun and crashed into the ladder. The Everclear bottle and shot glass shattered onto the floor and wall in a splash of alcohol and glass.

Then one beast latched onto his neck with his teeth and ripped out the vein.

Nick screamed and saw his own blood spurt across the walls in a red arc. He fell to the floor with a groan, the devils squealing with delight, lapping up his warm blood. His world of pain and horror was fading fast.

"Goodbye, Nick," Peggy shouted. "They aren't *your* children, anyhow!"

He fought the darkness. Reached for his pants pocket. Bloody fingers wrapped around the butane lighter there. Peggy gasped as he pulled it out.

Nick flicked the trigger and ignited the Everclear and the insulation in the wall.

"Peggy," he whispered as flames rushed across the exposed insulation and up to the ceiling. Beasts scattered, squealing. Peggy screamed. Nick's eyesight failed him as the conflagration exploded around him.

The last thing he heard was the deep laughter of the demon.

Jason A. Kilgore

The Secret of Jeremiah James

Jeremiah's wracking cough echoed against the barren walls of his bedroom. He hacked to get up some of the thick, yellow phlegm that had accumulated in his throat and tasted blood as it came, then absentmindedly added the Kleenex to the pile growing next to the bed. It had been like this for the last week, the latest week of ten years of slow decline.

He leaned as far as he could to his right, but he couldn't reach the respirator. The coughing bout had left him too weak to get up, so he grabbed the call button hanging from his headboard. *Damned nurse! You'd think she wouldn't be so damned lazy for the price I pay!* he thought, pressing the button over and over, *I'm too damned old to be bothered with such irresponsibility!* He heard the muted buzzing from the nurse's quarters echoing through the dusty hallways and empty rooms of the house.

Jeremiah collapsed from his efforts. His noisy breathing rattled up from his throat. The cancer had spread before the doctors could do much about it. They had removed what they could, and most of his voice had gone with it. He pressed the button again and held it, noticing how the distant sound resembled the beehives he had maintained as a boy.

At long last he heard the stairs creaking as someone came up. He remembered when he was young, sick in bed and calling for his parents. The steps creaked then, too, and his father had peeked around the door. He had stood there, staring at Jeremiah for many minutes, ignoring his pleas for water. Jeremiah's throat had been dry and sore. A fever burned in his head, threatening to consume him, waste him. Then, silently, his father had turned and shut the door behind him, leaving Jeremiah to waste away -- alone.

Now the ghostly white uniform of the nurse appeared in the doorway and approached the bedside.

"Where the hell you been?" Jeremiah croaked. "I don't pay you so much to drag your feet when I need you!"

The nurse leaned over him and checked his pulse, exposing part of a pajama top under the uniform shirt. "What's the matter, Mr. James?" she said, slow and sleepy. "Problems breathing again? Do you need me to raise your head up?" Her light blond hair fell to obscure her smooth face.

"Don't butter me up, damn you! I've been ringing for a good ten minutes." The effort of talking started Jeremiah coughing again, but the spell was short. More blood on the tissue.

The nurse stood up and put her hand on her hips. "Mr. James, it's two AM. It's late. I'm tired. You've called me twice tonight for nothing more important than getting

215

Kleenex for you. And I have a guest tonight. Now would you mind telling me what you want?"

Jeremiah started wheezing again, but he pointed an age-spotted arm toward the respirator.

"Oh, Mr. James, I'm so sorry." The nurse walked around the bed and moved the respirator closer. Opening a valve, she placed the nosepiece on Jeremiah's face. "There now," she said. "Better?"

Jeremiah inhaled deeply. His lungs gradually reopened. "You're so damned slow," Jeremiah whispered, the words dragging. "I'm getting tired of your incompetence. And I don't appreciate you bringing that gigolo into my house." Jeremiah paused to catch his breath. "As of tomorrow, I'm docking your pay."

The nurse expelled a breath of frustration. "Mr. James, you can say whatever you wish, but my contract is binding. It's a full-time job taking care of you, and you never seem to appreciate it. In the two years I've worked here you've never said one nice thing to me, or even called me by my name. You haven't *ever* increased my pay or given me a bonus. And you make me live in that cold, run down storage unit you call my quarters instead of one of the three empty bedrooms.

She paused for him to speak. But he didn't have anything to say to her insolence. The thankless bitch. He paid her plenty!

She continued, "Just what sort of condition do you think you'd be in without me? You went through *six* nurses in less than a year before I came around. Now, do you have anything positive to say to me? Anything at all?"

Jeremiah bit his lip. He wanted so badly to fire this worm on the spot, but he needed her at least until morning. Damned straight he'd call her supervisor in the morning. He'd had enough. No one talks to him this way!

"Go away," is all he said, the words rasping from his throat.

"Fine, Mr. James. Be that way. But I refuse to go out on a limb for you anymore tonight. And don't try pressing that damned button, either. I'll just get my 'gigolo' boyfriend to unhook it!" She walked stiffly out of the room at that point. Jeremiah heard her padded footfalls fading until a door slammed at the other end of the house.

She'll change her tone when I talk to her supervisor, Jeremiah thought. *I won't stand for this sort of back talk.*

Jeremiah lay in the darkness for a long time, unable to fall asleep. The heavy velvet curtains had been pulled at his request, but now he found himself longing for them to open. The barren tree outside and the stars beyond would have been far more interesting than the blank ceiling, colored a dim orange by the faded night-light in the corner of the room.

momma....

Jeremiah paused his breathing, straining to hear what he thought he had. His eyes darted side to side. His breathing was rattled again. His pulse jumped. *I'm dreaming,* he thought, yet he knew he was awake.

momma momma....

The boy's voice was high, panicked, far away. Visions of blood and mangled limbs flooded down through Jeremiah's memory. They came too quickly, despite his best efforts over the years to push them away.

momma....

"Damn. I'm hearing things," Jeremiah mumbled and pushed on the call button again. The distant signal echoed through the halls again. He kept it up, pressing again and again, but the buzzer silenced suddenly, leaving the house to the incessant ticking of clocks and a drip from the bathroom sink.

That gigolo boyfriend, the thought.

Jeremiah pushed again at the button, but his efforts were in vain. He might as well have pushed on the wall for all the good it did.

help me....

Jeremiah heard distant screaming. High, shrill, full of pain. The mournful sound filtered through some unknown barrier to his ears, took him back decades. A memory of guilt and death. The boy had been thrashing about, his guts spilling out of his belly and head shaking back and forth in an effort to escape the fire burning at his nerves.

Jeremiah shook his head to dispel the memory, but he failed. His wife had left him that morning, twenty-three years ago, and took the kids with her. So he had gone out to Harmen's Bar on the other end of town for a drink or two to get that overbearing bitch out of his mind. Five hours of drinking later, he had gotten back into his car and headed down the lonesome back roads toward home. He was probably going eighty when he crested that fateful hill. The car jumped a good two feet and came down into the boy and his bicycle.

momma momma momma....

"Shut up!" Jeremiah croaked at the walls. The nightlight seemed to increase in intensity, becoming redder. The walls and ceiling started to warp, like plastic heated in an oven. He pressed again on the button. Silence.

He had staggered out of the car after the accident. His head had hurt. A slow, steady stream of blood wound its way down his face, hot and thick.

The boy had lain just off the pavement. His shattered body was wrapped around the twisted blue frame of his bike. Perhaps eight years old, he had dark hair and blue-gray eyes that looked directly at, and through, Jeremiah. *Help me*, the boy had murmured.

"Oh my God," Jeremiah had said, fighting dizziness. Buried beneath had been a desire to do something. But everything had been too confusing. He hadn't known what to do.

The boy had looked down at his body and screamed. His left leg lay three feet away, and his right arm hung from him by nothing more than thin ribbons of flesh. Blood flowed freely from his body and down the hill to separate into rivulets, steaming in the chill, November air. The boy looked up to the cloudless sky and shook his head, coughing and spitting up clots of blood. *Momma....* the boy had said, his voice rising, *Momma!* His torso started shaking, then the boy wailed, his head thrashing side to side. *Momma momma momma!* It was the screaming of a hare caught in the jaws of a wolf, an end-of-your-life cry that reached the high pitches heard with torture.

Jeremiah drove away then. Maybe it was the alcohol, he didn't know, but he had sped away as fast as he had come, trying in vain to outrun the guilt. The boy was found dead by another motorist minutes later. The news gave his name: Johnny Pearson, age eight. Picture of his grieving parents. Hit and run. Appeals for the killer to come forward.

Jeremiah never told anyone, and no one witnessed. He purposely ran his car into a pole the next day as an excuse for the damage. He was never suspected in the crime.

Momma momma momma!

The sound was closer. The screaming intense. With growing horror, Jeremiah saw the walls and ceiling warp more and more, bulging in some places like waves in the ocean, swelling and falling. The night-light now bathed everything in the room a bright, blood red.

"Nurse!" Jeremiah tried to scream. "Nurse!" But his voice was as dry as October leaves.

"MOMMA!"

Jeremiah turned to his right and saw the boy standing there next to the bed. Intestines fell from the boy's ripped belly, laying on the bedspread and coating it with a red slime of congealing blood. His right arm hung from shreds of vein and flesh. "*HELP ME!*" the boy rumbled, his words now firm and deep, rolling like a low thunder, but wet with blood that dribbled from his mouth.

Jeremiah screamed and rolled off the other side of the bed. Plastic tubing flew with him, ruptured at the oxygen tank on the other end. Gas hissed over the constant screaming.

The floor rolled and bulged. The heat of what should have been cold tile burned at Jeremiah's skin. He pulled himself against the rolling floor toward the door, his breath escaping with a wheeze.

"Go away!" Jeremiah wheezed. "Go away! Leave me alone!"

The red light was blinding. He moved another foot forward and grabbed hold of something soft and clothed. Looking up, he screamed again. The dismembered leg lay clutched in his hand, blood seeping under his fingernails and into the sleeve of his robe.

Jeremiah threw the leg aside and rolled over onto his back. His heart surged against his chest. White-hot pain fired through his back and arms. He arched his body.

"I'm sorry!" Jeremiah yelled against the rattle in his throat, fighting for breath. "I'm so sorry, Johnny! I didn't mean to kill you! I didn't mean to do it!"

The mangled corpse of the boy hovered over the dying man, his hair whipped by an unfelt wind. Jolts of blinding pain shot through Jeremiah's body as he clutched at his chest. "Help me...." he gasped to the boy, fearing his voice lost against the boy's screams that filled the room. But the boy stared down at him, eyes black and cold like winter pavement, blood dribbling from his mouth onto Jeremiah's face.

The floor around Jeremiah burst into blue flames. Then the boy shoved on Jeremiah's chest and pushed him into Hell.

Jason A. Kilgore

Corporate Spirit

Alex Ravin sneaked glances around at his co-workers. Tracy was on the phone with a customer. Patel had walked away from his desk. None of the others were looking, so Alex turned back to his computer, minimized a spreadsheet, and navigated to the internal "Careers" webpage of his biotech company, Incytomix. The second position on the list, "Advanced Services Supervisor," was still marked "open" next to a red button labeled "Apply Now!" A sidebar on the page read, "Need a Personal Growth Mentor? Take charge of your career and contact HR today!"

Alex had already applied for the job, though. It had been almost two months and still no peep from Human Resources other than an email acknowledging the application ("You're actualizing your career!" read the subject heading). The most recent round of layoffs had booted one of his two supervisors, leaving his boss, Cindy, filling both positions in the interim until it could be backfilled. Not that she complained. Like all management around the company, she always wore one of those pasted-on smiles, even when she delivered bad news. She had announced the layoff of her co-supervisor and two of Alex's fellow workers with the same sort of oh-shucks tone she might use to let you know they were out of organic coffee in the break room. If he got the job, he swore to himself, he wouldn't be another "Cindy."

Alex re-read the job posting for the hundredth time. The deadline had been extended another month. Did that mean they hadn't found his application suitable and were still looking?

"Hey!" said a voice to his left. Alex jumped, quickly clicking back to the spreadsheet on his screen.

It was Patel, standing there with a steaming mug in his hand – his afternoon Darjeeling with milk. On the side was printed, "It's magic until it's science!" He took a sip, seeming to savor the surprise. Alex gave his friend and coworker a glare. "What is it, Patel?"

"I saw what you were looking at." His voice was low, spoken with his characteristic mix of colonial English and the lilt of Hindi. "Applying?"

This wasn't a good thing. Alex didn't want the weirdness of potentially being Patel's boss to get in the way of their working relationship. "Just looking."

"You won't catch *me* applying. The last thing I want is to sell my soul to this place."

Alex picked up a customer matrix form on his desk and put it in a file, trying to look busy and end the conversation. "Well, we can't do tech support for the rest of our lives."

"Uh uh uh!" Patel said with a sarcastic inflection, wagging a finger at him. "Not 'tech support!' It is 'Advanced Services' now! Medical Instruments Division!" The name change had been the bright idea of the last upper manager who'd come and gone. They all had to make their mark, somehow.

"Whatever. A decade of doing this should be enough relevant experience – *if* I wanted to apply. I could use the pay raise."

The founder of the company, P. Gerald Chapman, had a reputation as a greedy bastard. He was brilliant, but dark and brooding, and rumored to be dabbling in taboo, cultist pursuits. When he sold SpecMedTek Inc. to Incytomix the year after Alex started, everyone celebrated, thinking a publicly traded, international company would surely offer fair wages. The old man had died soon after, under mysterious circumstances, hardly living long enough to spend his millions. Incytomix had started introducing little perks here and there and talking about positive things like diversity and fairness. But wages barely rose. Now, instead of one "greedy bastard" running the company, there was a cadre of penny-pinching upper management and a board of directors who weren't approachable at all.

Patel shrugged and turned back to his desk. "I would not hold my breath, my friend. You know what the motto should be for Incytomix, right? 'Praises, not raises!'"

Alex nodded. Just that morning he'd gotten a "Certificate of Thanks" from his boss's boss, "Manager Mike" Blackwell, in his email. It was the only acknowledgment of Alex's months-long side project to streamline the process of replacing faulty medical devices they did tech support for. In some companies you'd get a bonus for such a massive undertaking. Instead, Alex got a digital certificate in his email that read, "Thank you for accelerating excellence and evolving our business acumen!" whatever the hell that meant. It wasn't even on paper unless he printed it himself.

He sighed. Every time one of these things happened, he felt a little bit of his self-respect ebb away. But he couldn't leave the company – there weren't any other biotech jobs in the area – and the needs of his family required he stay in town. It wasn't easy to build a network of support for a low-functioning and nearly non-verbal autistic child. Money was tight. Though he was middle-class and his wife worked, raising a special needs kid was pushing their finances to the breaking point, even with the meager funds the state provided.

A support worker was really needed by his son's side every waking hour, and they had a good one, but given how little state funding there was, he didn't know how much longer they could afford a worker to aide his son with everything from basic communication skills to calming his emotional outbursts. Alex had been forced to cut back the support worker to only ten hours a week, and only on weekdays.

Maybe it was a side effect from his little moment of career scheming, but Alex felt watched. He turned back to Patel, expecting him to be standing there again, but he wasn't. Patel was at his desk analyzing data from a customer. The others were working, too. And yet, he couldn't shake the feeling. He held his breath. It felt as if someone was right next to him. Staring at him. Reaching for him.

His computer pinged and he jumped again. He turned back to the computer, then clicked on an incoming chat message on the screen. The moment of being watched passed, but he looked around anyhow. Still nothing. The chat message was from his boss, Cindy, even though she was sitting in her office with the door open twenty feet away. It read:

Cindy: *Alex, did you update the PPI board today?*

Alex groaned. She was referring to the latest corporate craze, which stood for Practical Process Improvement. Patel called it "Another example of CBS – Corporate BullShit." Everyone was supposed to do something for PPI, such as "Just Do It" projects updating key documents or spreadsheets, or larger-scale improvement projects, called "kaizens," even though no one seemed to know what the word "kaizen" actually meant. Some Japanese thing. PPI was developed for manufacturing processes, but the corporate uppity-ups thought it should apply to everyone and everything. So now they all had more work to do, above and beyond the normal job duties.

Alex: *Not yet.*

Cindy*: Don't forget it's a deliverable on your goals. You've got 15 minutes til your next phone shift. Keep up the good work!*

She always added that last bit in chat. It was her way of ending a conversation. If you tried to continue the chat session anyway, she became non-responsive or terse.

Fine, he thought. He grabbed his customer matrix sheets and headed down the hall to the PPI whiteboard.

He was busy putting the sheets on the PPI board when two people, talking in conspiratorial tones, stepped out of the neighboring meeting room. Alex peeked around the corner and saw the Human Resources site director, Alicia, talking with Manager Mike in the corridor, their backs turned to him, so he pulled back out of sight. Since the new position would report to Manger Mike, he was the hiring manager.

"I'm not so certain about this," Manager Mike said. "I think we should keep looking for better candidates."

"Insourcing is the only way this makes sense," Alicia answered in her matter of fact manner. "Our lead candidate is a team player but is no longer consistent with his, um, *returns*. And he's not a flight risk. Low hanging fruit. I feel he's at a point where we can insource him."

There was a brief pause, then Manager Mike stated, "Okay. Ask the Asset to test him."

The two stepped away from the door, still talking, but Alex was too far away to eavesdrop further.

Were they talking about the supervisor position? Was *he* the "lead candidate?" The thought gave him a quick burst of excitement. He knew what "insourcing" was – hiring for a position from inside the company – but he didn't understand what they meant by "no longer consistent with returns." What *returns*? And who was "the Asset?"

Alex glanced at his smartwatch. He had only a few minutes before starting his phone shift with customers, so he hurriedly organized his papers on the board and stepped back to his desk.

* * *

The next morning, after dropping his son off at school and fighting traffic to get to work, Alex found a glossy pamphlet on his desk, along with a cheap, reusable water bottle and one of those little step-counters that you clip to your pocket. Everyone else had the same things on their desks, too. Printed in bold letters on the pamphlet, over a picture of a smiling model in gym clothes holding what looked to be a membership card, were the words "Permit To Be Fit!" Opening the brochure, a little punch-card fell out. He groaned. He knew what this was without reading another word of the pamphlet.

"Can you believe this nonsense?" Patel said, standing behind Alex.

Alex sighed and raised an eyebrow. "Let me guess.... The company is making us exercise in order to qualify for lower health costs. Right?"

Patel's eyes grew wide and he drew back so quickly his morning coffee sloshed out of the mug he was holding. "You read about it already!"

"No," Alex said, turning back to his desk and plopping the pamphlet onto his stack of customer complaint reports. "I guess I've just come to expect it from this place." He shivered, wondering why he'd left his coat at the front door. *Why is it so cold in here?*

Tracy chimed in from the next desk over, flipping her head to get her blue-dyed bangs out of her face. She was easily 300 pounds and not shy about it. "They'll punch my card if I meet my step goal. Do I *look* like I can walk 8000 steps a day? This is nothing more than discrimination against big people!"

Patel nodded. "And how the hell are we supposed to find the time to do all that walking?" He threw a hand up in the air, again sloshing his coffee in his other hand. "Sure, they'll cut our premiums by 5% if we meet their 'step goal' for us, but most days I eat at my desk, and I am *still* behind in work."

"Plus we have to get below what *they* consider to be 'obese.'" Tracy added finger quotes to the last word. "I ain't goin' to get below 'obese' anytime soon."

Alex had stopped paying attention. A movement had caught his eye. A shadow. It wafted between filing cabinets like a wisp of smoke. Crept up by Patel's desk. Then, as he and Tracy were complaining, seemed to settle over Patel like a mist.

"Pate.l..." Alex started. But what was he to say? He couldn't make the words come out without seeming somehow paranoid.

The shadow darkened, seeming to form a humanoid shape, hugging Patel from behind. Cozying up, head to head, as if whispering in his ear. It even seemed to have arms that reached around his chest. Patel, for his part, only heightened his rant, but his eyes became droopy as if intoxicated, his words slurring. "And don't get me started about the web portal we're supposed ... to log ... them ... on...."

"Patel!"

Patel snapped out of it, opening his eyes wide.

The shadow lost its humanoid shape and flitted away, hovered briefly over Tracy, then dissipated around her desk.

"What, man?" Patel asked, annoyed.

"The.... I saw...." Alex started to point toward Tracy's desk, but she thought he was pointing at her.

"What?" she said, eyes narrowing as if to say, *You think I'm 'obese' too, don't you?*

"Uh, nothing." How could he explain it? A trick of his eyes? Recovering, he blurted, "It's certainly lots of steps," and scanned the room, looking for a reappearance of the shadow. But it was nowhere to be seen, and everyone else was working at their desks without seeming to have noticed.

Everyone was working, that is, except for Cindy, who was standing in the doorway to her office, the new water bottle in her hand, half filled, and her step counter clipped to her pocket. She watched him, a look of curiosity on her face.

Alex looked away, but too late. He glanced back as she went in her office, but a moment later his computer pinged with a new chat message:

Cindy: *Can you come meet with me in my office if you have a few free minutes?*

Alex scowled. It wasn't really a question, now was it? And when did he ever have a few free minutes?

He clipped on the little step counter, just for show, and stepped the twenty feet to Cindy's door. The empty office, to the left of Cindy's, would be *his* office if he got the position. Everything but the desk, chair, phone, and a framed copy of the company mission statement had been removed. Even the little nameplate next to the door was empty. He wondered if *his* name might soon be posted there.

Alex looked into her office. "You wanted to see me?"

Cindy was reading something on her screen. Without looking up at him, she gestured to close the door and take a seat in the chair beside her desk.

This wasn't a good sign. He closed the door and took a seat. The chair was one of those rolling office chairs which looks comfortable enough, but when you sit in it, it suddenly tilts back too far. It was also too short, forcing average-height people to bunch their legs up a bit, and it couldn't be adjusted. Other chairs had come and gone in the office, but she always kept that one right where it was.

Finally she finished reading, then looked at him, putting on her smile. "Are you looking forward to your step challenge?" Then, before he could answer, said, "Isn't it great that the company is investing in our health this way? Rewarding us for healthy behaviors?"

Alex shrugged. "Apparently, we can get 5% off our healthcare premium, but then again, they raised our premiums by 8% over the last couple years."

She flashed a sly grin. "There's that insightfulness we've come to expect in you, Alex! How is work going? Are you keeping up with your PPI duties?"

"Yes, of course. It's the highest priority, outside of customer needs."

"Good, good." She folded her hands on her desk, still smiling the same smile. "Tell me, have you heard from HR yet about the position?"

Alex raised his eyebrows. "No. I keep meaning to inquire...."

"I'm sure it's fine," she said, breaking him off. "You know I'm on the hiring panel. After all, the position *is* lateral to me. At the end of the day, it'll be me that the person works with most closely."

"Yes," he said, "certainly." He didn't like where this was going.

"So...." She let her smile down just a bit. It was still there, but her eyes were all business. "Tell me what you really think about the 'Permit To Be Fit' program."

Uh oh, he thought. *Did she hear all the complaining? Will she blame me and use it against me for the hiring process?* He had to choose his words carefully.

He tried to act nonchalant and put on a smile of his own. "Well, it can't hurt for any of us to be more fit. And if it's industry standard for premiums to be raised, then we should thank Incytomix for giving us an opportunity to reduce them, however difficult."

Her grin didn't falter, but there was a dangerous gleam in her eyes. "It doesn't seem too popular out there. You didn't join in the complaining though. Why not?"

Alex briefly considered his options. He could toe the company line and state his support for the program. But he had promised not to be another "Cindy," hadn't he?

He dropped the smile that had crept onto his own face. He leaned forward, the chair tilting too fast and almost throwing him against the desk. "Well, Cindy, I think the program is another way to get workers to think the company is serving our needs when it isn't, really. Only a small percentage of us will actually walk 8000 steps a day, now won't we? With our sedentary desk jobs and complicated home lives, we're lucky to walk 5000. How do I know this? Because we already tried this as a company five years ago." Alex could have stopped there, but something spurred him to keep going, talking in a smooth but assertive tone. "It just gives a false sense of morale – a hope that the company is thinking of us – before tossing it into the shredder, only to have another inane program on our desk the next week. So I have to ask you, Cindy, do *you* think it's worth complaining about?"

He stopped, watched her face, waited for a reaction.

But her smile never died, and the same gleam remained in her eyes. An uncomfortable moment passed where they just sat there, unchanging, each waiting for the other to react. Then finally she grinned further, her eyes relaxed. "I like you, Alex. I like plain speakers. Let's put a pin in that topic for now." She turned back to her computer monitor and hit a few keystrokes. "On another note, it looks like you need to bolster your metrics, Alex. Your customer satisfaction scores have taken a dip."

He sat back again, this time controlling the tilt better. "I'll work on it. Tomorrow I...."

"Right. Keep up the good work!"

Her eyes didn't leave the monitor. She started typing away at something. The meeting was over.

Alex walked back to his desk, puzzling over the little meeting with Cindy. He shouldn't have spoken his mind like that, given she was on the hiring panel. *She's so "corporate" she probably has the company logo tattooed on her ass.* He may have just cost himself the new position.

Or was she sincere when she said she likes "plain speakers?"

He couldn't be sure. The fake grin did a lot to hide her true thoughts. *At least the room has warmed up,* he thought as he sat at his desk and logged into the phone shift system to take customer calls. With a huff, he unclipped the step counter and stuck it back in his drawer.

* * *

"No ma'am, the WhispAir XL is not intended for that usage. It's a CPAP device. It's meant to help you breathe at night while you sleep."

Alex adjusted his headset in irritation as he listened to the customer on the other end, a woman with a thick Chinese accent.

"Yes, ma'am, I understand. But I told you, it is for sleep apnea. It is not intended as a daytime breathing aide. For that you will need to speak with your doctor and...."

The woman cut him off, speaking Mandarin to someone off the phone.

"Ma'am? Mrs. Chen? Hello? Ah, yes.... Did you hear what I said? No, it is not to help you breathe as you walk. You are thinking of a portable oxygen concentrator. For that I can transfer you to a specialist who...."

She cut him off again, but the cell connection was poor and kept cutting out. He only heard maybe every third or fourth word she said.

"Yes, I understand you. But I cannot offer any discounts. I am not in Sales. You will need to contact your sales rep." Alex turned up the volume on his headset, straining to understand her past the accent and fuzzy connection. "I can't offer a discount, ma'am, but we have our Allegiant loyalty program, which includes a one-time discount on our instruments. Would you like to hear more about that? .... Hello? Mrs. Chen? Hello?"

The cell connection had been lost. Alex hung up and tried the number she had given him, but it went to a message that said the voicemail was full.

Tracy and Patel sat at their desks smirking at Alex.

"I do not understand why you try so hard, my friend," Patel said. "That customer was truly clueless. You should have just hung up and blamed it on the phone connection."

Alex re-situated his ergonomic keyboard. "Wouldn't be the first time. Though there was a time I would have frowned at your idea."

"Here's what you do," Tracy said, poking a fork in the prepackaged salad she was holding. "She obviously wasn't listening, so you just 'upsell' her to the latest model of CPAP machine. She gets what she was calling for, you get credit for making an 'opportunity' in our database, and our group metrics look better."

Alex shook his head. "It was the wrong device for her. I'm not going to do that."

Tracy shrugged. "Says the man who lags behind me in sales opps." She stuck a forkful of lettuce and dressing in her mouth and gave Alex a smug wink.

"And why are you plugging that loyalty program, anyhow?" Patel asked as he pulled the lid off a package of hummus. It was lunchtime, and, as usual, they all ate at their desks while they worked. They were technically supposed to take off at least a half hour to eat, but doing that would put them all behind on work, forcing them to stay late anyway. "It is a great idea, but we do not get anything from directing customers to it, and it sucks for product offerings."

Tracy nodded. "The Allegiant program is just a ploy to get their information so we can spam them."

Alex shrugged. "Well, it has its uses...."

Then, from the corner of his eye, Alex saw it again – the shadow creature. It was more humanoid this time, moving across the room toward them, stopping at each of the employees along the way. This time he could make out the torso, head, arms and legs, albeit still smoky in appearance. Each time it moved near an employee, it seemed to extract some wisp of smoke from them as if pulling off a veil.

Alex rubbed his eyes, thinking he was seeing things again. A trick of the fluorescent lighting, perhaps? *No*, he thought, *I'm losing my mind.*

No one else seemed to see it. Tracy was still talking. "And when a customer *does* sign up, it's their sales rep who gets a commission. *We* don't get anything at all! They keep talking about changing that, but...."

Something about that last comment attracted the shadow creature. It quickly stepped over to Tracy.

Alex felt his eyes widen. His heart raced. He raised an arm and pointed at the shadow as it leaned over Tracy, its head only a few inches from her, its arm raised over her chest.

"Tracy..." he muttered. His voice had gone hoarse. "A shadow...."

Tracy and Patel looked at him quizzically. Patel turned the way Alex was pointing. "What shadow?"

The shadow creature was taking on more form, becoming less translucent. The veil of dark 'smoke' seemed to shed from Tracy's body and coagulate into the shadow creature, and Tracy reacted with an eye roll and momentary nod, yet she seemed not to notice the creature.

"Honestly, Alex," she said, her words slurring. "Sometimes you creep me out."

But Alex hardly heard her. The creature turned what could only be described as a head and seemed to look at him. The room grew cold as it stared, its "eyes" a darker shade of black, then it took two more steps over to Patel.

Alex leapt up, finally finding his courage. "Patel, watch out!" He lunged toward the shadow.

"What?" Patel yelped, jumping back from him.

Alex threw his arm into the shadow. Tried to push it away. His hand passed through. Only cold air met him.

"Have you gone mad?" Patel asked, wielding a piece of hummus-covered pita bread in front of him as if it were a weapon.

The shadow flitted away toward the other end of the room, then out through the door, leaving Alex standing there in shock.

"Didn't you see that?" he asked.

Tracy huffed and stabbed at her salad again. "Alex, you've been working too much. There's this low-stress diet I read about that you really...."

"You didn't see that?" Alex repeated. He looked back and forth between his coworkers. "A shadow. It stood right here where I am. It ... it *did* something to you."

Alex's headset was beeping. He had another customer call coming through, but he ignored it and let it "bounce" to another tech person. Some of those other coworkers were watching him now, too.

"Okay, now you are really freaking me out," Patel said. He stood and put his arm on Alex's shoulder. "My friend, you need to take a break. Go outside and get some fresh air." He gestured toward the door, but since that was the way the shadow had gone, it was the last place Alex wanted to go right now.

Alex shook his head. "Um, yeah, maybe you're right." He forced a chuckle and pulled off his glasses, cleaned them on his shirt. "Just a trick of light, I think." But he didn't believe it. *I'm going crazy*, he thought.

* * *

"Geez, man, you look awful," Patel said when he saw Alex walk into the office the next morning. "What happened? Do you have a cold?"

Tracy turned and then drew back. "You got a cold? You should call in sick! Every year there is at least a 26% loss in worker productivity because people like *you* come in sick, and a 100% chance that I'd think you suck."

"I'm not sick," Alex said as he put his laptop bag on his desk. "I ... I just didn't get much sleep last night."

"Because you're sick," Tracy insisted. "Just look at you!" She leaned forward and scrutinized him.

Alex grumbled as he got situated at his computer. He hadn't slept at all the night before. Every shadow had seemed alive with an imagined creature. Every creak of the house had triggered him. And when, at last, his tired eyes would close, he'd see the shadow hugging Tracy again and sucking out some sort of essence from her. Even now, as he entered the room, he was watching for it, just as he had the rest of the day before. *Hallucinations*, he thought. He would need to get a therapist or something, though he couldn't afford one. The company's low-end insurance likely wouldn't cover it.

"I'll be fine," he insisted, without really believing it, and opened his email.

Of the nearly one hundred emails he'd received since logging out the day before, two were marked as "high priority." One was from HR with a subject heading of "How many steps did you take yesterday?" He realized too late that his step counter was still sitting on his desk where he'd left it, unused. With a groan he clipped it to his pocket.

The other "priority" email was from Cindy to everyone in the group. The subject heading read "Please get your PPI paperwork done COB today." Yet another acronym the company forced everyone to use.

"I've got an acronym for ya," Alex muttered under his breath.

Patel overheard and scooted his office chair toward Alex. "CBS," he whispered.

Alex nodded and smiled. "CBS."

He spent the next couple hours whittling down the slew of emails. About a quarter of them were from customers. Another quarter were from internal salespeople and engineers related to his customer cases. The rest was a toxic mix of corporate notices, conversations he had been cc'd on that didn't really involve him, online journal notices, and spam.

Alex opened three different database programs, none of which "talked" to each other, as well as his phone shift software, the Incytomix public webpage, and Google's search engine. Incytomix's webpage was so convoluted and the company so huge that it was nearly impossible to find anything on it or direct customers to any particular page. Doing a Google search was the quickest way to find information on their own pages. Before he knew it, it was time for him to log in to his customer call shift.

The precise moment Alex logged in, the phone rang with a customer call, causing him to flinch. He shook it off and pressed the button on his headset to pick up the call.

"Incytomix Advanced Services, Medical Instruments Support," he said into the mic, adding a 'smile' to his voice. "My name is Alex. May I have your name and phone number please?"

At first no one answered, but there was an odd windblown sound on the other side, as if the speaker were standing in a windy wasteland. He was about to hang up when a raspy, male voice come from the other side. "You have been chosen...."

Solicitor? he thought. It happens once in a while. "I'm sorry," he said. "Do you need support for an instrument?"

"You..." the voice said, drawing out the word in a thick whisper. "You are chosen. Accept ... the invitation."

The voice chilled him, set his arm hairs standing on end.

Alex glanced around to his coworkers, checking to see if this was some sort of prank. They were busy working. "Sorry? What invitation? Are you wanting...."

Then his computer pinged. A new email just arrived in his inbox from HR. It was an invitation for a meeting. The subject heading read, "Supervisor position."

"It is time..." the voice said. "You must join ... the team...."

Then the line went dead.

Alex frowned in confusion and hung up, then instinctively checked the room for moving shadows. Nothing. He clicked on the meeting invitation. It was marked high priority, started in only ten minutes, and was in the Executive Board Room -- a room he'd never stepped into in his long tenure at the company.

Alex blinked. *That's it! An interview, surely!*

But then a shiver ran through him. The voice had sounded sinister. And how had the person known about the meeting invitation? Was it someone calling from HR?

That's what it was, he thought. It must have been someone from HR tipping him off about the meeting. They must have had to whisper into the phone lest they get in trouble.

His spirits brightened. The voice had said he'd been chosen. If it was someone from HR, it had to be a good sign. He clicked the button to accept the meeting invitation.

Alex logged back off the phones and looked over toward Cindy's office. From his angle, he couldn't tell if she was in there, so he sent a message:

> **Alex**: *Urgent meeting invitation from HR. Have to log off phones.*

But there was no reply from Cindy, even after several minutes, which was odd since she *always* monitored her messages and emails, even from her phone while she was at home after hours. Then he realized: Cindy was on the hiring panel. She was probably in the meeting, too.

He gathered his resumé and application materials, then spruced himself up as much as he could. Using his cell phone camera as an ersatz mirror, he combed his hair with his fingers, straightened his shirt and collar, and checked for any bits of food left in his teeth. Then he got up to go.

"Where are you going in such a hurry?" Patel called after him.

"See?" Tracy answered him. "Sick. I told you so."

Alex ignored them and hurried down the hall and into the elevator, pressing the button for the fourth floor – the top of Incytomix's sprawling building. The Executive Board Room was the all-glass part that extended out of the building like some fancy hat on an otherwise piebald brick edifice.

His heart was beating so fast it thumped in his ears. He hadn't prepared. Didn't know what to say. Quickly he tried to make a mental list of his strengths and weaknesses.

But then the elevator dinged and, when the door opened, he was across the hall from the oak doors of the Executive Board Room. Behind it he imagined would be a long table with the hiring panel, including Cindy, Manager Mike, and Alicia or some other HR representative. He'd be situated at the other end, clasping his hands, looking eager, and answering their questions concisely.

But shouldn't these things be scheduled ahead of time? he thought.

For a moment he hesitated, holding his breath. The next few minutes could change everything. His career. His income. His ability to care for his family. With a pay raise he could keep a support worker for his son. Success was the only option here.

Then the elevator doors started to close, forcing him to catch them and force them back open lest he should take another trip downstairs and be late.

Clearing his throat, he stepped out of the elevator, crossed the hall, and pulled open one of the doors.

What he saw made his heart skip a beat.

All of the company managers were there! They formed an aisle of sorts for him to walk through, at the end of which stood Cindy, Manager Mike, and the director of site HR, Alicia. Even the Site Manager, just two steps below the CEO, watched from a corner of the room. The room was full of business suits, except for his own rumpled "business casual."

Alex just stood there in the doorway, not quite knowing what to do or say, myriad thoughts rushing through his mind. Would he have to be interviewed by *all* of them? Why were they all so grim-faced instead of the painted-on smiles?

"Come in. Come in," Manager Mike said, gesturing. He was the only one smiling.

Alex stepped in, letting the oak doors close behind him, and slowly walked through the aisle of managers until he was an arm's length from his bosses. A few of the other managers stepped in front of the door as if to bar further entry ... or escape.

"We've reviewed your application for the Advanced Services Supervisor position," Alicia said, her face carefully neutral under her bobbed haircut. "The hiring panel has agreed that you meet the qualifications. Do you still want the job?"

"Yes, certainly."

"Alex." Manager Mike gave a toothy smile and put a hand on Alex's shoulder. "Alex," he repeated. "We've been watching your progress for quite some time, my man. You've shown skill in your work, but we can tell it's grown ... stale ... after a decade. And why wouldn't it? It's time for a new challenge, don't you think?"

Alex nodded. "Yes," he blurted, then composed himself. "My metrics are consistent. I'm very familiar with the company processes. Over the years I've worked with every department on a number of projects and...."

"Yes, we know," Manager Mike said, cutting him off and chuckling, a sort of good-ol'-boy joviality in his tone. "We're aware of your accomplishments. No need to elaborate." He stepped closer, pulling Alex toward him and turning him to look down the aisle at all the other managers, his arm around Alex's shoulder as if they were best buddies. "You see all these excellent men and women, Alex? Most came up the ranks, just like you. We call it 'insourcing.' We're a *team*, you see? All part of one mind-share. We want success for the company in a way that most of the rank and file do not. We've all made sacrifices to be here, just like you." Then he reiterated, "*Sacrifices*."

"But Alex," Cindy added, "what we're about to ask of you requires a mental paradigm shift. A more holistic approach toward how you consider our work."

Alex nodded. "I understand. I don't expect the job requirements to be what I had been doing."

The managers glanced at each other, muffled titters of amusement passing between them.

Alicia cleared her throat. "But before we go into the, um, *special* arrangements of this position, Alex, let's talk about your compensation. In return for a promotion and supervisory duties over half of your group and a corner office, you will be compensated with a 50% increase in salary and twice last year's bonus. You'll also be given an increase of 20% in employee stock options."

Alex perked up. With that much, he may even be able to afford *two* support workers to aide his son!

"But Alex," Manager Mike said, "you will never truly be 'off-work.' Do you understand? At any point of the day or night we can call you if something comes up. It's just part of the job."

Alex nodded. "Yes, I understand." Though *the never truly off-work* bit made him wince.

"And there's another stipulation," Alicia said. "And it's likely to be the hardest for you to accept."

A murmur passed through the other managers.

Manager Mike sighed and gave his toothy grin again, slapping Alex on the arm. "Alex, you know all the programs we have here? The PPI process with its matrix sheets. The 'Permit To Be Fit!' program with the step counters? And all the buzzwords we use all the time. And so forth? Well, it's all part of a special plan...."

Alex raised an eyebrow. He was getting the feeling he was about to be let in on some sort of cabal. And then he noticed something. The room was getting colder. And over by the door, the shadows were starting to move. *Oh God, not now!* he thought. *Please, no hallucinations right now!*

"You see," Manager Mike continued. "Every time we send out another email about a new program, with corporate-speak about 'accelerating productivity' or 'appropriately synergizing best practices' or some such, what do you *feel*?"

Alex knew very well what he felt, but what he felt wasn't exactly the company line. He didn't want to dis the company in front of literally *every* manager. "Well, we need corporate programs to ensure inclusion of all employees and to make...."

"No, that's not it," Manager Mike said, a humorous glint in his eyes.

Alex paused. "It, um, also is important for shareholders that we...."

"Wrong again."

Now Alex was certain of it. The shadows were moving, forming a figure over by the oak doors, coalescing like smoke leaking in through the hinges. And it wasn't just him who saw it. Many of the managers noticed, too, turning to look and stiffening as if at attention, but not really surprised.

"Alex," Cindy said, "I told you I like that you're a plain speaker. So speak plainly. What do you *feel* when you hear talk like that?"

Alex's heart was thumping again, this time in abject fear as the shadow creature turned to look at him. He hardly paid attention as the words tumbled from his mouth. "I despair," he said. "The jargon is mind-numbing. Day after day." He turned to look at Manager Mike. "You have these programs as if you were helping us in some way, with words that make it sound like you're improving the human condition and working as a team. And yet, every time one of these programs rolls out it winds up pulling us back down. Like giving us unlikely goals for our step counters in the name of our 'health,' yet really making it less likely to get a cut on our premiums. Or running the PPI program in the name of improving our efficiency and organization, yet making more work for us that in the end increases the chaos."

"Yes!" Manager Mike said, with sincere excitement. "Exactly!" It wasn't the sort of response Alex expected.

The shadow creature was now fully formed and taking steps on translucent legs up the aisle toward Alex. The managers to either side watched, turning to face it as it passed, reaching out to touch it as if for good luck. Alex dropped his resumé and considered bolting out of the room, but he'd have to run past the creature to get out.

Manager Mike continued. "You see, Alex, every employee with at least a sliver of good conscience hears these things, they feel at first a surge of interest and expectation, even excitement. And when they realize that things aren't what they seem, they despair. That disappointment is like a little bit of their positive spirit pulling away from them. That positive spirit is something we *harvest*, Alex. It is a deliverable. A 'return,' as we call it."

The shadow creature was now within touching distance. The hair stood up on Alex's arms as prickles of coldness washed over him.

"And when an employee's returns dwindle, *as yours have*," Manager Mike continued, "we lay them off – or promote them."

Alex turned to move away, but Manager Mike put his arm around him again, tightened, held him in place.

"It's okay, Alex. We all see the entity that stands before you. You aren't imagining things. He isn't here to harm you."

Alex's blood was rushing through his head, pulsing in his ears. He had to run. Yet fear kept him rooted where he was.

Cindy stepped forward and stood by the side of the creature. "Alex, I would like to introduce you to the spirit of our founder, P. Gerald Chapman. We refer to him now as the 'Asset.'"

The creature tilted its head in response, and with a serpentine voice rasped, "Alex."

It was the voice from the phone.

Manager Mike massaged Alex's shoulder. "You see him now because he allows you to. The Asset is always in the office, Alex, unseen by employees. He patrols around, makes sure all is well, and when those emails go out, he harvests the 'returns' for us. Afterward, he makes the rounds to us managers and delivers our share of the returns, along with whatever sage business acumen he wishes to share. You will reap this reward, too, Alex." Manager Mike's eyes grew suddenly serious. "In fact, he'll give you a taste of it right now...."

The creature took one more step and came face-to-face with Alex. The air was frigid between them. Its eyes were deep wells of darkness.

Alex fought against Manager Mike's arm. Pulled back. But the creature held his gaze. Came closer still.

And then the face seemed to open up, peel apart, issue forth a golden-glowing essence that rushed into Alex's body as he whimpered and closed his eyes. But the energy seeping into him was warm. And the warmth spread throughout his body.

And suddenly his fear was gone. In fact, he felt terrific!

Alex opened his eyes and saw before him not the shadow creature, but an older man, well-dressed and groomed – and glowing with a golden light. The founder, P.

Gerald Chapman. And all around, the managers were similarly cast in a shining golden aura.

But beyond what he saw, it was what he felt. Alex was full of energy and bursting with ideas. Gone was the bedraggled workaday slump. He saw in his mind how each of the departments worked together. How the employees formed an interconnected web. How their work intersected to manufacture product, advertise and sell, and make profits for the company. It was a transcendent moment.

Manager Mike patted Alex as the managers closed ranks around them, smiling at him.

Alicia handed Alex a clipboard with a form and a pen. "We would formally like to extend to you an offer for the position. Do you accept our terms?"

Alex took the clipboard and pen. It was all so clear now. He realized he would no longer be in the trenches, slogging through the daily mud of the company. And his family! His family would have what they needed. Manager Mike had said the only two choices were to be laid off or promoted. He couldn't be unemployed!

A flicker of doubt crossed his mind as he realized Tracy and Patel, and all his other coworkers, would still be "harvested" for "returns." But it would happen even if he didn't accept the position, right? And it's not as if the Asset was somehow hurting them.

The whole situation was so surreal, so unbelievable, yet he couldn't understand now why he'd feared it. The positive energy filled him with such confidence. The future seemed so much brighter now. It was a win-win situation.

He looked down and signed the form, ending with a flourish, and handed it back to Alicia.

"Welcome to the management team," Cindy said, and extended her hand.

Alex shook it with gusto. "Thank you, Cindy. Mike. It's time to leverage our competences and upsize our resources."

And as he turned to walk out of the conference room, the spirit of the founder stepping behind him, Alex already had an idea for another new program to roll out to his team.

ENDNOTES

Thank you for reading *Around the Corner from Sanity* by Jason A. Kilgore.

If you enjoyed this book, please visit the book's page on Amazon.com
and
leave a rating and comment. Then please tell a friend.

You are also invited to visit and follow the author's social media pages for more of the Strange Worlds of Jason Kilgore:

Twitter: https://twitter.com/WorldsKilgore
Facebook: https://facebook.com/WorldsKilgore
Blog: https://jasonkilgore.blogspot.com

ABOUT THE AUTHOR

Jason Kilgore lives in Eugene, Oregon, with his two children, Ben and Anna, loving the nearby Cascade Mountains and the Pacific coast. In addition to writing horror and paranormal stories, he enjoys penning science fiction and fantasy novels. When he isn't scribbling speculative fiction, Jason is a career scientist for a global biotech company, and enjoys staring off into space, deep in thought with his four cats, Dudley, Cirrus, Akela, and Jake.

Made in the USA
Lexington, KY
29 November 2019

57836513R00140